JUN   2002

YA   MIL
Miller, Mary Beth   *SCH*
Aimee

aimee

aimee

A NOVEL BY

Mary Beth Miller

DUTTON BOOKS

NEW YORK

YA

SCH.

This book is a work of fiction. Names, characters, places, and incidents are either the product of the author's imagination or are used fictitiously, and any resemblance to actual persons, living or dead, business establishments, events, or locales is entirely coincidental.

Copyright © 2002 by Mary Beth Miller

CIP Data is available.

Published in the United States by Dutton Books,
a division of Penguin Putnam Books for Young Readers
345 Hudson Street, New York, New York 10014
www.penguinputnam.com

Designed by Heather Wood
Printed in USA • First Edition
ISBN 0-525-46894-3

10   9   8   7   6   5   4   3   2   1

For Nathan, Ben, Tess, Luke, and Jake

I'd like to thank all the people who have helped make this book possible. Thanks to Sian Packard, Ronnie Schenkein, Brenda Bonczar, and Jaimi Bonczar, who read the manuscript and gave me hope that it would eventually be a book. Thanks to Andrea Brown, Nancy Ellis, and Linda Meade for believing that aimee *would succeed. I'd also like to thank Stephanie Owens Lurie for turning that belief into a reality. I am especially grateful to my husband, Jake, and my kids, Luke, Tess, Ben, and Nathan, for all their patience, support, and understanding during the writing and editing of* aimee.

aimee

I DON'T KNOW WHAT THEY EXPECT. My psychologist—I call her Marge because it seems to fit her—she gave me this notebook and told me to write it all down. She's the fourth one my parents have taken me to since the judge proclaimed counseling to be part of my sentence—My Plan to Become Normal Again, as I call it. My parents think that everything "these quacks" have tried is psychobabble, *garbage* in other words, but that's because they want to pretend nothing's happened. We're a perfectly normal family with one child, no divorce, a large income, and three cars, counting the SUV, and they don't want anything to rock that boat. It's unstable enough as it is.

So I wrote out a bunch of stuff last night about how pissy it is to go to shrinks and to have the parents I have—ladder-climbing kiss-ups. I had to write something. I didn't want to look too uncooperative.

But today Marge told me that I need to write about what happened, about my past. Not just go on and on about how mad I am at psychiatrists and my parents.

"That's not going to help. It's not the useful stuff," Marge said. She handed back my journal, which I'd given her to read when I arrived. Actually, I dropped it on her desk and then went and sat in the corner of the room, my legs pressed against my chest, my back to her. I didn't want to watch her read it.

"You also don't need to show me your journal every time you come," she added. "In fact, you don't need to show it to me or anyone else at all."

I didn't meet her eye when I took it back.

"Just write about what it used to be like with Aimee, Chard, Kates, Jason, and Kyle. Write what you felt, what you thought, what was important to you."

I still didn't say anything, so she leaned across her desk. Without looking up, I could see one of her boobs resting on her fancy blotter. The other was sitting on her mouse pad. When I remained silent, she sat back in her chair and studied me. I can always feel people's eyes on me.

I was tempted to look up, but I didn't want her to see the doubt in my eyes.

I don't know if I can write about what happened and come out whole—alive. I don't know if I can look back.

Besides, if I tell it, who will listen? No one believes us—the kids, that is. They all think we have it so great and that this is the best times of our lives. When people tell me that, I want to puke. If this is the best time of my life and I'm going to spend the rest of my life looking back at this with fondness and all that crap, then I should just end it all right now.

Oh, Aimee, I didn't mean that.

Aimee, I'm sorry, but Marge may be right. And since I've been so uncooperative with all the other psychologists and there's no one left on the short list of acceptable shrinks the judge gave my parents, I'll give it a try. I kind of like writing—it's easier than talking to Marge—especially if I don't have to show it to anyone. So I'll start with the way it was.

———

We used to watch a lot of zombie movies, along with a bunch of other horror movies—mostly at Kyle's suggestion. I never liked them, and Chard and Aimee made fun of them, always pointing out how the makeup and props were designed to make it look real. They'd go to one of those super bookstores and browse the movie magazines for articles or pictures showing how the movies were made. Once they even created their own set, with Aimee lying on the couch, fake ax in her forehead, blood everywhere, and Chard crouched behind the La-Z-Boy, waiting to scare us half to death. Kates didn't speak to them for a week after that.

I was never sure if Chard and Aimee exposed the movies' secrets because they found the photography a bit too believable, or if they just wanted to kill Kyle's morbid love affair with them. He'd talk on and on and on about the latest horror flick until we told him to shut up or pay. We had some interesting ways of making him pay, like setting him up with Mandy, a blind date that turned out to be a dog—literally. That was Jason's idea. Instead of making out with some girl dumb enough to agree to go out with him, Kyle ended up dog-sitting for a trophy-winning Shih Tzu that was due to have puppies any moment. The dog was such a purebred fluff ball, she couldn't seem to get the puppies out, or at least that's how it looked to Kyle. So he loaded her and about fifteen blankets into a wheelbarrow, since he didn't drive, and started rumbling off to the vet's. Jason happened to see him, and he had to drive both Kyle and the dog to the vet's, help with the delivery, and then explain to the ticked-off owner why Kyle was watching the dog instead of him. So it all sort of backfired on Jason.

But later, after Aimee and everything, while I was rotting on the shrink ward, I kept thinking about Kyle's zombie movies. It was the feeling of unreality, of being the only one with any sanity, that haunted me.

Because that's how I felt during the trial—like I was the only one alive. The only one who knew the truth. All the other people who could have helped were dead or changed. Aimee was obviously gone forever, but Kates, Kyle, and Jason, even Chard, had returned as zombies. My parents were always borderline zombies, but they and everyone else I knew had turned into real zombies.

They stood when the judge came in; they hadn't changed that much. They listened to the testimony of the first people to find Aimee and me—Aimee's family and neighbors, then the police. They listened while the doctors talked about what was wrong with me. Of course, the defense's and prosecution's shrinks had different diagnoses, but neither considered that I was okay, at least before all this happened. They never thought that if something was wrong with me it had to do with the trial and why it was taking place.

It's hard to act normal when you're accused of murder and no one believes that you didn't do it. Not my parents. Oh God, no. That would be a social gaffe—to support your daughter when she's on trial for murder. Not my friends. They didn't even come to the trial, except when they had to testify, and maybe when the verdict was read, but I didn't see them there. They didn't stand up for me or meet my eyes once during the whole thing.

The closest anyone came to really looking at me was

when Chard had to point at me, which he did with a red face and anger in his eyes, whether at me or the way the prosecutor had phrased his question, I may never know. But he didn't meet my eyes. Not even when he left the stand. I think Kyle winked at me as he left the stand, but then again he's always twitching something when he's nervous. Could've been that. Kates cried, but she didn't look at me. Jason sat so stiffly I thought he was held in place with a backboard, but it was probably just his father's eyes on him the whole time that made him try so hard to look respectable.

So I stood alone. I stood without Aimee because she couldn't stand with me.

But I guess if I am going to do this journal crap I should do it and not rant and rave like my father after I've broken curfew yet again and he's too dumb to do anything about it.

There were six of us in our group. Me. Aimee. Kates. Kyle. Jason. Richard, whom we called Chard because he hated his real name and because his parents hated the nickname. None of us were getting it on—at first. The monkey mambo came later.

"Six little monkeys, jumping on the bed, one fell off and bumped her head. Mama called the doctor, and the doctor said, 'No more monkeys jumping on the bed.' "

And none of us believed the doctor.

We lived *There*. I don't want to say where, because four of us are still *There*. Where I want to be. But I'm *Here*. Alone. We moved *Here* after everything fell down and my parents had nowhere else to turn but away. As if that would make things better. No one ever welcomes a new kid, especially a senior.

Being *There* meant playing soccer and video games, going to movies and dances—whose idea were those anyway? Hanging out. Three of our moms didn't work, and we actually liked hanging out at their houses because of the food. Chard's mom stayed home, but not really. She was a shopaholic, which meant she was always good for a ride to the mall. Kates's mom was a health freak, exercising nonstop in their basement workout room that rivaled the gym at Jack La Lanne's. She was ugly, too. All bones and stringy hair, pimples from sweating and not showering, and skin that was perpetually tanned. For a health freak, she sure loved the sun. I guess there must have been a few 'shrums mixed in with all the sprouts she ate, because she sure missed the skin cancer reports there. Jason's mom just stayed home, except when they were short-handed down at his dad's car dealership and his dad needed a warm body to act like a salesperson until he could get his hands on the victim. But that didn't happen often.

We didn't hang at my house much because both my parents work, my mom is a clean freak, and my dad doesn't trust us in his house unchaperoned. Mom's never home because she's a lawyer. If she's around, she's in her office working on a brief. When I was little, I thought she sewed Dad's underwear in there, but I know better now. His underwear is multicolored and skimpy, unlike his belly, which grows bigger and bigger every time the phone rings and it's for them. That means more trouble—from me.

Dad's really not that bad as long as I toe the line. He's some kind of plant manager for the local car factory, and he asked for and got a transfer *Here*, which is a long ways from *There*, but looks just like it—same pizza, same hamburgers, same clothes, same kids.

But they're really not the same. No one *Here* ever played kick-the-can long into the night, listening to the sound of shoe connecting with metal ricochet off the houses on an otherwise silent street. We knew every possible way to get out of our houses undetected, and it wasn't hard. Parents think they're such light sleepers, but they're really dead inside, and that's why they never hear us. If they were alive, they'd care more about midnight games on lonely streets and wonder where their kids were heading.

———

Chard's dad found out about his mom's shopping habit one day when we were all there. He came home sick from his store to find her slumped at the kitchen table, a heap of bills sprawled in front of her. She had been there when we crashed through the house, raiding the refrigerator, the cupboards, even the liquor cabinet. And she said nothing. Just slouched there. As if inertia would fix it all. She'd been so busy before, maybe a little sitting still would make it all go away.

"Mom," Chard said, tapping her on the shoulder with a bottle of Gatorade. "My friends are over. Going to the mall in a while?"

He waited, but she only hiccoughed. You know, like she'd been crying earlier and still hadn't stopped all the way.

Chard shrugged and tilted his head toward the basement. They have a rec room down there that would blow your socks off. Deep-red carpet, black leather couches, a fireplace bricked from floor to ceiling with a hearth wide enough to sleep on and not get singed. Pool table in one corner, Ping-Pong in another. Bar to the left, kitchenette to the right. Card table over here, dart board over there.

Chard's house had to be the best to hang out at for the rec room alone, but I suspected it was all on credit and would vanish one day. Chard said no, it had been this way forever. His older brother said so, too, and he would know, being eighteen and about to graduate. We ignored him, though, because he ignored us. We weren't even sixteen, after all.

Anyway, we were all there with the Gatorade and Doritos and vodka—the only bottle left in the cabinet that wasn't sealed. We didn't drink the sealed stuff, figuring that was way too obvious, but I think we were careful for nothing. We weren't getting smashed, and we weren't doing anything that involved motorized vehicles, so we were pretty safe. Besides, we were together. What could happen?

What could happen was Chard's dad screaming, "Jesus F—ing Christ," when he came home.

Aimee, who was brought up Christian, hopped on the couch with her hands over her ears, as if she didn't hear the seventh-graders saying worse on the bus every day.

Chard, though, was white and still, lying on the floor at my feet, his eyes fastened on the ceiling as if he was waiting for it to fall on him.

I nudged him as his dad really got rolling, and he turned over.

"You know what?" he said.

"What?" we echoed.

"I have some garbage that needs to be taken out. Wanna help?"

We knew what he was talking about and without a word we headed for the laundry room where Chard's mom stashed her purchases.

We all grabbed a couple of bags and headed up to the garage, then back. Then up. Then back. Then up. Then back.

Then up. Then back. We filled the rear of their Suburban and piled things around the seats. Then, while the deadheads screamed over everything from who drove the last car pool to who did the dishes and who earned what where and who was more worthy and who was lousy in bed and who really was the bastard and who the bitch, we took the car and drove off. They never even noticed, and if they did, they must have thought it was their eighteen-year-old holier-than-thou son going out.

We tried to sort out the bags before we arrived, but then gave up, just grabbed what we could carry, and swarmed the mall. We met every half hour to see what progress we had made.

"No, I don't have the card, but the number is on the receipt. All I want is for you to credit the card. No cash, no store credit. Definitely not store credit."

The cashier reaches for the phone.

"I wouldn't call right now."

Wait while he does anyway and gets a hoarse "Go to hell if you're a creditor!" from the man of the house.

Then back to me. "They're fighting? Will you put it on the credit card now?"

The kerchunk of the machine.

"Hey, weren't you just here? About an hour ago?" The salesperson blinks rapidly as though I'll disappear if he keeps it up long enough. He's a little guy with big glasses hanging on a chain around his neck. Maybe if he put those on I'd go away, but I have a job to do, so I stay and smile.

"Yeah," I say. "I got a little lower in the pile and found another bag of stuff from your store."

Pause while he looks it up in the computer. "It's on sale now."

"Well, isn't the receipt here? Says the purchase price. Don't you have to give customers the purchase price if they have the receipt? Not past ninety days? Cut me some slack. Call them up and see if they're still going at it. See if she's still alive. You know whose stuff this is. Just pull a few strings and screw the computer."

The kerchunk of the machine, but the best he can do is 25 percent off instead of 50.

"Hey, you'd better go there. The sales guy remembered me," I say at the next meeting.

"Anybody got some money? I'm starving."

"Think they miss the car yet?"

"Only if they wanted to run away from each other."

"How much is left? That all? What's left in the basement?"

No answer. Chard chewed his hamburger and stared at the girl across the food court who'd waited on him. She had a ring in her nose, but that wouldn't bother him. He left his meal half eaten and headed over, pants slapping softly as he walked. I wondered if his mother was okay, but didn't say anything.

Aimee had pulled out some stuff from the last of her bags. "I mean, what did she intend to do with this?" She held up a gadget that none of us recognized. "You'd better return this one, Kates. You look the cleanest cut today, and I went to that store already."

"Only if you take my Victoria's Secret bag."

"Girl, you gotta be nuts."

"I'll take it," Kyle said, his hands already on the silk in the bag.

"Get your mind out of the gutter. We looked already, and it's one of those virginal things, not kinky at all, unless you think a woman forty pounds overweight in a white nightie is kinky."

"Lay off my ma." Chard was back. A quick glance at the girl across the food court told me he'd failed. Her mouth was tight, and her nose was a funny shape, as though she were holding in a snort.

Poor Chard.

We, of course, were grounded when we were dropped at our houses, one by one. Our parents greeted us with, "Where the hell have you been?" and "I heard from Chard's parents. You're lucky they didn't call the police and report him for stealing the car. See if he gets his license in November now!"

And my special greeting, "Get upstairs and do your homework. I can't figure out what we did wrong! Why do you think it's funny to flaunt our authority and our rules? Can you tell us what you thought you were doing? And don't lie!"

How could I tell them? I'd be betraying Chard. I didn't care about his mother. She'd be back shopping in a few months when the bills were almost straightened out and the therapy seemed to be working and his dad relaxed. But I cared about Chard's feelings, the ones he hid behind, and his oh-so-casual reaction to that girl's rejection.

He deserved better than her anyway.

———

We hadn't always been a group. First there was Kyle and Chard. Then Aimee and me. Then we picked up hitchhikers, as it were, and found Kates and Jason. But they made the group right. If they hadn't come along it would have been too much like double-dating with the wrong people for the rest of your life.

Chard had this thing about Aimee, and Kyle sometimes went after me, like the night we girls were sleeping at Aimee's house and the guys came over for a little while. Her parents were gone for the weekend, and the guys intended to stay as late as they could without getting busted and ruining the next two weeks. Our parents' groundings never seemed to last longer than that.

This was when we were fifteen, around the time of the shopping fiasco, and just when things began to speed up. Somehow four of us paired off and left Jason and Kates to stare at a stupid late-night movie on HBO.

The thing was, I was with Kyle, and I couldn't believe Aimee had finally considered Chard. Not that she knew I thought he always picked the wrong girls and that there was only one girl right for him.

So I was stuck with Kyle. I'd drunk a bit too much Boone's Farm wine and was very mellow. Very pliant, my dad would say, because I was doing something he thought I should know better than to do, but I was doing it because someone else suggested it.

Anyway, we were making out on the floor of Aimee's little brother's room, and Aimee and Chard were in her parents' room. (She couldn't listen to swearing, but she could lie down on her parents' bed and make out!) So there I was, kissing but thinking of what was going on in the next room, when Kyle gets it into his little head that I'm okay with all of this and tries to lift or guide—or whatever the hell he was doing with his hands under my arms—me onto the bed with the stupid superheroes of the month fighting the stupid bad guys of the week bedspread, and I'm thinking this can't be happening. He isn't serious.

But he is, because he's got his hands inside the waistband of my pants in back, but they're pulled taut because I'm not helping him at all. I'm trying to slide back down to the floor from the edge of the bed, and then, like an idiot, I'm crying, and everything stops.

First, he stops kissing me. Then he tries to figure me out, like anyone, including Marge, can do that. Then he leaves, and I go back downstairs, down the same stairs we were shrieking and laughing and sliding on an hour ago, what with the liquor and all.

And I find Chard sitting on the couch with Aimee on the floor by Jason and Kates, who are playing video games, and I realize I'm the only idiot in the bunch with a tear-streaked face and kiss slime on her tongue, and nothing happened between them at all. Aimee says so later, too. So I go upstairs and cry and cry and cry. And Kates is there, what's the mattering, and then Aimee comes in smoking and sends Kates out.

"The guys left."

"So?"

"No one can figure you out." She blows a long fern of smoke in my face.

I roll over.

"I can, though," she says. Then she stubs out the cigarette in the ashtray she keeps in her sock drawer. She was supposed to return it to the electronic gadget store with the rest of the stuff from Chard's mom, but she didn't. It looks like a makeup container. It has a false bottom, and inside is a condom Aimee's stepmother actually gave her during The Talk. That was in fifth grade.

Anyway, I asked Aimee what she meant, that she could figure me out.

"With you it's all about Chard. Always has been. But he doesn't see it, and now you think you've blown it." She paused. "Right?"

"Lot you know," I mumbled and forced my last tears into the pillowcase before facing her. "It's not about Chard at all." I thought a moment. "It's because I wanted to so bad, but I knew I wasn't ready." I stuck out my chin and waited.

She just stared back, then drew one leg up under her and leaned back against the wall. "Pitiful," she said, shaking her head. "It's still all about Chard."

And that's where we left it.

Aimee was the only one who could read me, the one who knew me best. But even you got it wrong sometimes, Aimee.

I'm sick of this crap. Now they tell me to quit messing with their minds. Mom, wonder snoop, found the journal and asked good old Marge what she thought she was doing. Intended to fire her on the spot.

"We," sharp intake of breath and D-cup chest swelling impressively, "feel it is in our daughter's," quick glance my way and tiny smile, "best interest if we terminate your care of her."

Marge, looking a bit like a fish with too-frizzy hair and oversized glasses, opens her mouth, but The Lawyer is giving her closing arguments.

"We feel, my husband and I—" They're sitting next to each other so they can squeeze hands at the appropriate times. I'm slumped on the couch like a good patient and a bad daughter. "We feel our daughter would have been better served if you had helped her to forget all of this."

Mom rises to her full five feet nine inches without heels. Judging from the angle of Marge's head, I'd say Mom has on four-inch heels at least. My arches and square toes ache at the thought.

The journal, a plain, red spiral-bound notebook, is waved in an arc so that all present can see it, then it is plopped on the desk.

Marge raises her eyebrows. "Then why did you bring her here?"

Mom colors and sits, Dad's eyes twinkle, almost like they used to, and I gag.

"Sit up," Mom commands. She knows a laugh covered by a cough when she hears one. She sits tight-lipped and stares at Marge without answering.

"It is, after all, the main thing we do here. Discuss things of great importance in our clients' lives. Psychologists have been known to focus on the past," she adds. She picks up the journal and, without opening it, hands it back to me.

I admit it. I started to like her then.

"It was part of the agreement," Dad says, as though he just discovered his voice. "The judge ordered it."

"I see. And did you think I should be told about this judge and why he ordered psychological treatment?"

"Absolutely not," Mom says, crossing her legs, her arms. She'd cross her eyes if she thought it would stop Marge from getting in. "It would prejudice you."

"Well, it hasn't. It's made me curious." Marge eyes me, her irises too blue behind her lenses, her lip color too pink. "Runaway? Drug addict? Pregnant? Promiscuous? Raped? Abused?—"

"How dare you—"

"I was trying to let you know that everyone has a story and a problem. I've seen them all. Getting to the heart of the problem isn't my goal. That's an easy riddle to solve. I could look it up in the court papers whenever I wanted. They sent them over, by the way. If a judge orders psychiatric treatment, they have a way of making sure it occurs." She smiles sweetly.

I've underestimated old Marge.

"My goal is entirely different. I try to get to the heart of the kids I'm dealing with. That's where the answer is. It's not in whatever action or actions brought them here."

She glances at her watch. Mom sits dumbstruck. Dad is nodding like one of those dolls whose heads wobble on pencil-thin necks, only he is broken, and the up-and-down, up-and-down motion won't stop.

At home, before we came, he was stuck on the side-to-side motion. "I just can't see what harm there is in her keeping a journal," he'd said to Mom then.

"And you couldn't see the harm in sending her to public school and letting her wander around with those kids either."

"No, I didn't, but that doesn't mean—"

"In my book, it means everything." I could hear what she didn't add. If I wrote something incriminating, like the truth, she probably thought it could be used against me.

"But we don't have any more options left," Dad had said. "The judge only gave us four names."

Mom had sighed and looked at him like he was a dog she hadn't been able to house train. "There are ways around things like judge's lists. We can go to another town if need be. Or something." ·

Dad shook his head, back and forth, back and forth, unable to come up with a quick answer to Mom's logic.

I said nothing during this pleasant breakfast discussion, and I said nothing for the entire session with Marge, but I did manage to slide the journal back into my duffel bag, the one I carry everywhere that has all the things in the world that matter to me. Some pictures. A yearbook. A razor blade. An ashtray with a false bottom. And now a notebook of where I've been.

Marge saw me hide the notebook.

"Next time," she said, "I'll see your daughter alone. Have her here promptly at four, and I think it would be good if we moved our sessions up to three times a week, don't you?" She smiled a caramelized smile, just as the little timer on her desk dinged. It's a neat timer. You can set it for an hour or two. When the time is up, two little figures, a boy and a girl, slide partway down a tiny slope and kiss, then one drops a bucket—guess which—and they both tumble the rest of the way down the slope.

The well, of course, is at the top, and as the two figures finished tumbling, Mom gathered her purse and other props and Dad extended his hand to Marge. I watched the two figures slowly pull apart and jerk back up the hill to the well. And I wondered, Is that well deep enough to swallow a person?

———

Aimee rolled over on her bed. "Let's go for a walk. I can't stand being in this house anymore."

"Where?" I asked. Not that it mattered. Not that I cared. It was sunny, warm, and a breeze shook the trees just budding green. I stood before she answered and dragged my shoes from under her bed.

She was still wearing her shoes. "I don't know where. Anywhere but here. It stinks in here." She shoved her window open and stuck her head into the screenless space. She sighed.

"Ready," I said. She pulled her head in but didn't close the window, and we slouched out the door, neither wanting to appear too eager.

We walked for two hours before she found the Dracula teeth from last Halloween in her pocket. She pulled them out and shoved them in her mouth.

I never saw what she had in her hand, so when she grinned at me, I snorted, then rolled my eyes. Aimee didn't crack a smile. Just kept walking. We wound up on the civilized side of the field, which was all built up with superstores where they sell everything from nylons to Jell-O to tires. I followed her through the automatic doors without blinking.

She smiled regularly during the next hour, watching people's reactions to her teeth. Little children either crumpled into tears or shouted with laughter, and their mothers either looked horrified or chuckled. I tried not to think of what would become of the scared kids with the shocked mothers, and I grinned at the women who liked our joke.

One old man popped his teeth out, and Aimee laughed so hard, she dropped hers. He darted for them, but she was faster.

"Sure you don't want to swap?" he asked, holding out his glistening, wet dentures. His lips were sunken, but his eyes danced.

"Thanks anyway," Aimee said and swished her hips while strolling away. His eyes twinkled more as he watched her go, then he headed toward Automotive.

"Where next?" I asked.

She shrugged.

"Got any money?" We were passing some snacks on sale, and my stomach growled.

"Only if we sell my teeth."

"Should have thought of that before you let that old guy go," I said, digging through my pockets. Empty. I didn't have any money or keys to get into my house. Neither did Aimee, but that mattered less since someone would probably be at her house. We were wearing watches, so even if our stomachs weren't starting a revolution, we knew it was dinnertime. Time to go home and quit screwing off if we didn't want to be grounded. At least if Aimee didn't. I had another hour before my parents might come home from work.

Outside, we headed around the back of the store, toward a side street that cut through to the entrance to our subdivision. We walked by the stinking trash containers, then the delivery entrances, and finally came up between the wall of the store and a row of bushes. A car was roaring up behind us, going fast for the narrow road and showing no signs of slowing up. I watched it approach because I had the teeth finally, and I was planning to flash them.

But Aimee outdid me again.

She spun away from me, and before I had my mouth around the oversized teeth, she was running for the bushes, looking like she planned to hurdle them.

I was faster than her since I ran track, but I felt like I was in a dream, and I held back an instant. She had too big of a lead on me, so I didn't catch her before she reached the bushes. Next thing I knew, she was jumping, both feet off the ground, one flying before her, one dragging behind.

The one dragging behind didn't clear the bushes. She fell

in a heap, laughing. I landed on her and yelled, "Don't ever do that again!"

But before my words and the Dracula teeth were out of my mouth, a rabbit bolted from the bushes in front of us. It moved slow and fast at the same time. Time does that when you want it to stop—it slows down, or seems to, so that you can see and remember everything afterward and wonder at its significance, if there is any.

So the rabbit was running in long bounds away from the bushes and toward the road in a diagonal line, and I was sitting on Aimee's back as she watched the rabbit with her head on her arms. And the car? It moved on a straight path, and I could almost read the math problem in my book: If a car is moving at the rate of forty miles per hour and a rabbit is traveling at the speed of five miles per hour, will the two objects collide?

They met as the rabbit hopped under the car. Then, just when I thought the rabbit might make it, it caught its head on the car's underbelly and somersaulted until it landed in a heap, a little cloud of dust and fur settling over it.

The car didn't stop.

We didn't move at first. Then, after a minute, I stood up and said, "Maybe we should see if it's all right. We might be able to help it."

"It's not moving, is it?" Aimee said. "That means it's dead." She pushed herself off the ground, stepped on her Dracula teeth, and walked over to the rabbit. She nudged it with her foot. No response. "Lucky thing," she said.

"What's so lucky about being run over?"

"It was so quick, and it looked painless, don't you think?"

"What I think is that we killed it. It never would have run

out if we weren't wrestling in the bushes. If you hadn't—" I stopped.

She blinked at me, her face closed. After a moment, she pulled a cigarette from her coat and lit it. "If I hadn't what?"

I felt nauseous, dizzy. Like someone broadsided by understanding. "What?" I said.

Aimee looked puzzled.

I continued, "What were you going to do?"

She rolled her eyes and sucked on the cigarette. "Don't be an idiot," she said at last, dribbling smoke. "I would have stopped." She walked away from the rabbit's body, one hand moving methodically between her mouth and the side of her leg, the other hand shoved in a pocket.

I stood a moment by the rabbit, wondering if we should bury it or something, then Aimee yelled, "Come on! Let's eat at your house tonight." I glanced down at the rabbit, which looked like a stuffed animal twisted by uncaring hands. Then I followed her, trying to figure out whether the bushes tripped her or if she let herself be tripped, whether there was room to stop on the other side of the bushes or if she would have ended up in the road.

Aimee kept ahead of me as we walked, and I didn't try to join her.

I didn't want to know the answer then.

I will never know it now.

Home is a veritable palace compared with where we used to live. I don't know how my parents afford it after all the lawyer bills, and now the shrink who won't be shrunk by my mother. It makes me wonder who they really are. The parents from *Before*, who lived relatively modestly and enjoyed the people in their neighborhood? Or these people, slumped over their gourmet meal under a preposterous chandelier consisting of long dangling sheets of glass? Those sheets of glass are heavy. I took them down the first night because I couldn't see around the lowest tier, but my mother made me put them back up.

Tonight I don't mind being able to see only part of their faces. I pick a sun-dried tomato off my chicken breast, shove it to one side, and glance at them.

Mom is eating. She cuts her chicken into perfect squares and triangles, slices any broccoli that is too big, puts a sliver of red pepper on every bite of chicken, scoops the rice—brown rice with couscous tonight—onto her fork and inserts the perfect blend of tastes into her mouth. Chew. Chew. Chew. Chew. Chew. Swallow. Cut. Stab. Scoop. Pat. Insert. Chew. Chew. Chew. Chew. Chew. Swallow.

Amazing. I pick a hunk of garlic off the chicken. If garlic is big enough to see, it's too big to eat. Aimee said it gives you dragon breath, and people avoid you the next day, especially if it's hot and you sweat the least bit. These days I don't need to give anyone a reason to avoid me. So I shove another particle off to the side.

Dad's wolfing his food. Cuts the chicken breast into quarters, eats that first. Then the rice. Saves the vegetables for last. They're gone in three bites. He'd love a good pot roast with all the trimmings, I can tell. But Mom has another dinner party planned for the partners in her new firm—since she's a junior partner again, she has to suck up a lot. So she has to cook something other than pot roast, hence the new recipe. She also thinks Dad should trim down, hence the small portions.

We don't talk. We don't make eye contact, and when our food is gone, except for my little pile of undesirables, we stand and carry our plates and glasses to the kitchen. We set them on the counter, then Mom walks out. It's my job to clean up.

Dad hesitates, then sets his glass down too hard on the tile. I hate the tile. Crumbs get stuck in it, and then they grow, multiply germs, and Mom gets on me to wipe the counter again. I've already taken a toothbrush to the grout, but that made the crap come up, and we had to get a tile man in. I had to watch him show me the proper way to clean tile.

Like I care.

When Dad's glass clinks, Mom stops in the hallway, just within sight, then she draws a deep breath and moves on.

"Try to understand, sweetie," says Dad. "We only want what's best for you."

"And what's best for you, too. And as little trouble as possible. Go quietly. It will be better."

"I didn't say—" Poor Dad, caught between me and Mom, between doubt and assurance.

"Then don't go nosing around my room, and clean the kitchen for me tonight, would ya?" I sling the duffel bag over my shoulder.

"She didn't read all of it," he tries. "I didn't—"

"Not much to read." I push the strap higher on my shoulder. "I only got the damn thing last Friday. Six days to be exact, and you already violated it. I kept my end of the deal. I did what the shrink told me to do, and you read it." My voice is almost at shriek pitch, and his eyes no longer have the slightest twinkle in them. They look dead, as a matter of fact.

"I said, we didn't read it. Not all of it, anyway. Your

mother just thought it seemed like a waste of time, that's all." He holds his hands out, palms up.

I turn and walk away. A waste of time. A rotten waste of time.

Like I said, who's going to listen?

———

"So." Marge leans back. The little timer has been set, the secretary has left my file on the desk and closed the door with a muffled clunk, and now we're alone. "So," she repeats.

"Sew. Are you a quilt maker?"

"Excuse me?"

"Sew," I answer, but she doesn't smile. I see her hand move across the paper. *Avoidance*, she is probably scrawling. *Denial. Antagonistic.* What else is there to be?

"I see." She sets her pen down and tipis her fingers.

"When do you suppose that particular gesture began? Before or after the discovery of America?" I interrupt.

Again she writes, and I falter on.

"I mean, you do have to admit it looks like a tipi. An Indian's tipi." Like there's another kind.

"What do you miss most about your old school and home?" Wham! Like that. No warning.

Something tears loose inside me. Chard. Aimee. Kates. Jason. Kyle, even Kyle. Their names tumble past like waves skittering across a street. But I don't say their names. To do so would be to allow Marge in, to let her go where even I don't go anymore. "Animal, vegetable, or mineral?" I ask instead.

"Animal."

I'm surprised she's playing along, and now I have to answer. "An eagle," I finally say. That was our school mascot, and the only animal that I can think of. We don't own pets. They are dirty, smelly, vile creatures that leave hair on suits and sweaters and evening dresses when you can't afford to have hair on anything, even your skin, so you get a wax job.

When Mom first told me she had made an appointment for me to go and get a bikini wax, I freaked. Then I told Aimee.

She responded coolly. "Why not try it? It beats shaving. My mom would never take me to do that," she said. "She must want to bond."

"No, there's a party at the senior partner's house, a pool party, to be specific." I glance down at the brown hairs scattered across my arm, think of the coarse black hair growing on my legs, in my armpits. I don't even go *there*, where my mother wants to have someone else touch me.

"I'm thirteen," I said. "I don't have that much."

"Then tell her you don't want to go."

She makes it sound so easy. Just tell her.

I haven't said much about Aimee's parents, because I can't. Not yet. I still see the look in their eyes when they found us, that night, the last night. I see the blame, the hurt, the anger, the hatred, one after the other, racing through their eyes. And I'm the object of their rage. Which I'd never been before. But I don't care because I know the truth, something they won't fathom and would never admit.

And suddenly, it must seem to Marge, I'm crying. I say, "Eagle," pause a second, then lose it completely. I spend the rest of the session with a box of Puffs and my back to her. It's all I have to give.

I have begun a new game at school. I used to play Avoid Everyone, but now there's this girl in my English class who is hell-bent on making friends, so I have to play Avoid Her in Particular. I feel like kicking her or shoving her into her locker whenever I go by. She always manages to look up when I walk past. Always says hi. Always is there.

Doesn't she ever go to class? Doesn't she have any friends? Surely someone in this stink hole of a school is her friend. She's not ugly. Maybe there's some guy who could date her, and then she'd leave me alone instead of always smiling and trying to stick herself into the cracks of my life.

If she succeeds, I'll fall apart. Those cracks are, after all, stress cracks.

————

"Hey, JK."

It's Chard, his voice all soft and soothing like I remember it, but the words aren't soothing at all. I don't think of the risk he's taking calling me, only about those initials.

"Don't."

"What?" His voice hardens but doesn't get any louder. Is he dumb enough to be calling from his house?

"Those initials. Don't call me them again."

"Fine."

There's a pause during which all the emotions I have for him and the emptiness I feel for everything clunk into one another like Morse code. Emptiness, then dashes of emotions, then dots of nothing.

"Any news?" he finally asks.

"School stinks. I have to see a shrink. My mom has a new job. You?"

"Kyle crashed today."

"His car?"

"No. He crashed."

And I know what he means. Aimee taught me about the darkness and anguish and what ends the pain. "How?"

"He drank a gallon of whiskey in less than an hour. His kid brother found him, called 911."

"Is he—" I let it hang, not sure I want to know.

"Yeah, he'll be okay. I'm not allowed to see him anymore now either."

He stops on the "either," and we are both thinking of how many of us are allowed physical contact with each other, and I realize that it's zero. My isolation is enforced by court orders and my parole officer. Theirs is enforced by their parents, well-meaning, know-nothings that they are.

"I just thought you should know," Chard says, and his voice breaks.

"Thanks." I'm not sure he can hear me. I'm wondering if he can feel my breath through the phone or my hand on his, where I'm imagining it's lying. But I feel nothing, so he can't feel me either.

A tear slips down my cheek, and I set the phone into the cradle as softly as possible, even though I'm alone in the house.

———

"You're quiet today."

As if I'm ever a motormouth, I think, as I turn from the muted print of some kids playing hide-and-seek in an old-fashioned sitting room. Their mother is sitting in a chair, sewing or something, and everything seems safe, happy, even gentle. We were never calm when we played anything.

Marge is sitting, as usual, at her desk. Her hair is pulled up and back, off her neck, and I can see a tiny mole just at the hairline. I see the edge of the phone bill Mom dropped on Marge's desk when she came in with me. It's peeking out from behind Marge's yellow pad, which is empty. Mom has the phone bill delivered more often than usual because I'm not supposed to be calling anyone, and this is her way, since she is absent more often than not from our home, of making sure I'm not doing anything wrong. She sees this latest bill as evidence that I'm backsliding. My life *There* is over. I shouldn't, therefore, even try to find out what happened to my friends.

But I had to know how Kyle was doing. The thought of losing him, too. . . . Well.

I didn't try to call Chard. That would be too obvious. Kates's mother doesn't let me talk to her. Besides, they've changed their phone number and e-mail address and access code a billion times to be sure there's no way the evil monster—i.e., me—can get through to her. I talked to one of my lesser loved acquaintances—those were the phone calls Mom saw on the bill and got hyped up about. But hey, no one said I couldn't call *anyone* back *There*. Only my friends, their families, and Aimee's family. I found out that Kates is being sent away to school anyway. What with Kyle and all, they'll probably send her away sooner than they had planned. This might be catching, after all.

"No thoughts? No comments?" Marge murmurs.

I like the sound of that. "Marge murmurs," I say out loud.

She strains forward in her chair to catch what I'm saying, but she can't.

"Do you have kids?" I ask to give her something to hear, and because I was wondering about it last night as I lay listening to my mother and father grunt on their exercise equipment. They have to be perfect, especially Mom, so that leaves no time for the kind of grunting they should do more of but don't, especially now.

I wait, but she doesn't answer. Instead she says, "I wonder why that is important to you?"

"Nothing is important to me," I say.

But she just nods and, for the first time that day, makes a note on her pad of paper.

I don't bother trying to read it. I go around and collapse on the couch. "I just thought you might. You're wearing a wedding ring, and you're plenty old enough."

"Thanks."

I shrug. "I'd like to know what you'd do with your daughter if you had an afternoon free."

"We go to concerts, ballets, and ice-skating rinks. Sometimes we shop or have lunch. We do puzzles and play computer and card games. I've taught her to ski. She's taught me basketball."

I stare at her. "Mom and I go for manicures and body waxings," I say. "But not anymore. Now we go to shrinks and court appointments." I listen to her pen scratching. "I knew you had kids." More scratching. "Don't you want to know why I called? My mom never even asked. Just blew up and locked me in my room. She consulted with our lawyers about the possible ramifications of this new twist in the story's plot, but she never asked why."

"Okay. Why?"

"Kyle tried to kill himself, and I wanted to know how he was. Is there anything wrong with that?"

"No."

That's it. No. A soft response for a hard negative. She waits, but I don't tell her he's still in the hospital and when he's well enough he'll have to go to some psych ward where they stare at you through little slits in the door and make sure you have nothing to hurt yourself with. They don't know about biting the inside of your cheek until it bleeds and swells and you can't stop biting it anymore because it's in your way all the time. They don't know about ripping off your fingernails way below the nail bed so that you can poke the raw flesh beneath. They don't know about jabbing the sharpened nails between your toes or gouging the soft skin there with whatever you can find so that there's an open sore to sear every step into your memory so that you won't forget why you're there.

To be punished.

———

I should address Aimee's accident-prone behavior. Everyone figured she was a klutz. After all, who could fall down a flight of stairs at school and crack their car up in the same month? No one thought it odd that she would be driving with her leg in a cast. She was Aimee. No one questioned Aimee. Straight A's, good parents, good behavior (at least at school), and kiss-up-to-the-teachers Aimee.

I remember once, when she got in this huge fight with her dad, which she lost, she went into the bathroom and slammed the shower door on her arm over and over. Until it broke. Yeah. Broke. She told her father she fell in the shower. He was so stupid, he never noticed that she was dressed and her hair was dry when she walked out of the bathroom with her arm dangling.

And the car accident? She was driving with a cast, but it was on her left leg and it didn't come above her knee. And the accident happened on this mostly straight road with only one curve, not even a forty-five-degree curve, more like a fifteen-degree curve, that sweeps up and across an overpass by the highway. She was going at least fifty, the cops said, when she lost control and went off the road. I don't know how she survived, but she was wearing a seat belt, so I guess that helped. And it always helps, if you're planning an accident and you want to survive, to remember to drive the car with the air bags. The car she was not supposed to drive. Ever. Hers was the clunker from prehistory with no air bags and no four-wheel drive. Wonder why she drove the forbidden car that day? She said it was because she could get in and out easier with her cast.

Believe it or not.

———

Mom's dinner party went off without incident, which means I ate, kept my mouth shut, and disappeared into my room as soon as I could.

Oh, and I talked nice to the boss's son, and he was the only one there who recognized me from the papers. It seems that if anyone is going to know who I am, it's the kids. The parents can't seem to remember where they've seen me before, if they even think they have. Someone once asked me if I was that young country singer who won every award possible by the time she was fourteen or something.

"No," I said. "And I don't even look like her either."

That was not talking nice, and I was grounded for weeks afterward. It was, after all, the partner's ancient mother I was speaking to, and right in the middle of my court case, when sucking up to influential lawyers and being on my best behavior at all times was what I was supposed to do. Not insulting their mothers.

But I didn't mind being grounded, since I had nowhere to go. I wasn't wanted at parties anymore. So I climbed up to my room, turned on my music loud, slid out my window onto the roof of the kitchen, and headed for the corner.

The corner. Blue street light washing our faces to gray, bleaching our clothes to nondescriptness, hiding our anxiety and making us seem brave. We weren't the only ones to hang out there. We didn't even invent it. Chard's brother had been doing it for years, and lots of kids before him. Back in the kick-the-can days there were kids lounging on cars and against the streetlamp, talking, and if you believe my mother, doing God knows what.

We didn't do anything, and, for the most part, we stayed away from the other kids.

That night none of my friends were out, which shouldn't have surprised me, given that we had been forbidden to see one another. The only kid there was a boy who lived four streets over, in a newer development, one of the ones that they plant in a farmer's field and call "country living." All the houses are massive and are built around the same four or five designs, customized to fit the owner's taste, which means some have a sunroom in back, while others have a three-car garage as opposed to a two-car garage.

This boy was friends with Chard's brother and usually didn't want anything to do with us younger kids, but tonight it was just him and me at the corner, so he tolerated me.

"Where's the rest of you?" he asked.

I hadn't thought I was that obvious when I looked around for Chard or Jason or Kates. Even Kyle, although he was grounded because his mother had found some girlie pictures printed off the Internet under his bed.

"Just me," I said.

He pulled a pack of cigarettes from his coat, opened it, and offered me one.

I tugged my sweater's sleeves over my hands and shook my head no.

"Cold?"

"Couldn't sneak down and get my jacket."

"Right," he said, nodding at my house, his right eye all crinkled up to avoid the smoke. "Party tonight."

I glanced back at my house, with the row of fancy cars at the curb, and shadows moving across the squares of light splattered onto the grass. Not a curtain in the house was pulled. "You don't have big to-dos to hide who's there," Mom would say, if she could figure out why she did anything.

"Just some people my mom works with. Boring."

"So why aren't you there?"

"I can't behave."

"I'll bet you can't." His smile made me uneasy. In two seconds he had his arm around me and was guiding me away from the lamp, toward the darkness.

I ducked. "I'm too cold for this," I said.

"That's what I want to fix. Come on. Just a bit of snuggling. You're growing up real fine."

His hand was on my breast, and God, did it tick me off. I smacked him.

Which was a mistake, because he belted me back.

I staggered back toward my house, my lip pulsing and swelling under my fingers.

"Don't dish out what you can't take," he said, drawing on his cigarette and leaning back against the post.

"Ditto," said a voice from beyond the circle of light. And before I recognized it, Chard had chopped him on the neck, snapped his wrist in a swift, wrenching movement, then dropped him on the ground. "Don't come back to this corner again," he whispered. "I'm growing up real fine, too."

The kid said nothing, just groaned and struggled to his feet. He looked as though he was thinking of coming after Chard, but his hand hung limply at his side, and, despite his larger size, he would have lost. So he left.

Chard looked at my face, then took me to his house to put ice on it while we stood in the darkness of his yard. He helped me concoct a story to explain my obvious fat lip, then walked me home and gave me a boost up onto the kitchen roof so I could get in undiscovered.

That was Chard.

I never did ask him what he was doing out that night.

━━━

Turns out this new girl in my English class is going to be a bigger pain than even I could imagine. She doesn't take hints, and now my mother is in on the act. Mom has started pushing me to get involved in school, join some group, organization, club, clique, or team. Get some friends again, even dates. Not that girls fall into the latter category.

As part of this campaign, she searches my clothes and backpack, looking for clues about what I'm up to. I caught her in my room last night with her hands in my still-warm pockets. I'd dropped my jeans on the floor and gone to the bathroom. I returned, and what do you know? Mom's got her hands in my pants!

"I'm going to do a load of laundry," she said, not a hint of red on her face except her lipstick, which hadn't worn off yet. It was probably a new kind that is completely smear proof and needs turpentine or something to get it off. Anything for the perfect look.

So what has this new girl started doing? Dropping notes, little want-to-get-together-sometime? notes, through the air vents of my locker.

I usually chuck them in the nearest trash can, but yesterday she was watching me. Actually standing at her locker farther down the hall and staring at me. So I glanced at the note, written on this pastel paper, saw that it was more of the same old stuff, then wadded it up and stuffed it in my jeans.

I didn't look at the girl, just turned around and went the other way, thinking I'd find a trash can before class. But the bell rang, and since I already have two tardies and one more will mean a note home and I don't need that kind of grief, I bolted for class. Ran right past her, too. She didn't blink. Just watched me go with this dorky look on her face like she couldn't figure out why I wanted to avoid her. Or if I was.

Of course, I forgot all about the note.

And guess who found it wadded up in a ball in my jeans pocket?

At least she didn't read the note with me standing there.

She pulled her hand out of my pocket when I came back into the room, slung the jeans over her arm, and said, "Any other dark clothes in your hamper?"

"You're standing right next to it. Look."

She opened her mouth, then clamped it shut again. Marge's command to tolerate a little sarcasm on my part was obvious in her face. She spun around and searched the hamper. I strolled to my desk, sat in my chair, and watched. She found a pair of socks and a T-shirt. She did the darks yesterday, and the pile of folded clothes still lay on the floor next to my dresser.

She straightened, thanked me, and walked out.

I chewed my pencil and waited, and sure enough, she was back in about two minutes. Long enough to have gone downstairs, read the note, and walked back up. I'd be willing to bet she just put the clothes in the laundry room hamper and didn't even stick them in the washing machine.

"This was in your pocket," she said from the doorway, the note waving in her outstretched hand.

"Throw it away. I don't want it."

"You might."

"I don't."

"You should be doing more socially."

"Just admit that you read the thing and get on with it."

"Is she a nice girl? Is she in your grade? Who are her parents?" (The real point to her questions.) "Why don't you call her? Or write her a note?"

I just kept saying, "Yeah, yeah," and doing my homework until she gave up, sighed, and closed the door none too quietly behind her.

God, where is my luck?

Oh yeah. I forgot. My luck is always bad.

Aimee was queen of the elementary school I transferred into in third grade. She decided who was invited to slumber parties and kick-ball games. She was the person to know. Of course, I didn't know her, and I didn't know, as I sat and watched everyone catch up on their summer vacations, that she was the girl I should get to know.

I just wished I could change my clothes. I looked like a mini-lawyer with a dark skirt, ruffled scarf, white blouse, and loafers. My hair was slicked back tight against my head and gathered into a French braid at my neck.

None of the other girls had their hair like that, and most of the girls, Aimee included, wore leggings or jeans and big comfortable tops that they could play in. Clothes my mother didn't think were suitable for school. But after a day of standing off to one side and watching every kid snicker at me and listening to every boy planning to get a peek up my skirt or comparing me to a teacher, I decided to do something about it.

Of course, in third grade your resources are limited, so what I did was quit eating, starting with supper, and proceeding through breakfast, lunch, and dinner the next day. I pointedly dropped my full lunch sack on the kitchen counter so that when Mom returned from her part-time job that was only fifty hours a week, she would see it.

At breakfast the following day, I appeared in my nightgown. "I'm not going to school."

Mom looked up, smiled, and said in this tight, I'm-trying-to-be-patient-here voice, "Yes, you are. I have a court appearance that I can't miss and your father has already left for work."

"My stomach hurts."

"Eat."

"I can't. I don't want to."

"Well, you should."

"If I do, will you take me shopping and let me buy whatever I like?"

"Ah, a little negotiator, just like Mommy!" She seemed so pleased, but I didn't know what she meant. Since she was happy, I figured I was on the right track. "If you get dressed and eat a bowl of cereal, I'll take you shopping after school."

"And let me buy whatever I want." It was not a question.

"Right, darling. Now, I have fifteen minutes to get out of the house, so you'd better hurry up."

So I did.

That day at school, I studied the girls' clothes for name brands and styles. I knew by then who was boss and who was nerd, so I focused on the cool girls. Then I took my mother on a nice–nice shopping tour, which meant as long as I was nice and let her talk on her cell phone, she let me buy whatever I wanted.

She still does it. Only now she brings her laptop along and sits outside the store, giving me money, checks, or credit cards and waving at any store clerks who question my right to use them.

———

Marge tried a new tact today. She gave me some of those corny psychobabble tests to see how I'd do. I tried to get the answers wrong, or at least in the realm of crazy, but nothing I said phased her. She just added another session with me every week. Pretty soon I'll be living with her.

Which Mom should like. Then she'd be free to pursue her career and not have to come home to my sad-sack face every day.

Mom thinks she's so quiet when she and Dad are talking in bed. She couldn't be quiet if someone told her the moon would go off course if another decibel of noise came from the Earth. She'd probably argue with the person, then explain, very nicely mind you, why it was his decibel of noise and not hers that made the moon veer off from planet Earth for the rest of eternity.

Anyway, they were talking about me.

"She's doing fine," Dad insisted. "What do you expect?"

"A few dates once in a while. A girlfriend or two."

"Would that be wise?"

"Really!" I heard Mom roll over. I could almost feel her jerking the covers off Dad. I wondered if he hung on for dear life and warmth to his share of covers, or if he let her have them all, kind of like he did in almost every other part of their lives. "She's not a monster," she said.

Interesting, I thought.

"I know that," Dad said. "I just thought she might not be ready to share her life after what happened. She's lost a lot, you know."

Rah! Rah! Rah, Dad. You couldn't have done better if you knew I was listening.

"Haven't we all?" Mom said. "She needs to make some friends. She needs to get out."

"Take her to the movies. Take her shopping. Take her wherever girls and their moms go so she can meet some friends. School is obviously not enough, and it's still early in the year. Maybe when track season starts—"

"Easy for you to say," Mom said. "You don't have to go

with her or watch her eat. God, if she would just eat her food instead of pulling it to pieces and examining every bite for whatever it is she's not eating anymore!"

"Give her time. She'll get over it."

"Maybe we shouldn't have moved. Maybe we should let her talk to her friends."

Now there's a thought. Me going to school with all the people I'm legally forbidden to see. Wouldn't that be fun? And I'll bet there'd be lots of guys banging down my door for dates, too. God, Mom.

"She's not allowed to talk to them, remember?" Dad reminded her, not so gently. "And their parents don't want anything to do with us either."

"What a mess." I could almost hear her sigh. But I only imagined it. She was probably flipping through a legal brief by now and only half listening to herself. She wasn't even trying to listen to Dad.

"It'll get better," he repeated.

Turn yourself off, Dad, I wanted to yell. You're stuck. But that would have ruined any chance he had of winning. I wanted to believe, like him, that things would get better.

———————

The first time Chard called me JK, he had gotten the prison/psych ward guard to let him in as my brother, even though there was no brother on my list of allowed visitors.

"How did you get in here?" I asked, sliding back in my chair to see him better.

"Bribes."

"Money?"

"I took back a few of Mom's new purchases. This time for cash."

"She's at it again?"

He nodded. "Listen, JK," he said.

But I couldn't listen with him calling me that. "What?" I knew what the papers were saying, and I couldn't believe he would bring that crap in here.

"Jack, or rather Jane—"

"Shut up!" I clamped my hands over my ears and ran to the door leading back to the prison.

The guard looked through and wagged a finger at me, like I didn't know I was breaking the rules.

"Let me out!" I kicked the door.

Chard reached me then, slipped his hands under my shoulders in a very unbrotherly way and tugged me back to my seat. I don't remember what else he had to say that day, and he never came again.

Aimee's parents, the soapbox-preaching, far-right Christians, are divorced. Her mother wasn't like that at all, but her stepmother was, and she was the one who raised Aimee. At least from fifth grade on. Her mother had her own set of problems and wouldn't or couldn't—depending on how charitable Aimee was feeling toward her—take Aimee on as a single parent, so she let her father raise her and her brother.

Mistake.

Aimee didn't like her dad. She hated her stepmother, who seemed no worse than any of our parents, so we just figured it was a you're-not-my-mom-and-I-don't-have-to-like-or-listen-to-you thing, which in some ways it was.

But in other ways it was worse.

Her dad joined this new church when Aimee and I were in fourth grade. By then I had solved my clothing problem and Aimee and I had become best friends. The church's preacher was a woman. A supposedly very beautiful and charming and oh-so-wonderful-in-her-insights woman.

Aimee's mom said the preacher was full of crap, and she wouldn't switch churches. She was Catholic, and that was that.

"But you don't even go to church," Aimee's dad said.

To which her mother said, "It would appear that you've started going enough for both of us."

I was staying overnight and thought the whole thing funny, mainly because my family changed churches all the time. As Mom moved up and her bosses changed, we changed churches. By that point, we had already been Methodist, Episcopalian, and Lutheran that I remembered. Dad drew the line at Baptists and Catholics and churches where people talked funny. No one was going to make him have a seizure and dance in the aisle; no preacher was going to whack him on the forehead, knock him over, then proclaim him healed.

So I looked at religion in a rather lighthearted way.

But Aimee's family got serious fast. First her dad joined the church, then he started taking the kids. Aimee liked it at first, until the fights started, and the disagreement I overheard was nothing compared to what followed.

Because as part of his church duties, Aimee's dad started messing with this preacher lady, and Aimee's mom found out in a not-so-nice way. The preacher woman called her up to tell her it was time she stepped aside and let her husband fulfill his destiny. Aimee's mom assumed that meant the preacher woman's bed and told her no way was she stepping aside for another woman, even if she was supposedly possessed by God and the Holy Spirit and whatever else was in her evil little heart.

But in the end she did, and she left Aimee behind.

If there's anyone I'd like to apologize to, it would be Aimee's real mother. At Aimee's funeral she stood up and said she was sorry. That if she hadn't left Aimee with her father and stepmother, none of this would have happened. She said this in the church that had stolen her husband away. That took some courage. (Of course, I only have the newspapers' version of the funeral to go by, since I wasn't allowed anywhere near it. I was, as a matter of fact, locked up.)

I wish she had had a little of that courage back when it mattered. If she had taken Aimee with her, maybe Aimee would have been all right.

Maybe.

—————

"Don't tell me you haven't read the court papers. I know you have."

The clock ticks, and Marge pushes her hair out of her eyes. She was almost dozing when I spoke. I've been giving her the silent treatment for days now—I go six, yes, count them, six days a week now, and this is Saturday—and she obviously didn't think I was ready to move on to the next stage.

But I was. I'd been thinking about the courtroom and all that crap, and how none of it was real. The judge didn't have a clue and neither did anyone else in the room, because Chard and Kates and Kyle and Jason weren't there most of the time. They'd had some teachers talk on my behalf, but no friends. No parent would have permitted that. The only testimony my friends gave had to do with the plan we had put in place the week before Aimee's death, what I said, and what Aimee told me. No character references from non-adults were allowed.

"I haven't read them." Marge sets her pencil down and stands up. "I'm tired of sitting. Want to go for a walk?"

I glance at the clock.

"No one is scheduled after you, and your mother is consistently late. We'll tell the receptionist to make her wait."

"Hah! She'll want to know when we're going to be back, and then she'll leave and return at the newly appointed time. But she'll be put out."

"Do you want to go for a walk or not?"

"Fine."

I lag behind her, surprised at her impulsiveness but not wanting her to know that I like it.

We don't go far, and luckily we walk away from my school, which is close by. When we sit down on a bench at the neighborhood playground, I feel silly and want to go back to the quiet, dim office. The kids' screams and shrieks, the mothers' warnings, the dogs yelping from where they are tied to strollers, the clang and creak of swing chains, and the incessant pounding of feet wear on me.

"Why here?"

"Why not?"

"Because I hate kids."

"You don't baby-sit?" She seems surprised.

"Would you trust me to baby-sit your daughter?"

She looks at me, then glances at the swings and says, "Point taken."

"I have no extracurricular activities anymore, if that's what you're trying to find out. No drama club, no band, no track, no volleyball. Definitely no cheerleading."

"I see. So what do you do with yourself?"

"I come here. I go to school. I sit around home. I work out at home."

"Not very exciting."

"No."

"Do you like it?" She still hasn't looked away from the swings.

"No. It's boring, but I've been told that I made it that way."

She looks puzzled, then nods at two empty swings. "I meant do you like to swing, but I follow your train of thought."

Without a word, I walk over to the swings and sit down, push my feet back against the dirt, rise on my toes, then let go.

I pump my legs. Soon I am stretched out and pulling for more height, just as I had done at my grandmother's years ago. She had an old tree swing that could go higher than any swing I've ever been on. The tree bordered a cemetery, which never bothered me until my grandmother began to die.

Mom hated going to her mother's house, even when my grandmother was well. Then Grandma became sick. The C-word was never mentioned, but even then, at seven or so, I knew. Cancer.

We started going to her house every Sunday afternoon. My grandmother lay in a metal hospital bed that was set up next to her dining room window so she could watch the world slip past. She would smile from her pillow, too weak to raise her head. Mom would sit in the chair by the bed and tell me to go out and play, as though I might catch something if I stayed.

The only thing to play on was the swing, so that's where I headed. The dining room faced the street, and the swing was in the back, so I was out of sight. Not that it would've mattered. Mom was busy reading *The Wall Street Journal* out loud to my grandmother, who had a pile of poetry books and novels by her bed that she had always meant to read. She would stare out the window, her eyes going glassy and vacant as the economic situation of a Taiwanese company passed over her.

I would swing, my eyes going glassy and vacant, too. Over my feet I saw the silent house, peeling and surrounded by flowers going to seed and weed. Beneath my knees, as I plummeted backward to an almost vertical position, I saw rows of headstones tilting this way and that. It was an old cemetery with no new graves. No one visited.

Sometimes, I would lean way back in the swing and drop my head even farther so that the cemetery became sky and the heavens became earth. I would swing back and forth, seeing the house and cemetery sweeping back and forth.

I used to wonder if I let go as I arced backward, would I shoot into one of the graves and disappear?

But I never did. Let go, that is.

One Sunday, Mom came to the back door and called for me. "Time to go," she said, her voice quick, her steps light, rapid.

When I came up the back steps, she said, "Just go around to the car, dear. I'll meet you there."

She did, about a minute later. My grandmother's nurse closed the front door, and we drove away. I waved at the dining room window like I always did, but since she hadn't been able to wave back for weeks, I didn't know if my grandmother saw me.

It wasn't until Dad came home and I heard Mom discussing the funeral arrangements that I found out Grandma had died while I was swinging.

I let myself drift to a stop, my legs dangling near the ground. I don't want to face Marge. Why does everything I do have to bring a flood of memories? I'd like to go back to living and forget everything from before the present moment.

Marge stands when I stop, my head still drooping backward at the end of my arched back, my feet stretched before me, my toes tapping the soft sand heaped beneath the swings. Beside me I see a kid fly through the air as he lets go and jumps. He lands at Marge's feet. He grins and runs off as I straighten, stand, and join her.

Even without the clock's chime, I know that my time is up.

———

"It's right here, so you can't deny it!"

I peer at the papers Mom is shoving at me. It's the school calendar, which I haven't seen since I tossed it on the kitchen counter after my first day of school. Apparently, my mother keeps these things. I nod at the words she is jabbing, then turn back to my book.

"Why don't you go? A dance is a good place to meet new friends. Surely you've met a few kids at school, someone you could call up and ask to go with you—not as a date—but as a friend? Maybe you could introduce yourself to the track coach? We've heard such good things about her, which is partly why we picked this school, for the track team. Then you'd meet some of the other girls on the team before the season starts." She pauses as she realizes that this won't help for this particular dance—unless it is sponsored by the team. "There must be someone you could go with." She silently taps her lips a moment, as if she's running through the list of kids who've been at the house in the last month and deciding whom I should call.

I roll my eyes. Yeah, I want to say. I've met people, lots of them. They walk away when I approach, or more often, they don't even notice that I'm there. All except that little mousy girl in my English class. She's the teacher's pet or something, and everyone avoids her, too. She's the one who leaves the notes in my locker and tries to act like we're the same, but we're not.

I'm not a mousy little girl, sitting quietly in the first row of class, hoping that at least the teacher will pay attention to me.

I belong in the back, slouching in my seat and passing notes to Aimee or Chard or Kates or Jason.

I itch to call Chard, find out how Kyle is, but I can't. My parents are here.

I walk out on my mother midsentence. Pass Dad in the hall as he's coming in, trying to be home at a decent time, as Marge has suggested, so that he can spend quality time with me. Instead, he picks up the mail on the hall table, mumbles something, and doesn't even notice Mom trailing me like a billow of smoke spewing from a candle.

She stops when she sees Dad, whispers to him, but by then I'm upstairs and the discussion of why I won't try to fit in doesn't reach me.

That is until he opens the mail.

"Where is she? Get her down here!" Dad's voice rumbles, starting low and rising. I've hit Dad's weakest point, although I don't know how yet. I must have lied, done something deceptive, because that's how to get a rise out of him. Before, when I was pissed that he failed to keep a promise because of his work schedule, I used to lie. Just to piss him off. But now, I'm not sure what I did to bait him.

"Wait. Do what the psychologist said. Count to ten—"

I can't believe Mom is actually saying that. But I'm hoping it works. I'm too tired for this.

"Maybe there is a logical explanation. Give her a chance to explain—"

But my door bursts open. I hear the clack, clack, clack of Mom's heels as she runs up the stairs. Dad greets me.

"I want to know why you think everyone is going to keep humoring you, playing games with you. We've done everything in our power to help you and this is how you repay us. With lies and deceit."

Mom's hand darts out, lands mosquito-like on his sleeve. He slaps it, and it falls away.

"Don't you know that this breaks your parole?" Papers slash across my nose. The phone bill. "We could have you sent back for this. It is a specific violation of the terms the court laid down for your freedom. Don't tell me you don't know what they mean. I'll repeat them for your benefit." He pauses, but I don't say anything. "The aforementioned defendant shall have no contact nor make any attempt to have contact with the following people in any way—written, verbal, or in person. Jason. Kyle. Katherine. Richard."

He doesn't have the terms exactly right. There were a lot more words, and more people listed, including Aimee's step-mother and father.

I remember the long string of phone calls to Chard's house that only connected with the answering machine. I don't leave messages. They're incriminating. They're a permanent record of a spur-of-the-moment thought, and if you say anything remotely wrong on somebody's answering machine, you can be charged with a crime.

Each call must have been twenty seconds at most. I give the machine a chance to say hello or whatever in the hope that Chard will answer, and I hang up immediately if I get someone other than Chard.

I've tuned Dad out, and I don't even care that Mom is crying. For Pete's sake, they're just phone calls, and obviously I didn't speak to anyone. Since this is Dad's first major blowup over a phone bill, I know she didn't show him the earlier bill with the calls to other kids back *There*. I feel strange, almost breathless, when I think of this. I suspect that her crying now is a ploy to bring him back to reality, but maybe she's tired of fighting too.

I don't say anything to either of them. I haven't told them about Kyle, although they might understand then. They might even do some asking around and find out how he's doing.

"Stupid! Risks everything we worked for," Dad says.

I don't want their help. I won't take their help.

And they don't offer it.

Instead, Dad paces back and forth, and finally stops in my doorway. "You are the most ungrateful child a parent could ask for. Sometimes I wonder if we were right to fight for you."

I hear Mom suck in her breath as he pulls the door closed. It slams on the last sharp sip of air drawn into my mother's lungs.

I wonder where all her fine speeches are now. Where do they go when he gets like that? How can such an argumentative person end up so quiet?

The door opens.

"Forget that dance," he says. "You're not going."

The door bangs shut again.

Mom scurries to the door. As she turns the knob, she smiles a thin smile at me, then darts out, closing the door quietly. "Honey," she says, "I think it might be good for her to get out."

"Where in the behavior plan does it say that? Where is it written that it would be good for her to be with other kids? Was it good for Aimee?"

"She can hear—"

"I don't care if she can hear! It's true! What good did she ever do for Aimee?"

I close my eyes. Waves of doubt shake me. I see Aimee's ever-open eyes staring at me. I jump up and throw the duffel bag at the door. "I hate you!" I yell.

He doesn't respond. He doesn't have to, because he's right. I didn't do Aimee any good.

<hr />

Jason's parents were the parents we all wanted to have. His dad was so light-hearted, never bothered about anything as long as his cars were selling and his business was thriving, which they always were. His mom never cared about what vanished from her cupboards or how many homemade pizzas we ate. Her counters were piled with papers and things that didn't seem to mean anything to anyone and were never put away. An ironing board stood in her living room, and she stood behind it, ironing heaps of laundry while watching her soaps.

Aimee and I despised soaps and made fun of Kates whenever she admitted to having seen one. Still, we thought Jason's mom was cool because she never noticed and never cared.

Jason's mom let him have a dance party in his basement for his seventeenth birthday party. He was the oldest of us. The first to drive, the first to date, the first to party. He had started kindergarten a year late because he was deemed too far behind in his fine motor skills. I never knew who was behind that decision. Neither of his parents seemed worried about anything, let alone his fine motor skills, but it was okay by us. He was dark-skinned and dark-haired, and he grew a mustache early. Sometimes he could even buy liquor because of it.

Jason's basement, even decorated, wasn't much to look at, just some flashing yellow construction lights stolen from the side of the road, his stereo system set up in one corner and the snacks in another. Crepe paper and rock-and-roll posters hung on the walls. There was an odd assortment of chairs, including two old school desks with the seats attached. When I walked in, I longed to sit down and play school. I imagined that if I opened the desk, there would still be some Play-Doh stashed there, probably dried up, and if I popped the neon lid, the smell of childhood would spill out and make us all forget the dance.

Instead, I saw Chard and Aimee talking and joined them. Whenever we leaned close to talk over the roar of the music, I sniffed his scent of aftershave lotion and sweat as it mixed with Aimee's more refined perfume and the pasty smell of makeup. More kids, mostly from our neighborhood, arrived, and Aimee drifted away, her cast covered in a psychedelic sock with toes stuffed with potpourri, and her crutches decorated with crepe paper stolen from the ceiling. She had a few weeks yet until they cut off her cast, but judging from the way her crutches never seemed to touch the floor, I figured her leg was mostly healed.

Chard watched her go, a small smile on his face. "She's amazing," he said as Aimee managed a moon walk between crutches.

I stiffened and waited, holding my glass—no alcohol, Jason's mom was not that cool—and running a finger around the rim. Any minute I expected Chard to head toward one of the clusters of girls around the room, but he didn't.

He stayed with me.

And he talked only to me.

And when a slow dance came on and everyone groaned, and the few people who had been dancing stopped, Chard took my hand.

"Someone's got to start this," he said, and he led me into the center of the floor.

Soon everyone was pairing off, and still we danced, jostled against old paint easels and a minipool table. Chard didn't let go of my hand or my waist—he pulled me tighter. I smelled the orange shampoo in his hair and thought, Jhirmack, and felt his shoulder tense under my hand when I moved it.

That's when I admitted Aimee was right. Everything was about Chard with me.

I only hoped he felt the same.

———

That girl followed me outside today at lunch. Most kids stay inside the school, except those who need to smoke to make it through the day. Even they wouldn't have me, although I've never tried.

Usually, I head for the track and sit on the bleachers and watch nothing. Sometimes someone is running. Sometimes a coach is there, usually the girls' coach. She's not a teacher, unlike my old coach, who taught a watered-down biology course and some of the health courses. This one's apparently part-time and only coaches the girls' track team. She's a not-so-twiggy thing—probably a reed when she was in school, but now she pushes a stroller. Somehow she gets away with bringing her kid to work, but then again, it's not track season yet. She probably won't bring the baby to practices or meets. At least, I hope not.

She's always in sweats—probably trying to get back into shape. She runs occasionally, but most of the time she's inspecting the equipment, like it's all new to her and she's not sure how to set it up or if it's the real thing. She rattles and shakes the hurdles and stomps on the high jump mats. She makes lists, but I don't know if they're lists of what she wants repaired or replaced, or lists of what's okay.

She never has to watch her baby because she attracts girls—team members, I'm sure—who scoop the fat thing out of its stroller and bounce it around and generally act goofy. They're baby-sitting, I guess. Something I've never done, nor do I have any desire to start now. I'm not that desperate.

In fact, I couldn't care less if I ever have contact with these people. I just want to be alone, like I'm not alone at this school anyway. But I mean Alone—someplace where people aren't trying to ignore me at the same time they're staring at me. Someplace where, when I look their way, people don't glance away and talk faster. At least when I caught this coach-slash-mom staring at me a few days ago, she didn't turn away. She waved. Then she went on watching me for a minute, almost as if she was waiting for me to come down and see her. Instead, I swung my legs over the seat backward and leaned against the railing—I was sitting on the top row. When I turned around again, she was poking something into her baby's mouth and talking with another girl. I got the creepy feeling they were talking about me, even though neither looked my way. So I left.

But as I left, I felt empty-handed for the first time since school started. Seeing the coach and feeling like she was discussing me brought back a lot of memories. Track events, particular races—some failures, but mostly successes—came flooding back. Dad came to most of my meets and rattled off in a too-loud voice a constant stream of ego-boosting, that's-my-girl monologues. Even today, he has the state championship trophy on his desk in our office. I threw it out after Aimee's death, and he saved it. Probably so he could prove he had some parental bragging rights left.

Mom came to a few of my meets. It had to be a big one for her to sneak out of work to watch me race, and even then she was late and missed my events more often than not. Once, right after I'd had a torn ligament repaired, she appeared in the stands during practice. She'd been convinced that the coach was not giving me enough time to heal just so I could run in states. She even thought the doctor and physical therapist were rushing things. It's amazing no one gave in to her, but I guess my legs convinced them. Mother Dearest wasn't convinced, though. There was more than just this one state competition in my future, and she didn't want the others screwed up. Dad kept agreeing with whoever was talking. He wanted me running, but he could see Mom's point, too: Don't screw up the future for a brief time of glory.

That day, I had been practicing my starts, and the coach finally told me to run the whole track to get the kinks out (or, more likely, to see how fast I could still do the 400 meters). I popped out of the blocks and rounded the first turn, taking it tight on the inside and not letting myself really rip it, because I planned on letting it out on the far turn. I didn't want to burn up too much too early, and I honestly didn't know what I had in me anymore. The stretch was hard and my breathing was off, but I wasn't whipped yet, so I came into the turn and opened the stoppers.

When I let it out, I heard a whoop that wasn't me or my coach. Something in royal blue and black bobbed up and down in the stands by the line, but I never focus on the stands when I run, but that day I did, just to confirm it was her. When I saw the excitement on her face, I concentrated on my running, ignoring my surprise and the warmth in the pit of my stomach. I stretched longer, pulled harder, and heard her answering whoop as I increased my speed.

"Still got it, kid!" the coach yelled. He clicked the stopwatch as I zipped past.

I dropped my hands to my knees, puffing worse than I did at the first practice of the year, but knowing I'd done far better than at the start of any previous season.

"Knew you'd never lose it." He thumped my back, which made me spit, and said, "Stand up and trot. You know better than to let your muscles cramp up." He was already finished with his praise.

I stood, almost expecting her to be there, shaking my hand and trying to hug me. Instead, I saw her back, straight and tall, but with an ease to the way she held her shoulders, heading away from the center of the stands. When she'd nearly reached the end of the metal bleachers, someone tapped her. She turned and smiled. She looked lit up, like she was in a play or something. She thanked the old custodian who had stopped her as if she had been the one running. Dad wasn't the only one who enjoyed bragging.

I shook my head and trotted back to my coach. Let her eat up the glory. She didn't want anything else from me anyway.

She never admitted to coming that day, and I never admitted to seeing her. If I had, I would've had to ask why she hadn't come down to the track to see me. If she had, she would've had to admit she was proud of me. At least with Dad I knew what he valued: my trophies, good behavior, an occasional hike or bike ride with him, a joke well told. With Mom, I had to guess.

The next time I needed to recover from a minor injury— the ligament thing was the only big injury of my cut-short career—she took the opposite tack: she pushed the doctors to lessen my time away from the track. Maybe she felt she could be competitive now without being too pushy.

Who knows?

Anyway, today, this pain-in-the-ass girl followed me out there and sat beside me. Offered me half a candy bar and talked about little things, didn't even notice when I replied in monosyllables or dropped the candy on the ground beneath the bleachers. Let the rats or mice have it.

After a while I looked at her, I mean really looked at her, and I couldn't figure out why everyone avoids her. She has beautiful hair, even if it's brown, which she wears pulled back into a long loose braid, and strange hazel eyes that suck you in if you gaze into them. They make you wonder about her. I know that look. The slight pucker between the eyes and a tension around the mouth, like she's holding in a story that's eating at her insides. She wants to tell it, but she's at a party and it would spoil the mood. I want to hear her story, and I almost ask. Almost fall into her trap of friendship. Then I pull myself up, reminding myself where friendship has led me before.

She's little, too. I feel big beside her—tall, broad, strong, even masculine, because in every way she's smaller than me. And I'm a size eight at my worst, a six at my best, almost a four right now, but that's heading out to another kind of worst. But I'm tall, like Dad, and I have a piano player's hands that stretch forever when I spread my fingers. It pisses off my mom that I refuse to practice and take advantage of them. Teacher after teacher has told her that I won't learn to play if she tries to force me, and several have called me a mule on a good day, but she still keeps trying to find some- one who can teach me to play.

The girl's name is Hope. She assured me that her parents aren't religious nuts, they just liked the old-fashioned ring to the name. Also they had waited a long time for a baby, and the name fit what she was, their hopes.

Imagine having to explain your name every time you introduced yourself, or at least feeling like you had to. I'd hate that. At least Mom and Dad didn't screw me up there.

But Hope wants to be more than bleacher pals. She's mentioned seeing a movie together or something.

How lonely is she? I've heard people whispering about me. The kids here all know my history, the whole gruesome story. Why is she courting me for a friend? She can't be that lonely, can she?

I sometimes wonder, when I'm home alone, what it feels like to let it all go, let it all fall away. At some point do you change your mind but know it's too late? Is it like going to sleep? Is it the relief some people imagine? Or is it the hellfire and damnation that everyone used to believe in?

Even the concept of heaven and all that spare time to do nothing but be good and sing sounds like hell to me. I mean, what do angels do? Is God really so musically inclined that He makes every dead person who was halfway decent play a harp for all eternity? It sounds vindictive to me.

"You there, Father Saint. You look like a good man. Come here and play for me."

Maybe heaven's just a huge corporation filled with kiss-ups like my mom. People who have always been happy doing what other people tell them to do.

But if that's so, where does Jesus fit in, or Buddha, or Muhammad? They weren't exactly order takers, now were they?

So what do I believe?

Do I believe that my best friend in life is rotting in some inferno? Or do I believe that she's nothing now? Or reborn as a frog or cow somewhere?

Should I try to join her when things here seem a bit too much like hell to stand?

But I have the same problem Aimee had for a long time. Even though the jail and psych ward had me on suicide watch, I'd never be able to do it. I'm lacking in the department that gives a person the ability to make such a final decision. I can't even decide whether I want to eat supper most days. How can I decide on whether to live or die? That's how a person like me, with no reason to live in this world, manages to go on, even with a straight-edged razor that I took from Aimee one time when she was telling me The Lies.

Or what her family called The Lies.

She had been holding the razor open in the palm of her hand while she talked. Occasionally, she switched hands, pausing over each wrist and making quick, small slicing motions in the air before dropping the razor into her other open palm.

I had stared at the razor's glinting light the entire time her words pattered about the room. The incredible yellow-and-white room her stepmother had designed for her as a consolation prize for losing her mother. Aimee had matching sleigh beds so that when a friend stayed overnight, i.e., me, there was a bed for each. Her room was that big.

But she hated it.

Once I found her sleeping on the couch in the basement. She claimed sleepwalking. I figured she had done just that, or at worst, my snoring had driven her from the room.

But it wasn't her dislike of the room that led her to the basement—if you believe a dead girl's lies.

It was someone at the door.

Chard and I never really dated.

Everyone assumes otherwise. We were a couple, and I would say to this day that there is no one else in this life for either of us, but still, I never wore his ring, jacket, letter, or any other sign of his affection. We danced at parties, close. We necked from time to time, and one hot night we even made love.

It was during Aimee's incredibly klutzy period, right

before it came to an end. She still had her cast on, and her hair hadn't grown over the scar on her forehead from the car accident, but she was up and about mostly. But not that night. That night she couldn't go out. She was watching her little brother or something. And Kates, Kyle, and Jason were all on real dates.

Me, I was home moping. Wishing the phone would ring, but knowing that if it did it would only be Aimee complaining about having to baby-sit again, or my mother's boss forgetting that it was Saturday night and that even she sometimes took the evening off.

But when the phone rang, it wasn't either of them. It was Chard. Hanging out at his house alone in that big rec room, no brother, no parents, and grounded so he couldn't leave.

But I could go over there. Grounded means you can't go anywhere, not that you can't have friends over, so over I went.

He had lit a fire in that big fireplace, mostly because it was a basement and it was cold, and he knew, with his parents in the "paying off bills" stage just then, that he couldn't turn up the heat.

We started with Ping-Pong. I beat him two games to one, so he suggested pool. He won two games, and I won none. Barely even sank a ball.

He flopped on a black leather sofa and stretched out. "I'm bored."

"Thanks."

"No offense," he said, rolling on his side so he could see me standing by the pool table, still holding my cue stick.

I bent down and tried to sink one of my many balls that remained on the table, feeling uncomfortable with his eyes on me. I scratched.

"Come sit down." He was chuckling and flicking through channels. He stopped at a music video station. "Want something to drink?"

"Sure," I said, thinking about a Diet Pepsi, but he brought wine coolers. Now, there's a drink. Malt liquor, but called wine. And it tastes as smooth as grape juice, so you can drink a bunch fast.

Which we did. By eleven, we were drunk—giggling, wrestling, drunk. And I had forgotten about curfew, Aimee's promised call, even about whether Chard's parents would be home soon. Heck, I had forgotten I had a brain. I was just one big hormone tickling a boy I'd known a long time and to whom I was very attracted.

And he was no better.

So when we started kissing, then petting, neither of us had the brakes that we always had used before. And in the middle of it all, but before we got undressed, Chard's mother came downstairs.

Now it was dark, but she must have known that Chard was not alone. The television was playing, and there were more bottles on the end table than he could possibly consume, and we hadn't actually been quiet, though we weren't making a whole lot of sense. So when she came downstairs, I was embarrassed and tried to slide out from under him. But Chard held me fast, leaning harder on me, squashing me into the cushion.

"Get out!" he said.

His mom stopped. "Chard?"

"Get out, Mom!"

"Are you all right?"

"I'm fine, Mom. Leave me alone." Not *leave us alone. Leave me alone.*

She hesitated by the stairs, then turned on her heel and went back upstairs. I half expected to see his dad next. After all, if you are told by your almost-sixteen-year-old son to beat a retreat, you'd send down your stronger half. But she didn't. Maybe she was into avoidance. Surely her shopaholic behavior showed she was avoiding everything—her problems, the bills, what it did to the family, why she did it.

But I wasn't thinking clearly about it that night. I wanted to ask him how he managed to make his mother obey him, or if he thought he'd get in trouble later. But he was kissing me and touching me, and I didn't think of making him promise to love me forever before giving in. I figured I didn't have to, that this was all the proof I needed, and that everything was going to be perfect from now on. So after only a brief hesitation at third base, Chard ran home, and I let him score, all aglow with the knowledge that at last he loved me.

So there was a bit of monkey mambo going on, but it was just that once, and he apologized for it later.

Apologized.

Zing. Zap. Sizzle. Fry.

Watch all my dreams die.

What a poet I've turned out to be.

Aimee and I used to have this talk, a kind of game when we were drinking, about what we were most afraid of.

"I'm afraid of nuclear war," I once told her.

"Naw, that's sissy stuff. Never going to happen anyway. A random country or leader going nuts, dropping a bomb on us and frying half the world, that could happen, but all-out war? No. It'll be a mess afterward, but I'll bet we'll all just fry, and there'll be nothing much left to worry about, besides the basics—eating, sleeping, surviving."

"Terrorism," I said next. "That's a good one."

She nodded and took a drink.

"Sitting in a café in Paris after finally getting out of this hole," I continued, "and having a bus bomb go off outside and you're blown away."

"Or you're only partially blown away," Aimee said, "and you have to live with some horrible disfiguring injury."

"Or a madman arrives at the post office at the same time as you do and poof! You're history. Gone postal."

"Very funny." Aimee never liked it when I joked.

"How about acid rain? Leaking toxic-waste dumps?"

"Good. But what about an earthquake that sets all that stuff loose in the environment?"

"Meteor striking Earth?"

"Tornadoes?"

We giggled and drank. Then both of us started singing "Over the Rainbow."

"That used to be my favorite movie," Aimee said when we were out of giggles. "I'm not afraid of witches anymore, though."

"Speak for yourself." I laughed. "I'm certain there's one casting spells on me. Explains my lack of a date for the Sadie Hawkins dance again this year."

"You never ask anyone."

"No. I don't. I don't think anyone would say yes."

Aimee stood up, pulled me to my feet, dragged me to the mirror. "Look at you," she said, tilting my head back. "You're beautiful." There was no humor in her voice.

"Growing old," I said. "Turning into my mother. Having

dysfunctional kids that kill their classmates in a frenzy because I won't let them hang out at the video arcade."

"What?" Aimee dropped my chin.

"I'm afraid of growing old."

"Of dying?"

I hesitated. "Yeah. Of dying."

"I'm not." She raised her glass to the girl in the mirror. "To dying." And she drained it.

"Not funny, Aimee." I flopped back on the bed, refused to drink.

"It happens to the best of us." She shrugged. "Now a rapist, that might be something worth being afraid of, don't you think? Especially a date rape or one of those pill-induced comas that allow some pervert to take advantage of you and you never know it. Just find out a couple of months later that you're preggers and don't know how. You'd be hailed as a new virgin mother. Aren't you afraid of that?"

"Cut it out."

"What's the matter?"

"Just cut it out. Let's talk about something else." Because things had gotten too close to the truth.

I was late with my period. I was drinking, exercising, not eating, cooking myself in Jacuzzis so hot they almost killed me, but I didn't tell anyone, because my mother would have taken me for an abortion. Aimee would've helped me either way, but she would have advised an abortion. And Chard? He would have felt trapped, but he would have allowed it—either way, he'd have gone along.

It didn't matter, though, because I started bleeding that night. A bottle of vodka between us and two hours in Mom's Jacuzzi with Aimee did it, and if she knew, she didn't say a thing. If there was even a thing to say anything about.

After all, I was only a couple of days late, and that's if I was keeping track right.

And I didn't say a thing about Aimee's death toast.

Because she'd already asked Chard to the Sadie Hawkins dance without telling me. He was the one who told me he'd accepted. Might as well. Maybe he'd get her in bed, too.

———

That wasn't fair, that last entry. Chard only told me about the dance when I mentioned that since I didn't have anyone to go with maybe we could go together. Just so neither of us were left out.

But he wasn't left out.

"Aimee asked me two days ago. Said it was me or Kyle, and well, you know who'd win that one. Hands down." He flicked his head back and grinned.

I felt my stomach squeeze. I blamed it on cramps. He'll never get it, I thought. "How are you getting there?" I asked. Chard was still fifteen, he was young for our grade, but his birthday was in a week. Still, it was highly unlikely that his dad would give him the car. He was still holding a grudge over the shopping-mall incident, even though Jason had driven that time, and legally, too.

"Doubling with Jason and his date."

I sat there. There was still Kyle left, if I wanted to see Chard and Aimee together.

But I didn't.

I stayed home that night, listened to Mom lecture me on taking chances, asking out guys, if need be. She knew it was the Sadie Hawkins dance even though back then she never read my school papers. My mother never went to PTA meetings either. Never, God forbid, volunteered. Yet she always knew when there was some important social event coming up, and if I opted out, she'd nag and nag and nag. Like a cat in heat who sits by the door yowling until she drives you crazy. So you throw the thing out into the night, hoping she lands on her feet and doesn't have too many kittens as a result, and swearing that soon you'll have the stupid thing fixed.

But there was no fixing my mom.

As if finding the right social niche—or was it the right boyfriend?—was the be-all and end-all of life. This from a woman so power hungry and addicted to work, she took part of the bar exam while in labor with me and began working a week after she came home from the hospital. Thank God she had a mother who would watch me until the nanny parade started.

———

Marge was determined to find out about my life today, so I told her about bikini waxes with my mother and the time she dropped me at Aimee's when we were just becoming friends. While working on a trial, Mom forgot where I was—literally. She'd been so preoccupied with her case that she didn't pay attention to which house was Aimee's, so she couldn't come pick me up. She lost Aimee's number, too, so she had to wait for Aimee's parents to call and ask what was up.

It was Aimee's real mom who called, not the judgmental idiot Aimee's father later married. When Mom explained what happened as if it was perfectly normal to be so involved in your own life that you don't even notice where or with whom you dump your kid, Aimee's mom asked if I could stay overnight. She never commented on the appropriateness of the whole thing.

I was dumbstruck. Not that I wanted to go home, just that she didn't chew my mother out or report her to some agency for neglect. Aimee and I had a great time that night. It was the first time I had stayed at Aimee's house, and since it was before the matching sleigh beds, we slept on the floor and traced messages on each other's bare backs, our nightgowns wadded up under our armpits.

The next morning, Aimee's mom dropped me off at my own house early so I could change for school.

It was a fairly typical example of my childhood. Marge just nodded and asked, "How's your appetite? Your mother tells me it's not the best."

Like that matters. I ignore her question, but try to remember if I ate breakfast today. I can't remember, so I roll my eyes and sigh. I lean forward so my shirt bags out in front, but Marge isn't looking at me anymore. She has a different agenda. "What's happening at school? Anything new?"

As if that's possible. "Nothing."

"Something must be happening. You go to school every day."

"I said nothing is happening."

"You talk to no one at school?"

"Teachers don't even call on me, I have such a weird reputation, so no, I don't talk to anyone." I didn't say that I had gotten a note from the track coach welcoming me and my record-breaking legs to the school. Did I want to get together some time at lunch to discuss trying out for the team? Obviously, my mother had been busy making social contacts for me.

Marge wrote something down. Probably *antisocial* or *withdrawn*. Maybe *combative* or *depressed*.

"So no one talks to you?"

That's when I figured out she knew about Hope. What was she worried about? That I was going to kill Hope or be a bad influence on her? This was nuts, and I shut up.

Hope has been pestering me every free moment of my life for the last week. She even called me at home, but I hung up on her. Then I saw her at school when she had no idea I was around. She was with this guy, a cute guy actually, who was holding her elbow in his big hand as if he had no intention of ever letting go.

I slipped closer and caught a glimpse of her face. It was white and angry. There was more emotion on her face right then than I'd seen since she started to follow me around. People swirled around them, but no one much noticed what they were doing or saying, except me. Nosy me.

"I just want to know if you're okay. If you're ready to—" The guy stopped. "I never meant to hurt you, if I did, you know. I broke up with her a long time ago. I should never have dated her. My dating her didn't have anything to do with your—"

"Don't flatter yourself," Hope interrupted. Her voice had the edge of a samurai's sword. Even I felt the blast of air from her swing.

"Hope, I think you're the best. I just can't deal with it when you get like that—"

"You don't have to," she said. "No one does. No one even cares. I don't even know why you're risking talking to me. You never did before—or should I say since? Aren't you afraid some of my stigma will rub off on you?"

"Hope, I—"

"Let go or I'll scream, and then everyone will think you did have something to do with it, now won't they?" She jerked her arm, and he let go.

His face was sad, helpless, lonely as she walked away. He stuck his hands in his pockets and shuffled toward me for three whole steps before someone joined him, and then everything about him changed. His face took on the cocky look of the jock of the school. His back straightened and his shoulders lightened as though someone had stopped pushing down on him. His hands came out of his pockets, and his feet actually cleared the floor.

"She's the same frigid bitch, hey, David?" his buddy said. "Why bother? Let her slice and dice herself if she wants. I know a few girls we could have Saturday night."

"Yeah, right." He looked up and stared right at me. "No thanks. I already have a date," he said. He walked toward me, and I thought for an instant he was going to say something, but he had blown his cool enough talking to Hope. He wasn't going to risk talking to me.

His shoulder brushed mine as he passed, and he did it on purpose. Was it because he saw me watching, or because he knew Hope had been trying to become my friend? I felt the warning in his touch. Hope wasn't as alone as she had made it seem.

I also know what "slice and dice" means and wondered how I had missed the signs. I seem to be a magnet for these people.

But I want to be left alone.

Which is what I told Marge. Nothing more, nothing less. Then I stood up and went out to sit with her receptionist, who glanced at me in surprise. I barely heard the bell chime fifteen minutes later, signifying that my time was up. Mom was late again, so I went out and waited on the steps for her, watching the next patient arrive, breathless and anxious and late. He was over forty, which isn't what I expected since Marge specializes in miscreant kids. But then, as I sat there rocking back and forth and pretending I liked sitting on the steps of a shrink's office, another person sauntered up. He had the same slow pace as Chard, the same height and muscle mass, the same way of holding his hands not quite all the way in his pockets. But it wasn't Chard. Unlike Chard, who has gorgeous black curls, this kid was bald. He had a huge tattoo of a snake coiled and ready to strike on the back of his head. "Bite me" was tattooed beneath the snake.

Now he's more Marge's style, I thought as the door banged shut behind him. I wondered if he had chosen that spot for his tattoo because his hair would grow over it when he was done pissing off whoever it was he was pissing off. My guess was that it was the harried man who had gone in before him, but you never know. Mothers are good to tick off, too.

I wish I could tick off mine some more. But she's never around.

I waited an hour for her to show before I gave up and walked. I just wanted to take a shower and pretend to do my homework in my room. Alone.

———

I wasn't the only one Aimee confided in. Apparently, she told all of us some version of The Lies, Kyle included. That's what Chard told me during our latest phone call.

We've found a new way to communicate. Our parents have no idea. We use these phone cards that you can find or buy all over the place. I've gotten them off the backs of cereal boxes and under the labels of bottles. Dad picks them up as gifts at conferences and at clients' offices, and he leaves them lying around. I've bought them at stores like Walmart when I don't have any of his freebies handy. Chard mostly buys his.

So now we can talk, not long usually, but enough. We have a schedule of when it's safe to call. Since his mother now works as a receptionist to keep her out of the stores, build her self-esteem, and make money to pay off her debts, he's alone afternoons. I'm alone then, too, obviously.

"Saw Kyle today," he said this afternoon.

"How's he doing?" We don't leave many pauses. They're too expensive.

"He's in rehab. They diagnosed him as a borderline personality and alcoholic."

"Saw that one coming."

"Drinking much yourself?"

"No. No one to drink with."

"Ditto. I don't even see Jason anymore, let alone go out partying with him. He works for his dad now, when he's not in school," he says, and his voice sounds cut off, alone.

"No girlfriend?" I ask, unable to stop myself.

"Like who? I have a stigma, too."

"Not much of one."

"Everyone blames me. They say I should have stopped you or seen it coming."

"Did you?"

He hesitates, and I think about the Sadie Hawkins dance when he had all night to see it coming.

"Did I try to stop you or did I see it coming?"

"Well, there was nothing to stop, so did you see it coming?"

"She told me."

Now I hesitate. Told him what? That she was going to kill herself, or the reasons why? The Lies she told me, and I told the court? The ones no one else had supposedly heard from Aimee even though we were all so close, as the DA pointed out. The Lies that wouldn't have sounded like lies if Chard had admitted to hearing them, too.

"She told me," Chard repeated. "And she told Kyle. I don't know about Kates or Jason or if they just heard it from you at the end. But Kyle told his shrink that the fact he didn't stand up for you is partly why he did what he did."

"So now I'm responsible for him, too?" I can't take this. I don't need it, and I can't handle it. I almost hang up.

But I don't.

"No. He's responsible for you, don't you see? We should have told during the court case. Maybe if I had told my dad or mom, they would have made me testify about it."

I snort. Because I'm crying. Because I doubt they would have let him testify about The Lies. Because I doubt the DA would have let the question be asked, if anyone had told him about it. Because I'm crying so hard I can't talk.

"Are you okay?"

And I know that he means more than am I physically okay. More than whether I can handle this information. He means, how am I surviving? Can I survive alone? And I go from feeling completely cut off, from knowing that the people who loved me best in the world could have helped me and didn't, to knowing that they are worried about me, are sorry, and want to make amends.

I am not alone.

Aimee is. I believe that. We were not there for her, and now she's alone.

But I'm not.

The phone card cuts me off before I can answer Chard, and I don't have any more around.

He must not either, because he doesn't call me back.

We weren't angels, but we weren't really bad kids either. We didn't carry weapons. We weren't part of a gang, didn't gang bang or date rape (guys), didn't turn tricks (girls, but I guess guys could, too), and we didn't do the major drugs. We drank, yeah, but who didn't? We liked to hang out, but that wasn't so bad, though sometimes we ended up doing together what none of us would have done alone.

As developers continued to swallow up the woods and fields in our area, the houses they built grew exponentially. We didn't live in a poor neighborhood, but my house was a hovel compared to those going up a few twisting roads away. The roads for the fancy houses weren't connected to our subdivision, probably because the owners of these palaces didn't want to be associated with the more common folk who already lived here.

For us common folk, the mansions brought a new form of entertainment: voyeurism. It started out as a sort of hobby, encouraged by Jason—he loved anything to do with a power tool—but enjoyed by all of us. In the afternoons and evenings, we'd walk around the construction sites to get some idea of what the houses would look like inside as well as out. We'd watch from the almost roads when the workers were there, and pick our way over broken cinder blocks and scrap wood and shingles to peer in still-stickered windows when they weren't.

But it never occurred to us to actually go into one of these houses until the big man wearing a yellow construction hat and a suit and toting rolls of blueprints under one arm showed up. I guess he was the developer, but we dubbed him Suitman. He was the guy with the money and the vision, and his vision didn't include six punks waltzing around his development causing trouble and stealing things.

Suitman showed up one afternoon in midsummer, when the days were longest and hottest and we were the most bored and wearing the least amount of clothing. Which should have told him we were decent kids. There wasn't a tattoo or body piercing (beyond ears) on any of us, but our bare midriffs must have riled him up good.

Suitman marched down the driveway, his face all sweaty and purple, as if something was threatening to blow, and said, "You kids don't have a right to be here. Get out of here before I call the cops."

"City going to plow these streets?" Kyle asked. He had an uncle or something who worked in Sanitation, but why he was asking that right then, none of us knew.

"Yeah, so what?"

"Then this is public property, and you're harassing us." Kyle glared at the man a moment, then smiled at our surprise. "He can't do a thing," he whispered. "Let's walk around the block a few times, just to piss him off."

So we did, and every time we passed the house, the workers looked tenser and Suitman angrier. He had his cell phone out, but Kyle must have been right because he never made more than one call, which was probably to his lawyer, who I hoped wasn't my mom.

After about the fourth time around, the rest of us were getting bored. "Let's go swimming someplace," Jason said.

He'd been hanging his head every time we passed, so I figured he was embarrassed.

"My vote, too," I said to help Jason out.

"Fine with me," Kates said.

Chard spun around and started walking back toward the entrance of the subdivision, and we all followed.

Everyone except Kyle, that is. "Come on," he said. "This is fun."

"Nah," Chard said. "It'd be more fun if we could take it a step further and make him really explode without getting into trouble, but it's a stalemate like this. It's boring. I'm going swimming."

Kyle stood a moment in the middle of the road. I could tell from his slumped shoulders that he thought we were giving in. He was losing face.

"Come on, Kyle," I said. "Think of some other way to annoy him."

He looked over his shoulder, then at us. We hadn't stopped walking, although I was walking backward, watching him.

"Is he coming?" Jason asked me hopefully.

Kyle hesitated, then smiled a slow smile and started after us. He had thought of a way to get back at the guy, although we didn't hear about it until ten that night.

"It's not really breaking and entering," Kyle insisted. "We'll just go in and take a look around. We've always wanted to see what the houses look like on the inside, and I know the perfect house. The big contemporary one, you know—the one that looks like a barn. Aimee, you wanted to know what they were building over the garage, remember?"

Aimee shook her head. "This is wild, Kyle. What if we get caught?"

"We won't. There's no one living up there yet. They still don't have the windows in the garage of the house, so we can just climb in. We're not going to do anything but look—and get a little buzzed." He pulled out a bottle of schnapps and dangled it. "There's more by the gates."

"Which will be locked tomorrow, once they find out about this," Jason muttered. He clenched his hands. "I don't know—"

"You're right. The gates will be closed and locked tomorrow, and you'll never get to see inside any of the houses. But not because of us," Kyle said. "I saw a couple of guys working on the gates today. They didn't finish, but there's no guarantee they won't be done tomorrow. Then you'll never know what the houses look like inside. Come on," Kyle pleaded. He ruffled a hand through his blond hair. "It's more interesting than what we usually do."

"Do you mean drinking?" Kates asked. "But you plan on doing that anyway." I couldn't see her face, but her body had a worried posture—arms clutched tight across her stomach, head tilted to one side and turned away—like she was looking for a way out. All it would take to make her say no was one of us speaking against it.

"Yeah, but it'll be better," Kyle said.

Kates still hesitated, but Chard didn't. "Fine," he said, giving in abruptly. "But we get caught and I'm creaming you, Kyle."

I looked from Aimee and Chard to Kates and Jason, unsure of what to do. Then Aimee stood up. "Let's go if we're going to do this. Luckily the moon's out, because we can't use flashlights."

Kyle faltered in the doorway, then glanced at her.

"You didn't actually think you could walk around some-one else's house in the middle of the night with a flashlight, did you?" Aimee stared at him.

"Well—"

"You're lame," Aimee said. "We gotta go with him or he'll be in jail tomorrow."

Kates unfolded her arms and slipped up next to me, like I'd be any protection. Jason stood up slowly and brushed off the back of his jeans. He seemed to be hesitating, but the siren song of the houses and the knowledge that Kyle was probably right about the locked gates proved too much for him. He fell into step at the back of the group.

Which was how we ended up in a multi-million-dollar home, touring it as though we were thinking of buying it. Even Kates got into it. She designed wallpaper for most of the rooms and cut down the stone used for the fireplace because it was too countryish for the rest of the house.

The window wasn't as big as Kyle had made it sound. It turned out to be a basement window that wasn't in place yet, and we had to slither like snakes to get in. We made Kyle go first so he could break his neck and then serve as a mat for us to land on. He, the bonehead, went in head-first and did do something to one of his wrists when he landed. The rest of us slid through feetfirst and avoided that problem.

We toured the house from the bottom up, and while we never became boisterous, with each new floor (there were three after the basement), we grew louder in our praise or criticism.

"What were they thinking, sticking three skylights in a bedroom?" Kates said at one point. "Who'd be able to sleep past sunrise?"

"Kyle," Jason, Chard, and Aimee said. I slugged him on the arm.

"Probably," Kyle admitted.

We explored the bar and then a spiral staircase that went up to a loft lined with shelves. "Library," Chard said.

"Boring," Aimee added.

But Jason was touching the shelves and the carved woodwork trim. "So smooth," he murmured.

"Going to be a carpenter?" I asked him.

"Nah. Dad owns the dealership, you know."

Enough said, I thought. But I just nodded. Long before I finished elementary school, my parents started talking about, alma maters and degrees and what I'd become. I ignored them, but I knew what Jason was going through. I guessed his dad, despite his good humor in front of us, was leaning hard on him.

"You could do it for a hobby," I offered. "Dress up your home with lots of stuff like this."

"It takes years to get as good as this," he said. "Not likely to happen."

He turned away and headed for the stairs, where Martha Stewart, a.k.a. Kates, was pronouncing that the loft should be paneled and Aimee was arguing for green paint, rich dark green. "A very healing color," she said, sounding surprisingly prissy.

Jason snorted and pushed past them. I followed.

We ended the night in a huge, empty Jacuzzi, each sitting with a bottle of hooch and our feet pressed against each other and the sides of the tub. It was a tight fit for six pairs of teenage feet.

After some uncomfortable shifting, we invented a game called Who's Got the Giggles and tried to make somebody laugh with our feet. Whoever laughed had to tell some deep, dark secret or do a dare. A modified version of Truth or Dare, but no titillating sex questions allowed. This was all friends.

When Kates laughed, Chard asked her, "So when did you swap bodies with Martha Stewart?"

"Last Wednesday." She then ran her sandaled foot up Kyle's leg, which almost sent him out of the tub. We counted that as a laugh, although it was more hormones than laugh. "What do you want to be when you grow up?" Kates asked.

"A photographer," Kyle said. He was serious, too, but we all laughed at that one, knowing what his favorite magazine was and guessing what kind of photographs he planned on taking.

"Will you be taking your photos in unfinished houses, late at night?" I asked.

"I didn't laugh. You guys did," Kyle said. "I get to pick one of you and ask something." He glanced around the circle. Aimee was tipping back her bottle of hooch. "Aimee, want to be my model?"

She dropped the bottle into her lap. "I didn't laugh," she said.

"Sure you did," Kates said, but she didn't sound convinced.

"Nope. Didn't," Aimee said.

"Well, answer a question anyway," said Chard. "You haven't been asked all night. What do you want to be when you grow up?"

We'd all gotten that one, and any one of us could have answered for any one of the rest. But suddenly we all real-ized, even me, that we had no clue what Aimee's answer would be. Jason's "business owner," Kates's "nurse," Chard's "engineer," and my "anything not dealing with law" were as obvious as our hair colors.

But what would Aimee say?

She took another long drink, then lowered her bottle to chest height and looked at each of us. "I don't plan on growing up," she said. We froze into statues and stared as Aimee went on. "So I don't plan on working at anything." She chugged the rest of the bottle.

"A housewife?" Kyle said, the surprise and doubt obvious in his voice.

"Naw," Chard said, shifting closer to me, mostly so he could get a good look at Aimee's still face. "She'll marry money and travel the world in a yacht, but she won't be a housewife like what you're thinking."

"No kids. Definitely no kids," Jason added. He tilted his bottle back in a quick motion, then clasped it between his legs. He kept his head down.

Aimee, her drink finished, leaned across and took mine. "Definitely no kids," she repeated, looking me in the eye. "And definitely no growing up either." She finished my drink, too, then leaned back and belched. "This is as boring as drinking at home, and now we have to crawl out a window and walk home buzzed, which is much, much worse. Let's go."

Without waiting for the rest of us, she clambered over the edge of the slippery tub. "A lousy spa. A self-serving, ugly spa," she said as she walked toward the stairs. She was referring to the room we were in, which was the room over the garage she'd been so curious about. "I'd have thought they could have figured out something better to do with the view than that." She didn't even try to keep the disappointment from her voice.

When Hope approaches me the next day, I don't back off. I know more now, and I understand. I'm still not sure I can deal with her. Something inside of me is saying, Try. Try to help, while another part is screaming, Run! Run away as fast as you can! But one look at her deep, lost eyes, and I stay put.

It's hot, but she has a long-sleeved shirt on. Even so, I can see the scars. Ugly, shiny white ridges rising out from under her green ribbed-cotton sleeves. Marge material if ever I saw some, I think.

She sees me looking and pulls the fabric down.

I look away as though she had asked me to, hoping her embarrassment means she's not going to bring up what she tried to do or our shrink connection. She follows me silently to the bleachers, where we sit side by side. Today the coach spots me and nods. She doesn't have her kid. If Hope weren't with me, I might've joined her, just to see how much she knows about me. She obviously knows something about the state championship or she wouldn't have sent that note, but what else did Mom tell her? Does she know about the murder charge? For that matter, what do any of my teachers know about me?

But then, as we watch, some workers and the macho guys' coach show up, and the men parade around the track, noticing things the girls' coach had discovered earlier. The guys' coach acts like he's in charge, like he was the one who got the men down here, while she hangs back, just watching. When they march past the high-jump pads without stopping, she joins them over at the long-jump pit. She says something, the men nod, then write something in their notepads. I'm surprised they're worried about the track this early in the school year, but it probably has to do with requesting the necessary equipment before all the budget money is gone.

Satisfied, the coach goes back to the bench, where she glances my way again.

She probably thinks I feel comfortable here or I want to meet with her. But she acts like a zookeeper with a wild animal—afraid to approach me for fear I'll run off. Maybe she's right about my running off.

But I have Hope with me today, so there's really no chance I could go down and introduce myself. I came with Hope and I'll leave with Hope, but I nod at the coach and even smile—like an idiot—when she glances my way again. I imagine running with her as my coach, but the baby-sitting thing gets in the way. I can't see it happening.

Hope eats her lunch without noticing any of the activity on the track. I don't eat. I just wait.

"All right," she says finally, as though I'd said something first. She stuffs her yogurt container and sandwich bag into a paper sack. She stares at her hands. "I don't know how you heard, but yes, I did try to kill myself last Christmas. My dad found me and rushed me to the hospital. I was in the psych ward for a couple of weeks. I behaved myself, so I came home early. I'm fine now."

"Really? Then why are you seeing Marge?" When I see her blank face, I realize that "Marge" means nothing to her. It's my pet name, and no one else's. "A shrink? Over on Fifteenth Street. The one with the strange timer?" I don't say her real name, but still Hope gets it.

She nods.

"Told her about me, hey?"

"Well, I'm supposed to talk about everything."

"And you do?" I can't keep the sneer out of my voice.

She winces. "I'm trying to get better."

"Then why do you want to be my friend? It wouldn't have to do with a certain—unearned, mind you—reputation I have, would it?" I bite my lip. I just opened the door for her to ask questions.

"I'm done with that," Hope says. Her voice quivers. "I never want to do anything self-destructive again. I was so scared once I'd done it and the blood started coming. I just sat on the toilet and let my arms hang in the sink and watched it and cried. I couldn't think of how to undo it without getting into a huge mess. I didn't think I'd pass out and my dad would hear me. At least I hadn't made too much of a mess when he broke in. Most of the blood went down the drain."

"How considerate," I say, but I'm seeing Aimee, hearing Aimee, and I don't want to.

She pushes her sleeves up, and I see the scars like minia-ture mountain ranges on the white, paper-thin skin of her wrist. She went for the blue veins everyone can see, and her squeamishness probably saved her. The scars were wide, but I doubted if they were deep. How come these people who want to die are so squeamish? You'd think they wouldn't care a rat's ass about pain or what the person who finds them is going to see, but they do.

I turn away. "Pull down your sleeves."

She draws her sleeves over her wrists and stares out beyond the track field. I glance sideways at her and there are tears, two great walloping tears racing down each side of her face. Yeah, she's doing just fine. Really. I start digging for a Kleenex, even though I know I don't have one.

"How did she do it?" she whispers, wiping at the tears as

they dangle on her chin. She doesn't look at me, but she might as well have taken a knife and ripped my gut open.

"None of your damn business." I stand. Why am I here? I think of Chard and Kates, Jason and Kyle, and wish for their company, but all I've got is this screwed-up wound-picker who won't leave me alone. She needs help, but I don't have any to give. I turn away.

She grabs my hand. "I'm sorry. I shouldn't have asked. I thought it might help for you to talk. You obviously don't talk to—to Marge, did you call her?"

Is she serious? Talk to Hope? What does she know about Aimee? "Let go of me. Now."

She drops my hand, and I see her eyes darken and fill yet again.

"And you want me to believe you're done with all of that. She was my best friend! I'd give anything—your life even—my life definitely—to have her back."

"Then why—"

"Who has the strength to wonder why? Don't ever ask me about her again."

"But the papers said everyone was calling you JK for Jack Kevorkian—"

I spin around so fast I almost fall off the bleacher. "Don't ever call me that again. Ever! Do you hear me? Ever!"

People on the track are staring, and I don't look at the girls' coach, afraid of her reaction to my outburst. Hope lets a tear slip down her cheek before she puts her hands up and wipes her eyes. I could smack her, punch her in the face, but then I see what she can't hide from me. I've seen it before—the desperation, the agony, the need to find a reason to go on, and the inability to find it. It feels like Aimee all over again, but without the final act. There's still time, I think. Hope still has time.

I sit down, deflated. I try to think of what to do, what I can offer her. I feel the coach's eyes on me, and I sigh. I squeeze my trembling hands under my crossed arms. "Let's find a more pleasant topic, okay? One that doesn't hurt us both. We'll go to the damn movies on Friday if you want, but it has to be a comedy. It'll get my mother off my back, and you could use a laugh. I'm not allowed to drive. I suppose you know where I live?" I say it all fast, before I can back out, before my contempt returns. I remember David's face and I think of what Hope must have been like. I focus on that person, the one who's gone but could come back, the way I wish Aimee could come back.

She nods, straightening and wiping her face again.

"Seven sound good?"

She nods again.

I stand and walk away, knowing I should have left without wavering, without turning back to her, with everyone staring, and my scream still echoing.

But I can't. I couldn't then, and I can't now.

———

It's not until I get inside the school that I realize I've been followed. At first I think it's Hope, but when I turn around, it's the coach. I turn away. Let her make the first move. She's probably just chasing a state record anyway.

"Have you known Hope long?" is what she says, and it takes me by surprise.

"Long enough," I say. "But I suppose you've known her

longer. Don't tell me she runs track. It might end your plans to get me on the team."

We're standing near the locker rooms, and she tilts her head and walks down a side hall. "No, she doesn't run track." She unlocks a door with her name—Karen Walker—on it, and I smirk.

She sees me smile and says, "I got *Walker* from my husband. He thought it ironic, but I didn't."

I watch her move whistles and papers off her spare chair. Is this a local thing, where everyone feels compelled to explain their names? Or is it what I'll do later on, when people start with recognition at my name but can't remember why? I'll change it before I'll explain it, I decide as she waves at the chair, which still has a towel draped over the back.

"Your mother dropped me a line, but I knew you were here well before that."

"Who didn't?" I ask, but I sit. "Why did you ask about Hope?" I don't want to talk about me.

She frowns as she adjusts a picture of a baby who looks oddly like a puppy that hasn't opened its eyes yet, all wrinkled skin and anguished struggle to make sense of a world where so much brightness invades even closed eyes. Both of the baby's fists are up around its head, as though it's trying to block the light. Karen sees me looking and smiles. "My daughter. That's just a day after she was born." She holds the picture out to me and I look closer but don't take it or even comment. She hesitates, then puts it back. "All the teachers are aware of Hope's situation, just as we're aware of yours. We're trying to help her."

I wonder if she is implying that they want to help me, too. "She needs help," I say.

"Yes."

Again there is a feeling of omission, but this time it has the flavor of someone waiting for more. "When does the season start?" I ask.

"No one is running officially, but some girls train all year in a club I run. We're very competitive here, and when the season starts in the spring, the rules for being on the team are very strict."

A warning?

She's looking at me closely now, too closely. I uncross my legs so my kneecap doesn't look so bony. "How good a shape are you in?"

"Decent shape." I haven't run since Aimee died.

"Decent shape?" She lets it hang.

I don't bite. "Do you have to be in this club to be on the team?"

"No."

"Good."

"Why?"

This is worse than Marge's. Still, no one ordered me here and I could leave any time I want, but I don't. I like the sweaty smell, the feeling of teamwork in this room. I feel comfortable, and that's dangerous. "Are you a shrink?"

"No. Phys. ed. major with a minor in social work." She grins. "I'd have to fatten you up before you could compete again. You know that, don't you? Maybe I'll just save all the snacks I shouldn't be eating and pass them to you. And we could start getting back in shape together." She grabs a roll of flab on her belly and flops it up and down. "It's up to you. I'll start when you do."

I nod, then the bell rings, and I hop up. "Gotta get to class," I mutter and dart out the door.

First I break down and say I'll go to a movie with Hope, and now I'm invited to train with the track coach. I'm becoming a socialite.

———

So now Mom is happy because I'm going to a movie. And Dad is considering letting me take my driving test. I didn't tell them about talking with the coach. I don't know where that will lead yet, so I figured I'd better not mention it.

I couldn't tell them anything about Hope's parents, though, which was a strike against me. Telling them that they're older parents who so desperately wanted a child that they named her Hope when she finally arrived isn't the kind of information they want. I also saw no need to mention her suicide attempt.

We're on our way shopping, Mom and I, when she brings up what happened in her overly casual way, which means she has a point but that she's not going to make it right away. "We haven't done this since before we moved." She peers left then right at a stop sign.

Not true, I think. We did this when I was out on bail and needed courtroom clothes, the kind of clothes that say, I'm a good kid, a smart kid with great parents, and of course I didn't do this horrendous thing. Oddly enough, my mother kept all those clothes, as though she thought they might be needed again, even though I wouldn't be caught dead in them outside a courtroom. There's a vote of confidence for you.

What I say is, "No, we haven't." Dutiful daughter speaking.

"Does it feel good finally to be making friends, again?" There's a pause between the words *friends* and *again* that makes me want to puke.

But I say—without gritting my teeth, mind you, "Yes," and stop there. The less said the better, right?

"You don't still miss them, do you?"

"Them?" I want to hear her say their names, see if she can say all of them.

But she gets around it. "Your old friends."

I snap. I shouldn't, but I do. "You can say their names: Kyle, who just tried to kill himself; Kates, who's being sent to boarding school; Jason, who's God knows what; Chard, who's doing okay on the surface; and Aimee, who we both know is dead."

"Stop it."

"What?"

"Stop trying to ruin every minute we spend together."

"I'm not. I just want you to face what happened and not pretend like it didn't."

"I am. I asked if you missed them, didn't I? And I want you to see that you're making new friends, who can be just as wonderful and important to you as they were."

Message delivered.

"Thanks," I say.

What I think is, You still can't say their names, and you can't even comment on Kyle or Kates and especially Aimee. You can't even remember which is which, can you?

But I don't say any of that. Marge has been lecturing me about getting along with Mother Dearest, on not saying everything I think the instant I think it.

We shop for two hours, and Mom buys more things than I do. Things for me, that is.

"Wouldn't this look cute with your pink jeans?" She tosses a shirt I've barely seen over her arm. "Try this on." She swings a sleeveless sundress at me and tells me to pick out a T-shirt to wear under it. I come out in the floor-length sundress that makes me look too long, too skinny, and flat-chested to boot, and Mom says, "It's perfect. Add that to my bill."

She doesn't look at me. I know that now. I had picked a T-shirt that didn't match the dress on purpose, just to see if Miss Color-Coordinated-Every-Waking-Minute-of-Her-Life would notice. She didn't.

I tell the clerk to change the T-shirt for a blue one and hand back the putrid orange I had been wearing.

We eat in the nicest restaurant in the mall and manage to discuss fashion or politics the whole time.

Then we head home. What is it about cars and adults? Why do they always want to talk to you whenever you finally have a little peace and quiet and can block out your life by peeking in the windows of other people's homes and listening to some music?

"I'm glad we got along so well today."

She should add that Marge told her to do this. Or Dad. Or someone else who understands kids, like a partner in her firm.

"Where are you going Friday night?" she asks next.

"I figured I'd let Hope pick. I don't have any idea where to go."

She's quiet a minute. "Does she have a boyfriend?"

I see the cute guy, the jock who actually has feelings. The one who used to be her boyfriend, but isn't now. "No."

"Too bad. You could double-date with one of his friends sometime."

"Stop writing my life for me, would you?"

"I'm not writing your life. I'm wishing you would take more of an interest in it." She sighs and takes the plunge. "You seem kind of depressed lately, that's all."

"I wonder why," I mutter, then add, "Only lately?"

"I just thought that if that psychiatrist isn't working out, then maybe we should try another one before—"

She stops and has enough sense to blush.

"Before what, Mom? Before I kill someone? Or are you afraid I might kill myself?"

Her blush deepens, and I see the perfect tips of her manicured nails digging into her palms as she curls her hands around the wheel. She's so tense I don't think she could make a required left-hand turn. It flashes into my head that if I jerked the wheel, we'd probably both be dead, and for an instant this suicide-murder interests me.

But then it doesn't, and I can't even say why. It just doesn't.

We drive home in silence.

———

There is nothing unusual in our silence, though. At home, I hear the clatter of a keyboard or the shuffling of papers in my mother's room. Sometimes I hear the whirl of her exercise bike. When she's in the kitchen, I can't hear her—not that she's particularly quiet, just that it's too far from my room.

And I don't go out of my room often. Today, after our "bonding experience" at the mall, Mom says, "You didn't show me those essays you wrote. You know I want to review them before you send them out." This is her way of reminding me that I still haven't finished filling out my college applications. I've filled out the routine questions, and so far none has asked how many people I've killed or been accused of killing, so I guess I can get in somewhere.

I had planned on going to the state university. We had all

intended to go there, but now I doubt my application will even be considered. The university is located, after all, not too far from where I used to live. *There.*

But mother of mine insisted that if State U was my first choice, I should apply. She probably knows or guesses that Kates and Kyle won't go there. Jason is going to the local community college until he figures out what he wants to be, or so Chard said last time I asked.

Chard is a question mark. I don't dare ask him much about the future in our brief conversations. There's so much other stuff to talk about. Besides, I'm terrified that his future won't be mine, can't be mine. Or that he's thinking of someone else. So I keep the conversations focused on gossip and how his mom is doing (better, therapy is working, and she's starting to talk back to his dad and act more like a real person and less like a slave). Sometimes he tells me about Kyle, but information has been almost nonexistent lately because Chard isn't allowed to see him while he's recuperating. I'd like to know whose bright idea that is. Why, if he's depressed, is he being kept from his friends? Sounds like a familiar treatment, though.

So I applied to State U, because, with all of Mom's prodding and insisting, I actually started to think there was some hope I could get in. Now Mom's telling me to fill out backup applications. Does she know something I don't?

"It's better not to count too much on one school," she says. "There's so many to pick from." She flips the pages of *The Insider's Guide to the Colleges* and stops near the end. "What about Yale?"

"Do they have my major?"

"What exactly are you planning on studying?" Her voice is carefully neutral because I've mentioned majoring in creative writing, and she's made it clear how she feels about this journal. Besides, I can't make a living by writing. At the very least, I'd have to have a backup career, like lawyer or dental assistant.

She glances up from the book. "What about advertising or marketing? Or you could try public relations."

I snort and take the book out of her hands. "I'd be a public relations nightmare in any PR firm."

She opens her mouth and then shuts it, but I know what she was going to say. The court will close my records when I turn eighteen, and no one will ever know about my past again. That is, those people who don't have memories won't know about it.

"I have a few applications of my own I'm filling out." I want to add, "Besides the Harvard, Brown, and William and Mary applications you gave me," but I don't. I've been reading up on colleges in the school library when I'm supposed to be researching my science paper. I finished that days ago, which isn't surprising considering that I don't have anyone to gossip with, so I actually do my work when I'm there. I figure, if I fill out her applications, she might pay the application fees for the schools I'd really like to go to, like Northwestern in Iowa or Middlebury in Vermont.

"You do?" She shifts in her chair and keeps her jaw from dropping by clenching her teeth.

"Yeah." I don't tell her which ones. Instead, I walk out of the room, leaving her guessing. She doesn't need to know everything.

So now I'm in her office to type up yet another college essay with a stupid theme about the innocence of youth or the value of goals in your life.

If they only knew. Aimee had goals, didn't she?

The computer is still on, so I sit and flip through the documents, opening and closing several while looking for the other essays I've written. I want to pilfer some winning lines from them. I never remember what all those strings of letters and numbers attached to the cryptic abbreviations mean, so I have to open the files to find out what's in each. My beloved mother knows I am computer-challenged, so she locks the files that she doesn't want me to see.

At least, she usually does. But I'm staring at a letter addressed to the VP of Admissions at State U, and it's definitely not from me. I don't even think it can be from Mom. It's sappy and not at all condescending.

Dear ——

I'm a little confused by the recent letter my daughter received from your institution. [*What letter?* I think.] I understand that you have a lot of students applying to your school and you can't possibly take all of the worthy applicants, but my daughter is an exceptional student whose record in track alone should earn her a scholarship to the best colleges in the country. She, however, wants to attend your school, and while I know there was some negative publicity during the past year [*that's putting it lightly even for you, Mom*], she was acquitted of the crime of which she was accused. She has matured a great deal in the last year, and I'm sure that a recommendation from her new track coach could be sent to support this.

We've been friends a long time, ever since I was lead attorney on the Gilmore case, and I feel you should reconsider your rejection of my daughter. We are prepared to send her without a scholarship or financial assistance, if that is necessary or if it helps her admission standing.

Please call me so we can discuss this further. I hope that Debbie and the kids are doing well. Your oldest must be . . .

I can't read any more. It's all family drivel anyway.

So I've been rejected, and Mom is pulling strings to get me in. Am I such a loser as that? Will I get in anywhere?

I look at the applications in my hands, then drop them on the desk. I'll leave the letter open on the computer so she'll see it when she comes in. Serve her right to know I've read it. Serve her right if I never fill out another application in my life and live forever under her roof.

Talk about hell. Who would I be punishing in that scenario?

I go upstairs. The essays can wait.

I want to puke.

———

I never met my grandfather—Mom's father, that is. Dad's parents are little withered-up, prune-colored golfers who live down in Florida. Last time I visited them, they cut the visit short after I broke out of the gated community, hit the mall, found a guy to tool around with for a while, then tried to get back in without a pass. It caused a big ruckus and resulted in a tightening of the rules regarding grandchildren visiting, at least that's what Mother Dearest says. It was during the summer between freshman and sophomore years. If I could've taken Aimee along like I wanted, I wouldn't have been so bored, and none of it would've happened.

My grandparents haven't invited me again.

My other grandfather bit the big one before I was born. He might have even missed his daughter's admission to law school, but I'm not sure. Mom doesn't talk about him. His memory lives in a single, framed collage stuck on the staircase along with all the collages of me and Mom and Dad and their vacations. Grandpa smiles out of his frame right next to my first-grade picture, the one where I'm almost toothless. He would have appreciated that stage in my life, since he owned and coached a minor-league hockey team in his spare time. In his full-time job, he was the banker and investment guru of our town, the man to know, business man of the year, grand pooh-bah of all the right clubs.

All the pictures show him with his hockey team or at other sporting events. Not one shows him getting one of the big awards he supposedly won. I've never seen them, either. Maybe Mom doesn't have his trophies and plaques, or maybe she doesn't want to be reminded that she hasn't won any. Like I said, she doesn't talk about him. Mom even forgot to mention him when I did a family tree in fourth grade. I had to ask Dad about him.

But in this collage, Mom's always with her dad, usually shaking some sports hero's hand.

God, my grandpa wanted a boy. It's obvious in one picture especially. He's standing with a nephew and talking to a goalie. Mom, who's about nine years old, is in the background, holding a doll. I can't imagine her playing with dolls. Even in the picture she's holding it wrong. She's clutching its arm in her fist, and the doll is twisted and dangling with its dress riding up and a bootie missing.

And Grandpa? Well, he's got his hand on the little boy's shoulder. His eyes are lit up, and he's grinning.

Mom's standing off to the side, looking at the doll as though she wants to punch it or decapitate it. There's a hint of my lovely mother's determination in her face. She looks as if she's deciding something then and there, and it's important, too.

In the next picture, she's maybe ten, she's wearing a pleated wool skirt and a sweater, and is carrying a blazer over one arm. She looks like quite the little businesswoman. You can see her breast buds poking through the material, and all that blond hair, even braided and tied up in a bun, is shimmering golden. No one is noticing her new, businesswoman side.

Grandpa never did notice it. His car went off a bridge late one spring night. No other vehicles involved, not even a deer in the road to explain it. Dad said it was a massive heart attack. His partner destroyed the business shortly afterward. According to Dad, there were hints that the problems had started even earlier, with my grandpa, and the partner just made things worse. But there was enough money left from the insurance to pay for Mom's college and Grandma's little house by the cemetery, so he couldn't have screwed up too badly.

But I wouldn't know for sure because, like I said, Mom never talks about him much.

I think that must be what it's like at Aimee's house. There's a big hole in the conversation where she should be, and no one says anything about her.

But I'll never know.

Court orders.

———

"So what do you think makes people kill themselves?"

I'm halfway through another stare-down session with Marge. Neither of us has said anything beyond *hello*. She jumps as though I had dropped a real bomb instead of a figurative one. She coughs and sits up straight. She had probably forgotten all about me and was daydreaming or rattling off in her head all the things she had to do that night.

"Well . . ." She pushes back her hair, which is busting free of all its bobby pins in the humidity. The air conditioner is broken, so it's sweltering in the office, and Marge has taken off her suit coat and is sitting in only her thin, camisole-like shirt. I'm wearing oversized bibs and a baggy, long-sleeve T-shirt, not exactly suited to the weather, but Marge has started eyeing me in a way I don't like, so I'm hiding. She's assessing my body fat, I'd say, but she should talk. She's only about a size six herself.

"Well?" I prod.

"That depends on the person."

"What about Hope?"

Her head jerks up. "How did you—"

"Your fishing expedition last time about who I talk to made it perfectly clear that someone had mentioned me. So how about it? Why did she try to bite the big one? Her life seems perfect. Doting parents. Beautiful hair and eyes. Handsome boyfriend. Even if he is an ex, he still talks to her. She even gets good grades and made the National Honor Society. So confess. What drove her to it?"

"You know I can't tell you." She closes her eyes as though tired of my voice already.

"Then I'll ask her tomorrow night. We're going to the movies."

I see a slight wavering of her gaze as she tries to meet my eyes, which tells me she's afraid of this meeting. Afraid for Hope, afraid of me.

How did I get here again? Someone tell me how I

became a monster. Did anyone ever explain to that guy who woke up one day to find he was a cockroach why he deserved to be a bug?

"Should I cancel?" I ask, raising my eyebrows and lowering my eyelids slightly to let her know that I know what she's thinking.

"No." She says it slowly, then shifts in her chair. "No, it might be good for both of you. To be friends. You can learn about the consequences of suicide from her."

"Like I don't know those already."

"And she can learn how to live through anything, even with a bad attitude, from you."

So she sees me as a survivor—one with a bad attitude, but a survivor nonetheless.

But I'm not living. Living would be stealing Dad's car and driving back to Chard. Picking him up and taking off somewhere. Driving until we ran out of gas, or abandoning the car someplace and running in the opposite direction. Living on the street if we had to, just to be together. Feeling again what I felt when he touched my breast, the sudden turn of organs never felt before, the clenching and releasing, the shiver of anticipation and fear that I feel even now as I think about his hands on me.

But none of that is possible. For one thing, Chard is hours and hours away and I don't have my license. I've never even taken the driving test. Plus my folks, who trust me completely, don't exactly leave the keys lying around.

And none of that is possible because I am a survivor, not a true liver. There's a difference, and I long to point that out to Marge. A survivor lets life happen to them. They suffer through, get by, go on. A liver takes hold of life, shifts events into what they want, plows over obstacles, does things, gets into things, and if things crash, a liver can end them.

Like Aimee. She lived like that. For a long time, though, she couldn't plow over the obstacles in her path. I helped her do that. And I helped her end.

But Marge doesn't see that. No one does. They see only me, the survivor. And they think I'm worth saving.

Am I? For a second, I wonder if I might be worth it. I think of Karen's challenge and what it would be like to get back into training, to feel the satisfaction of breaking last week's time, of finishing first again, of hearing the crowd roar for and not against me. To feel like someone thought I was worth the effort, even if it was only so they could have another trophy for the display case.

Then I see Aimee again, stomping around school in one of her many her casts, laughing through it all, and I know I'm not the one who should have been saved.

The bell tings, and Jack and Jill go up the hill to fetch their pail of water.

As they fall down, I look at Marge. She's staring at my wrists. I stick my hands inside my bib front to hide them. I'll bet she's going to call my mother after I leave and set up a meeting to discuss my physical well-being. Like there aren't enough mental problems to talk about. I might as well drag this session on a bit longer. "You didn't answer my first question, you know," I say into the silence the bell has left.

"Time," she says.

"Why do people kill themselves? In your vast experience with juvenile cases you must have some idea of why."

"Next time." She sighs.

"There could be no next time, you know. I'm asking now."

There's a polite knocking at the door.

"Go the fuck away!" I scream.

Marge jumps up. I've never sworn before. I've never screamed. But I have to know this, and I have to know it now.

She circles her desk, goes close to the door, but stops just short of opening it. "It's okay," she says to the door, then turns back to me. "I think they do it when they can no longer find a reason to keep going. When nothing in their lives is good enough to balance out the bad. And they do it when they no longer have the courage to carry on past some recent painful experience. They commit what is, in the end, a desperate, final call for help, that is hopefully heard in time by someone else."

"And what if it's not heard in time?" I ask, although I know the answer.

"Then they die."

"Die."

"Yes."

"So it's always a call for someone to stop them?"

"I can't say that it always is, but in my experience, it has been. That's why suicidal people talk about death so much. To let others know they need and want their help. It's up to the rest of us to see that and help them."

"So I failed this basic human truth," I say, knowing that I sound sarcastic even though I don't want to. "I didn't help when I should have?"

"Perhaps."

"But what if I had helped, and she lived, and nothing changed? Isn't that worse? I think it would've been. She tried to make others believe her, and no one would. No one except us kids, that is. And because we did, because I did, I get all this righteous shit about helping and how life is always worth living. Let me tell you, surviving isn't the picnic you crack it up to be. Surviving is a piece of shit the size of Montana." I stop. My breath drags my shoulders up, then down. My head clears, then fogs. Yellow slides across my eyes, first in dots, then in waves.

Right before I hit the floor, I think, Thank God. I don't have to survive anymore.

———

That's how everyone found out I hadn't been eating. My mom, supersleuth of notebooks but firm believer that skinny is always better, didn't notice. Or she didn't think much about it other than how annoying it was to try to find something I would eat and how disgusting it was to watch me pick at my food. Marge had been too busy taking notes and trying to make me see the error of my ways—although lately she'd brought up or noticed my weight more and more. Maybe she might have said something next session. Maybe she thought my not eating was a grief reaction, but it's been a bit too long since Aimee died to use that as an excuse. And Dad? Well, he's been gone a lot lately. Business trips, he says. I say, part-time separation. Whether from me or Mom doesn't matter. Probably the former, given my track record. It must be nice to walk away when things get tough. Why, then, am I obligated to stay?

So I woke up in the hospital, and I missed the worrisome yet promising outing with Hope. I don't have phone privileges, but it doesn't matter because the only person I would call is Chard, and I don't have any phone cards. It doesn't matter because if I don't eat, I won't get the right to use a phone, move out of bed, have visitors, watch TV.

Let's see. Have they named anything I want to do?

———

"She needs it."

It's Marge, in the hallway, accosting my overdressed mother under the fluorescent lighting that makes even dear old Mom look bad.

I hear the click of Mom's heels. She has stepped away from Marge. "It's not necessary, especially now. She's getting help for this latest development, help here."

"The help for her anorexia—you can say it—ends at the hospital door." Marge's voice is hard. "And she needs her journal now more than ever. It's the only hope we have of understanding what she is feeling, thinking. Obviously whatever is going on in her head is bothering her. She's working through the issues, getting closer to the heart of the problem. She's in a lot of pain, and this is little more than a veiled suicide attempt in my opinion—"

"In your opinion? You don't know? Then you haven't read her journal? It was there in your office, and you didn't read it?" Way to go, Mom! Nothing like telling me not to leave the damn thing lying around.

There's a pause, and I imagine Marge shaking her head.

"So you don't know then, do you?" Mom's voice drops halfway through the sentence, and I hear the rattle of a cart, the whisper of rubber on linoleum.

"I haven't read it. I have seen changes, though—"

"That's the skinniness in her face. She hasn't changed."

"Don't you understand that this is your daughter's life we're talking about?"

"Yes. I do. That's why I don't think she should be living in the past. Help her move forward. Help her get over this."

My ass, Mommy Dearest. Get over this, my ass.

"She needs to understand her role in all of it. All of her problems, this latest one included, come from her past, from what she went through before, during, and after Aimee's death. She has to face what happened, and maybe you do, too."

I hear Mom scoff. As if there were no door separating us, I can see her toss her head, push her bangs back, cross her right arm over her purse, tightening her hold on it. "You don't seem to know where to stop, do you? She doesn't socialize. She doesn't participate in any school activities. She doesn't talk to anyone, including us. She doesn't need more help focusing on the past. She needs to move on. She needs to make new friends and forget all of this. When she does that, she'll get better."

"I've given it back."

The door had opened a crack, but it slapped shut again. "What? You did what?"

"I gave the journal back to her. I'd appreciate it if you do not take it away again." Marge is commanding my mother. Unbelievable. And there is some kind of threat in her voice that probably has to do with my being admitted to the hospital. Maybe she has some control over how soon I'll be released?

"And you didn't even read it before you gave it back?" Mother Dearest sounds horrified.

"No."

"Stupid. You're absolutely stupid. I should hire—"

"Thank you," Marge interrupts. "Oh, and you can't hire anyone new, and you know it. They court has picked up on your tendency to fire your daughter's psychologist whenever she gets close to addressing the real issue of Aimee's suicide. The judge is losing patience."

"She is an adolescent girl who's been through a lot and just needs to get on with her life. She's not a nutcase. Besides, she's my daughter," Mom says, "not yours."

"Not if the court takes custody away."

So this is Marge's threat. I imagine not going home to Mom, and I almost smile. But when I think of Dad, my smile fades. He really doesn't deserve that kind of stigma, that mark of failure. I'm not sure what he deserves, but not that.

Marge continues after a shocked pause, during which I would have liked to have seen my mother's face. "I think we're coming to an understanding, your daughter and I. I think that I know much of what happened, and I want her to tell me the rest. I don't want to sneak behind her back and betray her trust. To do so would be fatal. I will help your daughter, but it must be on my terms." She sounds so pompous, so sure of herself.

Miss Self-Righteous Marge, you don't have a prayer.

———

I have a brother again, or rather Chard has managed to slip past the hospital Gestapo by posing as my brother.

This time when he arrives, which is, amazingly, only the second night I'm in the hospital, he doesn't call me JK. He sits on the bed and caresses my collarbone, tracing its jutting path from shoulder to neck with a finger. His finger rests in the cradle of breath and heartbeat between the bones at the base of my neck, then he reaches up and strokes my cheekbone.

His breath grows quicker, and he averts his eyes and lays down beside me. He slides his fingers through my hair like a comb. "I'll stay. Or I'll come back. I don't care," he says, skimming his finger over my temple while I try to feel every part of him that connects with a part of me. "It doesn't matter what they say. I can't flunk or anything, since I am actually acing all my courses, and I can do the work here besides, so what can it hurt if I stay?"

I shrug, and my shoulder knocks into his. He sneaks a hand up to his eyes, wipes at them, then snuggles his face into my hair. I feel him breathing, wonder if he's smelling me. I must not smell right, because he gets up and moves over to his coat and bag. He digs in it a moment, only glancing once at me, then looking away quickly. He tugs a small plastic bag free of the backpack, from which he pulls a spoon, some napkins, and a quart of Ben and Jerry's.

"I'll eat a bite if you kiss me," I say, knowing that he brought it for me.

He bends down and brushes his lips over mine, gently, carefully, but still he jostles the tube in my nose. It bumps into my tender nose flesh, and my eyes water.

But I take a bite of ice cream.

Which makes me throw up, and my feeding tube comes out.

Chard hides the ice cream under the bed before the nurse comes in, what with me gagging and the beepers going. She shoos him out, tells me I can't eat yet, and not to try to get me to again. After he leaves, she tries to put the tube back in, but she has to call for a sedative so she can shove the tube past the back of my throat without my gagging and struggling.

Chard is back at midnight. He sneaked in the back entrance, which he said was depressing as anything because there were carts full of dead flowers waiting to be thrown out and half-filled balloons drooping and floating in the air currents like sick fish.

He crawls into the skinny, stiff bed with me and settles in to sleep. I hope we'll be left alone, but I know at some point a nurse will come to check some vital sign of mine, so I don't sleep. I listen for the sound of the nurses on their rounds, the doors closing, the soft commands and apologies as they move from room to room. Some people cry out in their sleep, others curse, some, like me, are awake when the nurse arrives.

But nurses check pulses, not window ledges where teenage boys fit neatly behind thick curtains. So Chard stays until dawn, when I wake him again. I feel the staff's shift change coming, the stretching in the muscles of the hospital.

"Chard, you've got to go. The nurse is in with the old man who's been groaning and coughing all night, so you can get out without being seen."

He rubs his eyes with the butt of his hand, like a little kid. A yawn blossoms on his face, then a smile. He tucks me in, kisses my forehead once. "I'll be back. You go to sleep."

Then he's gone. A brief cracking of the door, a light, a shadow falling against the wall opposite my bed, then the bleakest darkness of all, the darkness just before the dawn.

But I have the memory of his face, still groggy, still patient, still there.

Aimee was right.

I am all about Chard.

He's left a bagel on the cart next to my bed and two

ketchuplike packages of cream cheese. I ignore those, but eat the bagel, nibble by nibble, while I wait for him to return.

If he brings one later today, I'll eat it too.

———

Shocker number one: Chard's parents filed a missing persons report. Shocker number two: The police found Chard holed up at my house. Mom broke the law. For me. I still can't believe it. She called his parents, apologized for not telling them, but she had called him. She had driven him to the hospital. She had told him how to get in at night. A client of hers had done it once to try to steal drugs. And now she was begging his parents to let him stay.

What a surprise. Is this the same Mom who says I need to get on with life and not focus on the past? I'll have to check for signs of an alien body snatching the next time she's here. That and smile more. Who knows, maybe she'll call Kates, Kyle, and Jason if I do.

———

What a liar. Mom didn't beg Chard to come. She just accepted it when he showed up. Then she embellished the story when she saw how much better I was doing after Chard's visits (I did, after all, eat the bagel), and she decided to take the credit.

This is what Chard says happened:

"I called, you know, like we had been doing, and she answered. It was five o'clock. I almost hung up, but then I thought of how she's never home then, so something must have been wrong. All she said, though, was not to call again. And that me and my rotten bunch of friends had done enough damage to her daughter. She said you never would have gotten into this whole mess and wound up in the hospital if it weren't for us. I wanted to ask her if we had anything to do with—"

He stops, but I don't say anything because I know what he was going to say. They had nothing to do with the end, because I was there alone, with Aimee.

"She said," he continues, slicing little bits of cheese off of a hunk he's brought and offering them to me, but I'm too full of pumped-in food to eat the real stuff, so he eats the cheese. "She said it would have been better if your family had moved away from that godforsaken place like she always wanted to do, but your dad never wanted to. No, not even if it meant a huge step up in her career. Not even if you were charged with murder and no one would speak to you anymore. No, you had to stay put. She was really riled up by then." He stops and drinks water from the hospital pitcher.

How it came to be about her, I don't know, but Chard says that he asked her what I was doing in the hospital. "Your mother said you were starving yourself to death. Your psychologist told them you were committing a form of suicide by not eating and that this was not the typical anorexia thing."

I look away as he waits to see what I'm going to say, but I don't answer, because I agree. I'll never be a beauty—no sense trying for the unattainable.

But back to Chard's story. "I asked if I could visit you or if she would give you a message from me. She said no and not to go trying to sneak in through the back entrance either!"

For a second, I almost think she was telling him how to

get in. Life would be so different with a mother who did things like that. Then I remember who we're talking about and decide she'd never do that. Still, she got him in, intentionally or no, and I owe her that.

"I thanked her, hung up, and jumped in my car." He squeezes my hand, and we sit in silence for the last ten minutes of visiting hours. Now that he has someplace to stay he doesn't have to sleep here. When he leaves, he kisses me for real, on the mouth, long and slow and deep, and we even manage not to dislodge my feeding tube.

God, I wish he were here, lying beside me, telling me this story instead of me lying here alone—again—writing it down, trying to piece together the he-said, she-said part of it.

I hear carts jangling down the hall and smell the sickness of a hundred people, but I can't hear my own heart and I can't smell my own sweat. I'm sweating because I'm sitting up in the middle of the night after a particularly vivid dream of Aimee, and I'm trying like hell to figure out how I ended up here with a tube in my nose and straps that I've ripped off my arms in my sleep. They've left bracelet- or, rather, watchband-sized marks on my skin that burn.

And I think of my mother, who blames everyone but me—and certainly not her—for where I am and who I am.

———

A man is coding across the hall. People are trampling through my mind, shouting official-sounding things, shoving the family out of the way. I can hear the wife asking over and over, "What's wrong? What's happening?"

I want to shout, "Death, that's what!" But the images

invading my mind hurl me backward. But I won't go there. Not now.

What can I write about to take my mind off the man dying across the hall? Off Aimee?

But of course there's nothing. Everything ended with Aimee, just as everything started with Aimee.

My mother. But what about her? Shopping? Been through that a bit already. Home life? Hah. What's left?

"Stand back. All clear," echoes down the hall.

The almost-widow moans, "Oh God, oh God, oh God."

Isn't anyone with her, comforting her?

I race through my memories to find a good one. All I come up with is the one field trip Mom agreed to chaperone. I think she did it as penance for forgetting me at Aimee's. Okay. Stand clear.

Aimee's mom was supposed to chaperone this trip to a museum for our Girl Scout troop. Then she got sick and couldn't do it, and the whole thing was going to be called off. Somehow or other, Mom—through guilt or lack of prior commitments—ended up driving Aimee, Kates, and me in our car.

The three of us weren't exactly model scouts. Kates's mom was the leader, and therefore Kates had to be a model citizen. Aimee and I did it because it was something we could do together and because it was a challenge to try to liven up the meetings. Without us, Kates would have had to paint her Aunt Jemima bottle according to the directions handed out. We painted our bottles as reggae queens. Aimee's even looked like a guy in drag, although that may not have been intentional. Her artistic skills weren't the best.

Once obligated to doing the chaperone thing, Mom really got into it. She ransacked all my old kiddie tapes, which we'd listened to on long trips to keep me occupied in—say—my preschool days, and stuck them in the car. She also made a stop at the grocery store and loaded up on snacks that weren't even healthy. She bought Doritos and gummi worms, as well as chocolate up the wazoo, trail mix, chips, and pretzels. Just how much food she thought three girls could eat in a three-hour round-trip car ride, I don't know.

Fortunately, we brought our own music. We didn't think of bringing earphones for her, but she should have.

We met at the school, and when everyone was ready to leave, I climbed into the front seat and commandeered the CD player just as she was reaching for a Raffi tape. "No 'Baby Beluga,' Mom," I said.

She started to say something, then clamped her mouth shut, cutting herself off after, "But—"

We bounced, sang, yakked, and gossiped for an hour of regular driving, then our progress stalled in traffic, and we developed an urgent need to pee. Probably from all of those Diet Cokes and Mountain Dews Mom had brought. We had to get off at the next exit to find a bathroom, and in doing so, we lost the caravan of other Girl Scouts.

"Don't worry. I've got a map," my plan-for-everything mom said. She studied the map while we hurried through the two stalls at Mickie D's.

The car smelled of stale chips and Doritos when we got back in, and we had no sooner hit the highway again than Kates's lips turned this ugly gray color, and her forehead glistened.

"Kates is going to be sick," Aimee announced like she had noticed a new clothing store out her window. "Got a bag?"

"A bag?" Mom glanced at the bag of garbage at my feet, then eyed the bag holding the remaining snacks.

"Or a bucket. My brother does this all the time. Gets carsick," Aimee said. She cracked a window. "I didn't know you got carsick, Kates. Fresh air might help."

Kates looked at Aimee like she was a freak or something. Her breath had that funny holding-back rhythm you don't want to know more about but you know you're going to learn all about in approximately a half minute.

"Dump the garbage out and throw the bag back there," Mom ordered, hearing Kates's raggedy breathing. She rubbed the space between her eyes. "Is there anything remotely like a bucket in the car?" she whispered to me. To Kates, she said, "Hang on, sweetie. I'll pull over as soon as I see someplace."

I looked at the side of the litter-covered highway and said, "Anyplace will do, Mom."

She gave me a dirty look. "She can't throw up out there. I'll find a bathroom."

By the rules, Mom, live by the rules.

"Better hurry," Aimee said, as Kates, wild-eyed, jabbed at the window button and gagged. She got the window partway down, and, to her credit, she managed to barf at least half of her puke out the window. Some of that splattered down the side of the car, and I turned around to see if any hit the car behind us. Aimee mouthed, "Bingo," when the driver turned on his windshield wipers and slowed down.

"Oh no," Mom groaned, flicking on her signal and pulling over. "What now?"

"Home?" I said. "I think the museum's out."

"Obviously," Mom said. She glanced at Kates, who was shaking and stinking. Her shirt was speckled with splotches of yellowish vomit. Mom twitched the plastic bag I was still holding away from me and marched around the car. She opened the door and, using the brush side of the window scraper, pushed as much of the puke as she could out of the car. Then she tossed the scraper against the cement safety wall. Her lips were slits, her face white. Mom was never good around puke. Once, after she'd gotten a whiff of mine, she'd ordered Dad to clean me up. Then she ran for the bathroom herself.

Kates was crying. She took one look at Mom's gray face and said, "I'm sorry. I'm so sorry. I've ruined the trip and your car. I'm sorry. Let me help." She shoved herself upright, shaking.

Mom stood back a moment and watched Kates struggle to get out of the car. Aimee pressed against the opposite door, with the window down and exhaust pouring over her to cover the stench. I willed Mom to hold back her own vomit and find some pity, but I needn't have bothered. She must have seen what she looked like, either in the window's reflection or in Kates's eyes.

She dug deep and forced out, "Don't worry about it." Her voice switched from cold and practical to soft and maternal, like a singer dropping through octaves, each word becoming easier to hear.

I jumped like a dog does when its usually beloved owner talks harshly for the first time. Then I checked to make sure there wasn't a twin nearby that had switched places with her. But no, it was her. She leaned into the car and helped Kates take off her shirt, then rolled it into a ball, shoved it into the plastic bag, and tied a tight knot in the bag to hold in the smell. Next, she pulled off her own sweater, leaving her in only her turtleneck. She helped Kates, who was still shaking and stammering apologies, into her sweater. All this was after, mind you, Mom had produced antibacterial wipes and cleaned most of the mess off Kates's face, hands, and arms.

She fished the emergency blanket out of the trunk and wrapped Kates in it, depositing her filthy shirt in the trunk.

When she slid behind the wheel, I stared at her. Granted, I didn't get sick that often, and I asked for her help even less often, given her weak stomach, but when I did, the nicest thing she had to say to me was, "Make sure you hit the pan or the toilet."

I thought it was just me who was noticing this softer side of my mother for the first time. But when this new maternal being decided this would be a good time to hold my hand, I saw Aimee's jaw drop in the rearview mirror. Aimee glanced to see if Kates had noticed, but she had wadded herself into a ball in the center of the seat, away from the wet, disgusting side, and was sleeping.

Aimee shrugged and looked out the window.

I let her hold my hand for a long time.

Kates slept all the way home.

Back in our neighborhood, Mom drove straight to Kates's, turned off the car, and went around to help Kates into her house. She explained to Kates' dad what had happened, handed over the shirt in its sealed bag, then came back to the car. She didn't even ask where Aimee lived. She drove there without any input from me, explained again, then headed for home.

Safely within her own house, Mom reverted to type. She called the car cleaners first. Then she took a shower. When she came out, clean and powdered, she checked on me. I was sitting on my bed with earphones in. She slipped up behind me and put her arms around me as if she wanted a hug.

I jumped. I hadn't heard her come in. Besides, the last time we'd hugged we'd been posing for a picture in front of some character in Disney World, so I wasn't expecting physical contact.

Before I could gasp out a surprised "Oh, it's you!" she had snatched her arms back like they'd been burned.

I tugged the earphones out of my ears as she straightened.

When she saw I could hear again, she said, "Don't you think you should shower, too? And put your clothes in the hamper. I want to wash them. They stink." She turned on her heel and stomped out.

For a moment, I wanted her back. I wanted to apologize for not knowing how it felt to be hugged on the spur of the moment anymore. To know what it felt like to have her hug me at all. But then I thought of the ice in her eyes when she'd pulled away, and I let it go.

She wouldn't change. Even if she wanted to, she couldn't.

I thought of Aimee's surprise at my mom's sudden bout of tenderness in the car and knew I was right.

But what if I had heard her coming and hadn't jumped? Would she be here, hugging me now instead of leaving me alone in the hospital? Would I even be here now?

Across the hospital corridor, there's only the sound of whimpering. It's the final call for good-byes before they cart the body off to the morgue. The doctors have paid their respects to the widow, and the nurses have straightened the body, and now the widow's in there, crying over it.

I ring the bell for the first time ever. This remembering thing isn't working. My mind is still on death—the death across the hall and the death across my life, lying like a shadow over everything I see.

When the nurse comes, I'll ask for a sleeping pill.

And I'll take it this time.

Aimee, where are you? Some nights I feel you here with me. It's as though you are lying behind me again, my shirt rolled up and your finger tracing letters across my shivering back as I try to decipher your message. We only played that game after we had been told lights out and no more noise by one set of parents or the other. Only once, when we were at Aimee's real mother's for a night before she took off for Vegas, were we allowed to stay up talking uninhibited until we fell asleep. Aimee's mother made us popcorn and gave us soda and ice cream when we asked. She stayed in her room while we chattered. When we stuck our heads in, she was seated on the bed surrounded by papers. I think she may have slept with them, I'm not sure.

But that night, after we had turned off the lights and played finger messages until we heard her mother snoring and knew it was safe to talk, Aimee told me in whispers about "the divorce" for the first time.

Amazing that it should mean so much to a kid today that her parents were divorcing. I know kids who'd like nothing better. But to Aimee, it meant darkness. Her parents had tried separation with attempts at reconciliation. But those attempts were ruined by her dad's new flame.

It was always on the weekends that Aimee and her brother were staying with their dad that his lover showed up. Her father acted surprised, but Aimee couldn't act surprised, too. She hated the phoniness of it. The sudden knock as the three of them were sitting down to eat. The lo-and-behold of the woman appearing on his doorstep with some forgotten item or thing to tell him. The astounding way the loaves and fishes seemed to multiply, and there was enough so that a fourth person could easily join them for dinner, even when they were eating something like steak and baked potatoes. I mean, who makes an extra steak or even bakes more than one potato apiece, unless they're a binge eater?

One weekend Aimee's mother came early to pick up Aimee and her brother. Someone in the family, some close aunt or uncle, had died, and she had to take the kids back for the funeral. She had been trying to call all night, but someone had taken the phone off the hook so she couldn't get through. That's how she found out that her plans to reconcile were for nothing. Stepmother is already here. Go on home.

So she filed for divorce.

And Aimee filed for help.

But no one listened, except me.

Aimee hated her stepmother from very early on. At the beginning I think it was mostly because her stepmother was trying to replace Aimee's real mom. But later, the hate took on a passion that made me cringe when Aimee talked.

And that last night at her real mother's house, she had talked.

"I won't go live with him. She can't make me, either. Mom keeps asking me which place I want to live at, and I keep saying with her. But she keeps asking over and over, like I've answered the wrong way and she's waiting for me to give the right answer. She can't leave me with him. I won't live there as long as he lives with her. I won't. That would be like living in hell. And she can't expect me to go home with them willingly. I won't go. No one can make me."

"But Aimee," I said, "where would you go?"

She sighed. "I don't know. I can tell the court that I don't want to live with him, maybe even tell the judge why, I guess, but that would kill my dad. And he's so stupidly happy with her. That's what gets me. He loves her. Her! As though he can't see who or what she is. What she does."

I didn't want to know too many details. I figured it was safer to steer the conversation back to more general things. No one in my family ever talks about unpleasant things. They just disappeared, never to be mentioned again. But Aimee and her mom talked about everything, which used to be fun for me, but now was making me queasy. I didn't want to know "what she did" to Aimee. I wanted Aimee to be happy, of course, so I tried to find a solution. "Where does your brother want to go?" I asked. "Surely he doesn't want to stay with your stepmother?"

"He wants to go with my dad, of course. The brat gets everything he ever wanted there and with her, including free rein over me."

"Then why can't you divide and conquer? You go with your mom if he's staying there—"

"Everyone says we have to stay together. Besides, it's not about him." She sounded old. Like someone had suddenly replaced the fifth-grader in the bed beside me with a grand-mother. Someone who had seen wars and fires and floods. Someone who knew what horrible things the heart is capa-ble of and that evil cannot always be prevented.

Again I tried to tone down the drama Aimee was pre-senting for me, not knowing how close to the truth she was running. "I know, but she can't be that awful."

I nearly blew our whole friendship at that moment. Aimee eyed me in the ever-burning yard light slanting through the vertical blinds, then turned her back to me and stopped talking.

What did I know? I was in the fifth grade. My parents were never around, but that also meant they weren't able to hurt me in the ways some parents do. They had their quirks, but at that time they didn't seem unmanageable, something I couldn't live with.

I begged with her, pleaded with her, and massaged her back when she wouldn't answer. Finally I gave up, rolled over, and tried to sleep.

But I didn't. Because Aimee started writing the same words over and over on my back, under my shirt, and this time my shivers had nothing to do with the coldness of her finger.

Mom had tried hard to make the doctors keep me in the hospital longer, but they kept murmuring about insurance and length of stay for my condition and diagnosis, while Mom went on and on about not being able to watch day and night to be sure I was eating.

The doctors won, and I was going home the next day, when I received my first card in my two-week stay. It was from Hope. She'd scribbled a note about how she was still looking forward to going to a movie when I came home. She made it sound like I'd taken a little vacation. There was no mention of my getting better, no hint that I was in the hospital or that I had been sick.

It was a "missing you" card, the kind I might have sent Aimee if one of us moved away from the other.

The kind you can't send to dead friends.

I wanted to throw it away, but the nurse brought it in during my mother's lunch hour. Mom opened the card for me, trying to save my energy for other things, I guess, and she read it.

"She sounds so nice." She handed me the card.

"She's crazy." I set the card facedown on the wheeled cart you're supposed to eat or play solitaire or do crosswords on. Mine was empty except for the urine-yellow water pitcher they filled every morning and its matching cup.

"I'm not sure you're such a good judge of whether or not a person is crazy."

Wham! Incompetent, half-insane daughter no longer able to tell whether person she has met and mother has not is crazy.

As if the scars running over Hope's wrists are just some new fad. Soon we'll all be having them done when we realize how much before her time this marvelous girl is.

But my admirable mother is referring to my past. I should have known that Aimee was crazy—or not, however you want to look at it—and I should never have been with Aimee that night. I should never have listened to her Lies. I should never have loved her as much as I did. I should have known she was a loon and nothing but trouble. But if she was crazy, wasn't it right that I tried to help her? Even if I failed in everyone's book but Aimee's?

I never want to see Hope again.

But something tells me—perhaps it was Mom taking the envelope with its return address when she left—that I will be hearing from her soon.

———

When I first saw Marge after the hospital episode, she handed me a stack of books on depression and grief recovery, with a few about suicide thrown in to round out the program, and told me to start reading.

"Right now?" I asked, thinking that she was letting me off lightly.

But she said, "Later," in a cold voice that told me I had disappointed her. She tapped her pencil against the edge of her desk, a staccato rhythm that jarred my nerves and set my foot jerking against my will. I pushed down on my leg to stop its movement. Everyone was watching what I did, right down to whether or not my muscles were tense, because one of the doctors told my parents to watch for signs of passive exercise after I got home.

"What the hell are you talking about? Passive exercise! Can't any of you people talk in English?" Dad said.

The doctor patiently explained in retard language how some anorexic patients burn calories by tensing muscles when they are lying still. Or they might incorporate small, almost unnoticeable extra movements into their daily routine to add exercise to their schedule without really adding exercise.

"But she's not anorexic!" Mom snapped. "She's suicidal."

Like that was a whole lot better. To avoid adding the label "anorexic" to my many diagnoses, I forced myself into stillness.

Anyway, when Marge handed the pile to me, I stared at it and didn't even crack a binding.

She, as usual, had to speak first. "You haven't spoken much about Chard and your relationship with him."

"What relationship?"

"You must have some kind of relationship. He traveled quite a distance to see you in the hospital."

"That was nothing." I dumped the stack of books onto the floor and shoved them away with my foot. They fell over.

"No one else seems to feel it was nothing."

I kicked the thickest book under the couch. "Does that mean he's in trouble for it? He doesn't have a parole officer to answer to. I do. And I didn't invite him, so I shouldn't catch any crap for his visit."

"What did you talk about?"

"Crap."

She scribbles, and I can't resist a comment. "Drawing a picture of that statement to clarify your notes?"

"Actually, no. I'm doodling."

"I'll bet you wrote *defensive, agitated, combative.*"

"Then you lose."

I snort. A silence falls that lasts the rest of the session. I assume she's waiting for me to address the issue of Chard and all the ramifications of his still being in my life. I assume she figures it has something to do with Aimee's death.

But she's wrong.

Isn't she?

⸻

The books Marge gave me are junk. Drivel. The authors don't understand anything, and I refuse to read any more of them. I put them on the front seat of Dad's car and wrote him a note telling him to drop them at Marge's on his way back to work. He works so much now, he's almost as bad as Mom. But not quite. At least he still golfs and has something of a life outside of work. His life just doesn't include me— or Mom either, apparently.

He was home when I arrived, but only about a quarter of his things are here anymore, and he took more with him when he left. Which doesn't look promising. It seems I'm in the same position as Aimee—having to choose which parent to live with. But so far Dad hasn't offered to take me. Then again, maybe I don't want to go. He can't scream about phone bills and lying if he's gone, and I won't miss that.

There's a lot I won't miss if he's gone. Others I will. Things have gotten very quiet around here lately, but if it's just me and workaholic Mom, things will be simply silent. I slipped a cartoon into Dad's suitcase so he'd find it later. Not that he's laughed much lately. He used to, and part of me hopes he will again—maybe by the time I graduate and go to college. As it is, it doesn't look like he'll be here then.

But good old Mom, queen of denial, says not to worry. It's just that he has to travel so much with his new job that his living in a town forty miles away makes sense. Otherwise he'd have to drive an hour each way, without traffic, and that would be insane.

And let's not have any more insanity in this family, please.

Maybe he'll call when he finds the cartoon. It might be easier talking to him on the phone. Besides, it'd be nice to have a real phone call for once. One I'm allowed to take without worrying about being overheard. And maybe he'll laugh if he can't see me.

———

Marge is miffed. We're back to the same old stare-down stuff. It doesn't bother me, but I can see she's sick of it. She actually looked at her watch today. She's never done that before. I'm breaking her. Soon she'll be tame enough for a three-year-old to ride.

I could have told her that my first day back at school was even worse than the first day of school, but she would have asked me, What did I expect? I hadn't made any friends, so I shouldn't have been surprised that no one noticed that I was gone or that I returned—other than my homeroom teacher who handed me my accumulated homework and told me I could finish it whenever I had the chance, as long as it was done before the quarter was over. She patted my hand when I reached for the stack of papers.

I nearly puked. She's such an old thing, all wrinkled and beyond controlling her class or even hoping to, but she tries to teach. She stands in front of us and lectures about dead writers and their vast understanding of the human soul, but these people never had their souls ripped out and trampled, never reveled in the blasting, gutting, and blowing up of human bodies in darkened theaters and then had to go home to a dark and empty house.

Or maybe a few of them did. One old writer guy said something like, "Every happy family is the same, but every unhappy family is unhappy in a different way." I believe he's right. Not that I'm going to go out and buy his collected works to read about his unhappy families. I don't need more angst in my life.

New word, *angst*. Felt I had to use it. It is so right for my situation.

Aimee and I used to read together. We would read the same book at the same time, and then talk about it. The books we chose weren't classics. We weren't nerds. They were just books, whatever happened to be climbing the bestseller list, and usually we liked to trash them. Especially Danielle Steel's books. God, if my life ends up like what she writes about, I'm done for. I'll knock myself off. Romance, my ass. Tragic drivel is more like it.

———

I shouldn't have said my absence from school went completely unnoticed. Along with my homework assignments I found a little note from Karen. It said, "Gained five pounds these past two weeks"—which roughly coincided with my hospital stay. "Ate too much at several parties and it rained too much to walk with the baby. When are you going to start training with me and eating my extra snacks? Sent one to you. See attached. Best, Karen." The note was taped to a box. Inside was a fistful of Hershey Kisses.

I left the box in my locker, but I did slide a note under Karen's door.

"Mission accomplished. Snack devoured. Feeling thinner?" I didn't sign it. She'll know who it's from. Besides, I don't want to get too friendly with her. At least, I don't want it to become a habit. It might result in a baby-sitting job—or worse.

———

Speaking of baby-sitting, that's what Kates did almost non-stop when she wasn't at school or with us. If it wasn't her little brother she had to supervise, it was some group of monsters from her neighborhood. And if not that, her parents' friends always needed someone reliable to watch their precious brats when some big dinner or wedding came up.

Reliable. That's Kates. With her chin length hair, always brushed until the red highlights outshone the brown, and her neat, relaxed way of dressing—sweaters, turtlenecks, colored jeans or khakis—she always looked like a kid you could count on not to cause trouble.

And as far as I know, she caused trouble only once in her life of her own accord. Aimee and I—and sometimes the guys—led her on some pretty wild rides, but she never started the car, as it were. Only once did she initiate the action, and then it was Aimee and I who went along, at least for a little while.

Of course, the ride also involved baby-sitting. The only good thing I could see about baby-sitting was the money Kates was always rolling in it. She wasn't tight with it either. She willingly financed lots of stuff for us, including gas for tooling around in Jason's parents' old car and drinking binges, as long as we provided the entertainment. She rarely drank as much as we did, and her life followed a more predictable pattern than ours. At least it was duller than Chard's, Aimee's, and mine. Kates, Jason, and Kyle didn't have quite the same quality of home life we had. Maybe that was why they hung with us. Entertainment value.

Anyway, Kates's wild ride started with a call from a desperate mother who needed someone to watch her darling little nine-month-old girl while she danced off with a gaggle of friends to celebrate the fortieth birthday of a school chum. She'd heard of Kates through Kates's mother and called her.

Kates was available, but she told the woman when she agreed to take the job that she had two friends in baby-sitter training.

"Can they come, too?" she asked. We were sitting on her bed when she asked, and we smirked. We knew that all these women wanted to get every teenage girl involved in baby-sitting so they would have a larger pool of baby-sitter choices and, therefore, a better shot of getting out of their houses when they wanted. As usual, this woman said yes, we could come. It was the riskiest thing Kates did—asking to have us come with her on jobs. But the women were over a barrel—they'd have agreed to just about anything to have the renowned Kates sit for them.

Aimee and I rarely went with Kates at the start of the evening. We usually joined her later, when the worst parts of the job were over. We didn't want to shovel spoonfuls of green slime at a moving mouth or scrub the dirty little body afterward. We left that stuff to Kates.

This night was no exception. When we arrived, the mother had been gone for two hours and wasn't due home for another three. So we had a good chunk of time to try out different makeup and fingernail polishes—if she had any good kinds. Or we could raid the cupboards if they were loaded with sugared cereals, snacks, and treats.

Kates greeted us with a worried frown, the first sign that something was wrong. The second sign of looming trouble was that she was holding the baby. She usually had mobile babies occupied in some game, like dancing to music or finding stuffed doggies. The nonmobile ones she usually had asleep by seven-thirty.

"What's up?" Aimee asked. Sort of a routine question, but she must have also sensed a difference in Kates, because she didn't toss the question out and plop onto the nearest couch. Instead, she stared around the unusually messy room. A powder bottle, wipes, spare diapers, a sippy cup, pacifiers, toys, a washcloth, a towel, and the baby's clothes lay in disarray on the couch and floor. Kates was a fanatical cleaner, which was another reason she was so popular as a baby-sitter. She could play with kids, visit with us, and still leave a house a heck of a lot cleaner than when she arrived.

Kates's response knocked us flat. "Thank God you're here. I can call the police now."

"What?" both Aimee and I shouted. The baby started crying. But she wasn't really crying. It was more like a soft whining, like a puppy that's hungry but knows if it howls or barks, it will be kicked.

"See what you've done!" Kates said. She bent over the baby and crooned to her, swaying her whole body and brushing the little girl's cheek with a finger.

"Us?" Aimee said. "You're the one calling the police. What did you think we'd say when you greeted us with that?"

Kates looked at Aimee like she had proposed frying the baby in oil. She only assumed this I-know-more-than-you role when she was baby-sitting. She spun away and walked to the couch. She laid the baby down and began to strip the clothes off her, working quickly but gently.

Aimee and I glanced at each other, then shrugged. Aimee sat in the chair opposite the TV, and I headed for the kitchen.

"Wait," Kates said. She pushed her hair behind one ear and continued crooning to the infant as she undressed her. When she finished, she said in an awed whisper, "Come here."

I sighed and strolled over. Aimee heaved herself up from the chair, dropping the channel flicker as she rose. We glanced at each other. What was so new and different about this baby that she had to make such a fuss about?

A large black, purple, yellow, and green bruise across one shoulder and halfway down her back was what was different. Several other bruises, mostly older and yellower, decorated the skinny backside of the girl.

I stepped back. "Oh!"

Aimee looked away.

"That's not all," Kates said, her voice still low. She slipped her hands under the baby's armpits and turned her over. The girl whimpered. When Kates moved her hands, she revealed what looked like a long, slender burn on the baby's chest. It was angry and red and oozing.

"Okay," I said. "So calling the police might not be a bad idea. What do you know about these people?"

"They're friends of my parents." Kates said, covering the baby back up. "My parents will flip if I call. But this is awful."

"Did they say anything before they left?" I asked. Aimee retrieved the flicker from the floor and with glazed eyes, clicked through the channels. Music filled the room and she dropped the remote again. She wasn't looking at us, but I could tell she was listening.

"They didn't tell me to do her bath. I just assumed. Everyone wants me to give the kids a bath. Then they don't have to do it." Kates stopped. "Maybe I shouldn't have?"

"You'd have had to change her at some point, wouldn't you?" I said. "I mean, they stink up their diapers pretty regularly from what I can tell, and wouldn't you have seen some of it then?" Why were we justifying Kates's behavior? I wondered. She'd done nothing wrong. Aimee still said nothing, but an angry fierceness lit her eyes.

"I don't know if I would have noticed the bruises on her butt. It's pretty dim in her bedroom. The lightbulb by the changing table doesn't work. I might have missed them." Kates scooped the baby against her and cradled her head into the crook of her shoulder. The baby tried to snuggle, but after wriggling around a moment, she poked her butt out by tucking her knees under her hips. At last she closed her eyes. "In baby-sitting class they tell you to turn in cases of abuse to a responsible adult. But who?"

"Your parents," I said. "I vote for your parents. Tell them, and they can take it from there. Maybe there's a logical explanation for the bruises."

"And the burn?" she asked. "Explain a burn on a baby's chest. I think it looks like a curling iron did it." She shuddered and hugged the baby closer. The little girl struggled a moment, and Kates loosened her hold. But something was irritating the little girl. She began a series of small cries that never became wails, but sounded mournful.

"If I tell my parents first," Kates said over the baby's cries, "then I have to leave her here. With them."

"Give her to me." Aimee extended her hands. Her foot tapped the floor.

Kates and I both stared at her. She'd never asked to hold a baby before. If Kates asked for our help it was always me who caved—and then failed at whatever she asked.

"Give her to me. You're holding her wrong," Aimee said. She took the little girl from Kates's arms and wrapped her in a blanket. She shifted the baby's weight so that she lay curled against Aimee on her side, belly to belly, but barely touching. "You were holding her with all the pressure on her injuries." She sat back in her chair, the baby resting against her, and stared at the music video on TV.

Kates and I sat on the couch, while Kates idly folded and refolded the towels and dirty clothes. After a while, she carried them upstairs. When she came back down, she said, "I still don't know what to do."

"I told you what I'd do," I said.

"Pass the buck," Kates said, making it sound like what I'd suggested amounted to leaving the kid in a snowbank naked.

"Defer to a higher power," I said. "Don't you think your parents will do anything? Do you really think they'll wait and not call?"

She shook her head. "It's just the thought of leaving her with them for even a little while longer. I can't wake my parents up when I get home. It'll be too late."

"Why not? They won't care, given the circumstances."

"I don't know." Kates bit at the skin on the side of her index finger.

"So call the damn police and get it over with," Aimee said. "It's what you want to do. It's what you should do. It's abuse, isn't it? Do you doubt that? So call the police." Aimee lunged for the phone and dialed before we could get our jaws off the floor. "Hello," she said after a moment. She pulled the phone's base closer and read the emergency sticker on it. "Please come to 4678 Tulip Drive. It's an emergency. There's a baby injured here." She paused. "No, I can't stay on the line. I'm alone here. Just come fast."

She hung up. Standing up, she passed the baby to Kates, then grabbed my arm. "We'll be waiting down the block. We'll come back after the cops arrive, saying that we saw the lights and knew you were here. I can't stay, and neither should you." She faced me. "The fewer of us here, the better." Dragging me to the door, she said over her shoulder, "We'll be back."

But we didn't come back because Kates called her parents as soon as the cops arrived, and then the baby's parents had to be located, but by then the social workers had arrived. The paramedics were also there. The reporters were next. They listened to the police radio, I guess.

We went home before they took the baby away and before they arrested the parents, but it was on the eleven o'clock news, so I watched it then.

Kates stayed out of camera range and, with her parents' help and the police's, managed to slip out the back way. She never allowed her name to be used, even though X rays revealed broken ribs and other injuries on the baby. She was clearly a heroine, or rather, Aimee and Kates were heroines.

Kates's parents lost several friends over the whole thing. Sides were taken just like in a playground battle, and some people chose to support the abusers. Those idiots said that all parents have the right to discipline their children as they see fit. Some people suggested that Kates needed a little discipline, too. They viewed her as a meddler and home breaker. We learned a lot about what can be justified under religion's name. Aimee's father and stepmother, despite their right-wing religion, became closer with Kates's parents. They were being two-faced and should have stuck with their own kind, but they didn't. They went for the image of normalcy.

Kates stopped taking jobs with people she hadn't already baby-sat for, saying she was too busy, but she was just afraid.

And Aimee? She never talked about the baby or baby-sitting again. She wouldn't go with Kates anymore either. Sometimes people would plead with her to watch their kids, knowing she took care of her little brother a lot, but she never would.

She said the pay wasn't worth it.

But I remember the ashen color of her face, the hollowness of her cheeks, and the expression in her eyes as she took that little girl in her arms and cradled her against her belly. Sure, I felt sick at heart when I saw the poor little thing, and I even sniffled a little, but it wasn't the same for me as for Aimee. Nor was it the same for Kates, although it hit her hard.

Maybe that's why she called the police so fast. Only Aimee understood.

I have to visit my dear old dad this weekend, which is a relief because Hope has been calling me nonstop since I got home. Maybe she thinks she has even more in common with me now. I'm not sure she knows that my episode was diagnosed as a suicide attempt, but she knows that I'm officially nuts.

As if what happened with Aimee was a little bit of nothing.

Anyway, she keeps calling, asking to come over or if she can pick up my homework for me, as if I'm incapable of that on my daily jaunts to school. She asks if I'd like to study together.

My mother has been eavesdropping on these calls. I know this because Mom was not made for spying. She may have the knock-'em-dead good looks of women spies in movies, but she makes no attempt to hide her knowledge of my conversations. She simply picks up the phone and listens. Hope doesn't notice the click and new background noise coming from my mother's room, but I do.

I keep praying that Hope doesn't mention Aimee or her own suicide attempt. That would be too much of a clue for dear old Mom to miss, and she might catch on to why I'm avoiding Hope. But then again, if Hope slipped something about suicide into the conversation, it might spice things up. Mom would flip, and I wouldn't have to talk to Hope anymore.

So far, however, our conversations have run along the lines of:

Me: Hello.

Hope: Hi! How are you?

Me: Fine.

Hope: Are you well enough to come over? Or would you like some company?

Me: No.

Hope: Maybe tomorrow. I got a new fall coat today, and we're going to the beach tomorrow. It's beautiful this time of year, and much less crowded. We could go for a long walk, if you can come?

Me: No. I can't.

Hope: Are you grounded?

Me: No.

You get the idea. Why she hasn't taken the hint and what exactly it is that she wants from me, I don't know.

But since I have to go to Dad's and he has a computer that isn't locked, I should be able to e-mail Chard—if his parents have lightened up their control of his computer. They weren't too pleased about his disappearing to see me, and so they tried to block his access to the Internet for a while. They say he has to have some consequences for scaring them half to death. It's as if the time we were together in the hospital never happened.

Speaking of Chard, Marge won't let go of him. We've reached a real impasse in our almost daily sessions. I greet her, she greets me, then she says, "Shall we return to the topic of our last session?"

I stare at her hairline and wait for it to drive her nuts. Sometimes I ask, "What topic is that? It's been so long since we've discussed anything."

She never falls for that one.

But I think she's heading for a big blowup with me. Some type of confrontation. I can feel her exasperation just like I feel Mom's when she serves dinner and I shove it to the side and walk away. She bites her lip, but it bugs her. So I keep doing it.

I suppose I've always acted that way, tried to get my mother's goat, that is. I don't intend to change now.

I walk into Dad's new abode to find junk. He has no taste. I always thought some of the perfection of our home was due to Dad, but after seeing the brown plaid couch and lime green velveteen recliner, I know differently. Still, I don't miss the stiff feminine touches Mom apparently would've added. I wonder what our house would have been like if Dad had had more say in it. Maybe it would have been a less fashionable, more relaxed place, kind of like here, where there's a Far Side calendar in the kitchen and a Mickey Mouse phone in my room. Overall, it's not too bad—small, ugly, but comfortable.

The room I have to sleep in is little more than a closet, and it lacks its own closet to boot. I have to leave my stuff in my duffel bag, or stack it on a table with the computer and his work. I don't mind. I didn't bring much. Dad's so relaxed in his new home, he even walks into my room to fetch stuff whenever he needs it. As if he still thinks I'm seven or eight, when privacy was not an issue. Maybe he forgets I'm here, which wouldn't be hard since neither of us is talking much. We don't want to talk about the important things in our lives, like separation, divorce, and death. Talking about them might cause a scene. Not much else is going on in our lives, though, so we're mostly quiet.

But when he popped his head in my door the fifth time, I called him on it. "Don't trust me alone, Dad? Afraid I'm puking in the wastebasket? Don't worry. That's not my style."

"I never said that. I just forgot the figures on the latest upgrade at the plant. They're insisting we remove some of the machines we had to install only three years ago. Tighter government regulations." He shuffles through piles and slides folders around until he finds what he wanted. Everyone is a "they" to Dad. He never tells me who gave him any information. It's always, "They did."

I grunt an answer as he searches and watch his backside.

When he turns back around, he has this weak smile on his face. "Listen, I'll knock next time." He waves his papers at me but avoids my eyes.

I glance down and see that I am clutching my notebook against my chest as if I'm not wearing a bra or something. My knees are tucked up, too. I hadn't wanted him to see the notebook, didn't want him to know what I was writing, but come to think of it, it wasn't he who'd complained about the journal. No, he thinks I'm embarrassed about his seeing me in what I wear to bed. His shyness is almost too funny, but I don't laugh. I lower my knees and nod.

He still hesitates, and that's when I know he wants to say more. One hand twitches the papers against his thighs, the other keeps straying in and out of his pocket. "Listen, Pumpkin."

He hasn't called me that in years. Not since Candyland and Chutes and Ladders were my favorite games.

"I want you to know that we love you and that none of this"—he waves his hands around the room, but he means the situation between Mom and him—"none of this is your fault. Not the trial, not the move, not even this eating thing, whatever that is, is part of what is going on between your mom and me."

He stops. I'm supposed to thank him, I'm sure. But I don't know what for. Letting me off the hook for their problems? I'm not stupid or deaf or blind. I know my bills are adding up. I know what people say to them about me and their amazing ability to stand by me.

"Anyway, we love you."

It sounds lame and empty and hangs in the air for almost a minute before I respond. Even I know what I'm supposed to say. But talking about our emotions isn't done at my house, and now I realize it's my mother who dictated that rule, too. I grunt out an "I love you," and turn back to my notebook, my cheeks flaming with embarrassment.

"Hey," he says, again not meeting my eye, "there's a show in town. We could get tickets and go."

I consider this. It can't be a rock concert. We couldn't get tickets to that this late. Is it a play? Does he mean a movie? I'm almost afraid to ask, but I have to. "What show?" I don't mean to, but I sound wary, uncooperative.

"*Peter Pan*, I think. It's on tour."

I smile, but my cheeks feel like cold clay, difficult to mold. How old does he think I am? "That's nice," I say, but he's caught my hesitation.

"Not someplace you want to be seen with your old man, huh?"

I try to hide my relief, but my shoulders untense and my fingers stop clutching my pen.

"Okay, then," he says. "Maybe another time." He nods once, touches the door frame with his hand, then leaves, closing the door quietly behind him.

While at Dad's apartment, I e-mailed Chard, but it was returned by the server. I tried calling both with and without a credit card, but I couldn't get through. Their phone must have been off the hook part of the time. The rest of the time I think they used Caller ID or something, although how they knew Dad's new number I'll never know.

Dad did take me to a new "expert" to help me deal with my eating disorder. He's not interested in firing Marge, he explained on our way over Saturday morning. He just thought a little extra help couldn't hurt. He'd made up his mind about going to this newest quack and nothing I did would change it. "I'm not afraid of your firing Marge," I said, staring out the window at the passing strip malls. "I'd like that. All I want is for everyone to leave me alone."

"We're only trying to help, and, remember, your therapy is court ordered, not parent ordered." He sucked in a big breath and let it out slowly.

"Yeah, I know. I brought it all on myself."

"Don't sound so pitiful. You did." He stared straight ahead, waiting for the light to turn green.

I stared out the side window at the broken glass, dirty fast-food wrappers, and beer cans. At least he wasn't making me go to *Peter Pan*. Maybe if I played along with this "expert," they'd cut back on my appointments with Marge.

This guy's expertise turned out to be hypnosis. He thought he had planted a posthypnotic suggestion that I would eat three full meals a day.

He couldn't know that pretend hypnotism used to be one of our favorite games. All six of us would gather in one tent, long past curfew on the nights one sex was allowed to camp out in someone's backyard (usually Jason's or Aimee's; the other sex would sneak out and join them), and we'd play with our minds. We'd try to hypnotize one another, and we loved to see who could fake that they were hypnotized the longest. Aimee always won, although I still swear that she actually was hypnotized by Chard. At least, she went to another place. It was on a night when we'd had a séance first and since that failed, we'd moved on to hypnotism.

Chard had spun a cross on a chain in front of Aimee's eyes. She blinked funny and then closed her eyes. I think she either suspended her disbelief or allowed herself to trust

Chard for once. I don't know. But we couldn't wake her up when we tried.

"She's really out of it," Kates said, her voice barely above a whisper.

"What did you do different?" Jason asked Chard, who just shrugged.

"Ask her something. Ask her if she's ever been kissed," Kyle said. I swear, he was always a walking testosterone pill.

"Naw," Chard said. Then he leaned closer to Aimee, who was sitting cross-legged on her sleeping bag with a freaky smile on her face. "What scares you, Aimee?"

I would've been surprised by his question if earlier we hadn't been trying to raise the spirits of Jeffrey Dahmer and Lizzie Borden—the first to know why he did it, the second to know if she did it. We'd all been pretty spooked by it because we were so afraid it might work. After all, what if good old Jeffrey decided he liked the body he channeled into so much that he stayed and that person became a cannibal and a murderer? The idea of becoming a spinster who killed her parents was less frightening, but it was still gruesome.

Aimee's smile disappeared. A frown puckered her brow.

"It's okay, you can tell us," Chard whispered.

She looked so much like a scared three-year-old that none of us were surprised by her answer. "The dark, the night," she said.

We all giggled.

"Did you send her back in time, too?" Kates asked. "Or is this a current fear?"

But Aimee had slowly curled herself into a ball before our eyes, and now she was whimpering. "Mom, no. I'm scared."

"Make her stop," I said. "It's not funny anymore."

"Aw, come on. What's it hurting?" Jason said.

"Shut up, Jason. Chard, stop it. Wake her up. Tell her not to remember any of it, and wake her up!"

The fear I felt for Aimee filled my voice, and he stared at me a moment without saying or doing anything.

"Do it!" My voice rose above our normal night voices and echoed in the yards around us.

"Jeez, don't have a cow," Chard muttered, as Aimee's whimpering and cries of "no" shifted into real sobbing. He looked concerned, too, as he moved in front of her and said, "You will wake up when I count to three and clap my hands. But you will remember nothing of what has happened—"

"And no one will tell her either," I added, staring each of my friends into a silent nod of submission. When everyone had agreed, I told Chard to go ahead.

"One, two, three!"

With the clap of his hands, Aimee sat up. Knowing she'd be confused not only by the situation but also by the tears on her face, I threw my pillow at her in an attempt to soak up some of the dampness.

"Hey!" she said, falling backward.

"Don't ever act like that again," I muttered as I flattened her to the ground, then released her.

She looked confused, then, taking my cue, said, "Sorry, guys, it was all an act. Fooled you!" But she didn't sound convincing. Not to me anyway.

This shrink Dad took me to failed miserably in his attempt to hypnotize me. I played along but almost blew it and laughed at the trigger that was supposed to make me eat. He said to listen for the sound of my parents laughing or talking in the kitchen, then I would want to eat.

I guess Dad hadn't filled him in on all the details of our

lives. To get even with Dad, I told him all about it afterward, when it was too late to say anything to the doctor. I wondered how much the session had cost. But Dad couldn't complain. He was responsible for the whole fiasco.

———

Marge was sitting in her usual spot, with her usual hairdo and her usual glasses, but something was missing. It was the alarm clock. That's when I knew I was there for the duration.

"Sit down."

I sat.

"It has become painfully obvious that you don't want to be helped. We had been making progress before your illness—"

"You called it a failed suicide attempt before."

"Yes. I don't believe you want to be helped."

She waited.

What did she think I'd say? I'm a mess, and only you can figure me out?

"I don't need help."

"I see." She twisted her pen cap all the way around, then pulled it off. Very effective gesture. "Then why are you starving yourself? Why are you unable to make friends? Why are you still hopelessly clinging to the friends from your past? Why did you help your friend commit suicide?"

I could have peed my pants when she said that. "You said there was no reason to read the court papers, that you always got to the heart of the problem without them."

"Touché."

We sat for a full fifteen minutes without saying anything. I may not have been able to watch the alarm clock, but I do wear a watch. The whole time, she kept twisting that pen, pulling off the cap, then putting it back on, then twisting it, and pulling it off. It started to make me queasy, watching her. I was sweating, and, for a minute, I thought I was going to pass out again. But I'd had a bagel for lunch, so passing out probably wasn't an option.

Then it hit me. She believed it, too. She believed every word of the accusation. Why shouldn't she? I'd defended Aimee's suicide up to the point of passing out at our last "productive" session. I'd never given her reason not to believe it. What if she had some court-appointed power to reverse the sentence or commit me for being a murderer? I felt the bagel rise in my throat, but I only burped. Sweat seemed to own my palms, my forehead, my armpits. And I was shaking.

"Believe whatever you want, whoever you want. But only I know what happened that night. Only Aimee and I know what to believe. The rest of the world?" I shrugged, suddenly remembering Aimee as I always did in the end. I stood up. "The rest of the world, you included, can go to hell."

I walked to the door, but before I got there she had a new question for me. "What about Chard?"

I sighed, thinking she really had fixated on something irrelevant.

But then she added, "What does he believe?"

I spun to face her. My skin felt too tight. From my toes all the way up to my scalp, my skin had been burned and shriveled and shrunk. "He knows the truth. He always has. No one allowed him to testify about what he believed, or he would have said I didn't do it. They said everything he knew was hearsay. That Aimee lied to all of us and especially to me to get me to help her. But I know. We know. Ask Kyle! Ask him why he tried to pop himself off if he didn't know. And believe. And would Chard have come to see me in the hospital if he didn't believe and know the truth?

"You're all alike. You all think we're untrustworthy. We're just kids, so how can we know what pain or anguish or hate or love is? But I think the people who don't know or won't recognize any of them are the grown-ups, the oh-so-perfect, ever-knowing grown-ups with their noses so high in the air when they walk by us they wouldn't even see or smell the shit they were stepping in."

"And Aimee didn't lie. To any of us."

I stopped. I felt my skin expand as I breathed again. Then I slammed out of the room.

But as I stomped down the stairs, dragging my fingernails along the textured wallpaper and feeling it give a bit under my hands, I knew that we'd had a breakthrough of sorts and I'd probably had all I could take just then. I sat down on the steps outside to wait for Mom, knowing Marge would tell her to come.

I thought about Aimee and the assertion that she had lied. Aimee didn't tell us the same things, but she told every one of us the same basic story with the same backbone of truth. My version just happened to be the one with the most blood and muscle and nerve, the one that most resembled her life, because I was the person closest to her.

I'm right about that.

I've staked my life on it.

———

The second time Chard came to visit me in the hospital, I was a mess. I'd been there a few days already by that point. Long enough to think more than I wanted to. I felt as though I'd been left in a burning car with no way to roll down the windows or open the doors. I had to watch as all the blood and sweat was sucked from my body. More than food, I missed my old life, my old friends, Aimee. There was no point in eating. Or sleeping, for that matter. As quiet settled in the hospital that night, I couldn't sleep, so I plugged my headphones into my CD player and cranked the volume.

Every anti-rock-and-roll freak who wants to blame all of life's problems, especially teenagers' problems, on modern music would be disappointed, though, because I listened to Mozart's *Requiem*.

I also liked Maria Callas. I got hooked on her because of the movie *Philadelphia*. Aimee didn't. She said that Callas made her understand why people say opera is just a lot of fat people screeching at one another. But I loved the emotion in her voice. I can't stand watching opera, but I listen to it all the time in my late-night mental roamings. I listen for the singers' pain and tears, joy and triumph.

I recently asked Hope if she liked opera, but she agreed so fast, it was obvious she just said it because it was the first time I had ever asked her a question. She probably ran to the library to check out a copy of *The Magic Flute* to have something in common with me. I wonder if all that emotion pouring from her room—because I imagine she's not cool enough to listen with headphones on—makes her mother and father scared or nervous. Do they stand outside her bedroom door and whisper about her as they count the knives and razor blades?

Anyway, as I listened to Mozart that night, I began to feel connected again, as if someone out there knew what it felt like to be me. That parched, hot ache had begun to fade from behind my eyes when a hand touched me.

For one second, I thought it was the hand of God, and I was about to become a preaching born-again nutcase.

Then I thought it was Aimee. She owed me at least one visit before I went, too.

But when I rolled over, it was Chard.

I must have looked really bad, what with my expecting a ghost or God and being hooked up to tubes and having headphones on to boot, because he just said, "Oh, babe!" and slid into bed beside me.

That night I thought of how long it had been since I had been touched. Not in the tentative way he'd held me the night before. I mean touched like when we'd had sex. I was unprepared for how I felt as he pressed against me. I molded myself against him from my toes to the top of my head, which comes only to his chin. He rested that on my head, and I cried.

He didn't say anything, and that was good. Everyone thinks they know what is wrong with me, but they can't, because no one ever asks me

Aimee used to ask.

Chard, well, he always knew without asking.

Even on the night of the Sadie Hawkins dance, when he and Aimee had shown up under my window, pitching pebbles and *psssting* until I opened it to the frozen air and watched their breath mesh in frosty clouds.

"Come out," Aimee called. "We left the dance early."

I glanced back at my alarm clock. Ten o'clock. "Obviously."

"It was boring," Chard said. Then he nudged Aimee. "Sorry!"

"Shhh!" I brought my window down, thanking the Anderson Window Company for making their windows quieter than the wooden ones they had replaced. Besides, they were almost impossible to nail shut. I pulled on sweats and slipped downstairs, where I grabbed my coat and boots and was out the door, forgetting my key and locking myself out.

We laughed about that as we climbed into Chard's car—at the last minute his parents had let him drive Aimee to the dance instead of doubling with Jason. We drove to the back of an elementary school where we giggled and drank, then made angels in the snow. We gave each of the angels an empty wine or beer bottle, then drove off in search of food. None of us mentioned that I hadn't gone to the dance, and neither Aimee nor Chard told me whose idea it was to pick me up. We could have gone to the all-night diner, but we didn't want to be with other people, so we cruised through an Arby's instead.

Then we drove around, screwing up when we had to shift, and talking about nothing. Stalling out on some railroad tracks, and peeing on different sides of the car when we couldn't hold it anymore.

When Chard dropped us at Aimee's, I wondered if he'd go home or cruise some more. We watched the lights of his car as they moved up our street and then flickered in and out of houses until he turned up the block where he lived.

Aimee and I stood a moment longer, then she flicked my arm with her hat. "He's yours for the taking, you know."

"What?"

"You know exactly what I mean. Show some interest. Be his. Stop being his *friend*. Be *his*." She glanced up the street. "Come on. We'll figure out a story about why you're here in the morning. I'm cold and tired, and if I stay up much later, I'll puke."

I followed her inside, up the stairs, and into her room. As we slipped into bed, I asked her again what she meant, but she jumped out of bed and ran for the bathroom.

Almost a year and a half later, lying in a hospital bed, I know what she meant. I hold on to his shirt and press against him. I don't try for more. I can't deal with more. But I feel closer to him than on the night we'd gone too far. After that night we had both been scared of what we'd done. I'd been afraid that he thought I was a slut.

But Chard didn't see me like that. That night in the hospital he held me tighter than he had before, if that was possible. As dawn slipped through the tinted windowpanes, it revealed my skinny knees and protruding ribs, which he must have felt against him in the night.

"Don't lose any more weight, all right?" he said, rubbing his chin across my hair. "There's hardly anything left of you."

"There never was much of me," I said.

"How can you say that?" he asked.

And for a moment I hear Aimee again, holding my face up to a mirror and telling me to look.

But I never did look.

"What should I do? Lie?"

"No, tell the truth. Admit you're beautiful. Don't you know that? That night we were together, I never thought that would happen. I never thought we would even date."

"We didn't."

"No, I suppose not. We should. But that night, you were drunk and I thought that you would think I had acted like Kyle, taking advantage of you—just for your body. But it was never like that. Never."

For a second, I thought he was crying, but then he went on. "I never talked about this, 'cause I was afraid you'd turn tough on me and tell me to piss off and never come near you again. I figured you either didn't remember or else you had decided you didn't want to rock the gang's boat. Then you didn't ask me to the Sadie Hawkins dance, so I knew it had been a fluke, and I was glad to have kept you as a friend."

"But I didn't ask anyone else."

"You never ask anyone else. You hardly ever date. It didn't surprise me that you didn't ask anyone to Sadie Hawkins, but I always wondered why you didn't date more."

"No one worth anything ever asked me out."

"See! You turned all sorts of guys down. Good guys."

"I did not."

"Did so. There were even rumors that you and Aimee were . . . you know."

"Oh, God. That's a new take I hadn't heard before."

"Sorry."

"So we were talked about like that, you know, after?"

"A lot. I'm sorry, I shouldn't have said anything. I know it wasn't true. I told guys that it wasn't true."

"You didn't—"

"I never told anyone about our night—except Aimee. And I figured she already knew. She didn't, though. I could tell."

I stayed quiet.

"Why didn't you say anything to her?" He asked it like it was something that had bothered him.

"I thought you liked her." I could barely force the words out of my mouth. "She was so—everything. So popular. And you always talked to her."

"To find out stuff about you. She knew I liked you. I'd pump her for info on who you were dating." His arms tightened around me, and I thought the blood-pressure cuff or heart monitor or something would go off and warn the staff that he was there. There were more and more sounds outside the door. "I once asked if she knew whether or not you were a virgin."

"You did what?"

He grinned. "That was after that night with Kyle. When you cried?"

"That mess. That's what it was, too. A mess. But what isn't anymore?" I yawned without meaning to.

"Sleep, babe. It's almost light, and I have to slip out of here before we're caught."

"Don't leave me!" A sudden sharp pain drove through my chest, nailing my heart shut. The blood seized in my veins. I would die if he left. And I would lose him. If not immediately, then soon.

But he said, "I'll be back. I'll be back. I promise."

And he kept his promise for two more days.

Tonight I search our house for clues to who or what my parents are. After an hour or so, I find myself, still clueless, sitting at my mother's vanity table. She actually has one, and it's all laid out with makeup and crap on little silver trays with mirrored bottoms. It must be extraordinarily difficult to clean all these perfume bottles, one by one, then realign them in precise order, with the most expensive ones in front.

But she doesn't have to clean them. We have a cleaning lady. My mother works so she can pay someone else to clean her things.

And no one ever comes up here except her, so I don't know why she has the jars and creams arranged like this.

Who'd care? The cleaning lady? I doubt it. More often than not, the cleaning lady puts the bottles back according to size, then I hear the clinking and tinkling of the perfumes as Mom reorganizes them.

As I sniff her perfumes, Mom and Dad are having dinner together. I'm not sure if this is good or bad. Are they trying a reconciliation? Or discussing divorce? Or me? I can hear Mom now: "Should we recommit the girl? I mean, she's really slipping further and further. This eating thing, dear, it's driving me nuts."

I see Dad pat Mom's hand, see her glance up at him, hold his eyes with hers, those killer eyes, blue like forget-me-nots. Not at all a typical eye color. I've wondered if she went to some voodoo doctor to buy some eye dye to make them that way. They can't be real.

And if they are, why aren't mine that color?

I look up, clutch the edge of the table, rattle the bottles against each other, and face my reflection.

But I can't judge what I see.

"You're getting a little plump, honey," Mom says as she pinches my bottom as I stand at the sink.

Or—

"My goodness! I feel every rib. Haven't you eaten today? Let's go and get some ice cream."

Granted this last comment has come from my mother's mouth more often lately than in the past. Before Marge's attempts to enlighten her and the hospital episode, my mom would be delighted by my weight loss. She might have even taken me to the Ford modeling agency and asked if a nice cut-and-dye job, a makeover, and maybe a month at the spa wouldn't turn me into a suitable candidate for world-class modeling. I never know what price she'd pay for success.

The girl in the mirror. She's me, yes. But I can't be objective here. Aimee saw the good, envied my complexion, or wished for my hair. Dad sees both good and bad, but he sees them in terms of time. When I wear my hair in a ponytail, he's delighted. If I try out a new hair color, even the temporary kind, he freaks. Mom sees the bad—my too-straight eyebrows, the way I pucker my forehead and leave traces of wrinkles between my eyes, the gap between my two front teeth.

She had wanted to whiten my teeth, and after Madonna fixed her gap, she tried to have me do that, too. I wouldn't do either one. I'm a recalcitrant, ungrateful child. I don't see when someone is trying to help me. I only know how to piss people off. I look for and do the very things that would make them the angriest, my mother and father. Because he's part of the equation, too.

He's the part that hates the deception I had to use whenever I wanted to do something with the gang. If I want to tick him off, I just lie. It's the only way to get a rise out him that's not dictated by Mom. He's also the part that doesn't want me to grow up. He wants to keep me small, childlike—more manageable, I guess. If I act like a kid—smile and hop around and giggle (picture that!)—he's likely to give me what I want. If I get mad at him, he'll never give in. He's hopelessly stubborn when he's angry, infinitely flexible when he's not. Dad's also the part of me that worries I'll screw up somehow and not live up to my potential. He's scared I'll get knocked up before I graduate from college. At least Mom was almost done with law school when she blew it, and then she had the superhuman capability of sitting through her bar exam while in the earliest stage of labor. Of course, I took more than two days of putzing through her birth canal to arrive, but still. It was painful, not to mention annoying, that I had to come when I did.

She had lied to her doctors and everyone else, including Dad, about the date of her last period so that no one would suggest she hold off on the bar exams.

Nooo. She wouldn't have dreamed of giving anything up for me.

I lower my eyes. They're not her eyes. They're not Dad's either. They're from some relative I don't remember, maybe my grandfather, and the only thing I know for sure about them is that they are odd. Neither brown nor green, and with some kind of peculiarity that made one boy tell me that my eyes frightened him. What did he see? What in a person's eyes could frighten, if they're not evil?

"Aimee," I ask, "is that me? Is that who you said was beautiful? That girl in the mirror?"

I wait, but there is no answer. There is never an answer anymore. I finger the closest bottle. I feel my hand squeezing, squeezing, tighter and tighter until the cover pops off and perfume trickles over my hand.

It smells so much like my mother. I stare at the glistening liquid, think of how she's in cahoots with Marge to pry Aimee out of me, and I squeeze tighter, but the glass doesn't break.

So I throw a fit.

I throw the perfume bottles at the walls, the windows, the door. Then, when the mix of musk and jasmine and lily of the valley and rose and lavender has reached a crescendo of skunk stench, I start on the trays. They fly like frisbees across the red-and-cream-flowered spread, blanch against the wall, then shatter into fragments of light that shoot back at me in slow motion. The sound of breakage, of silver handles thumping into wall boards, gouging holes big enough for a mountain climber's toes, of glass splitting along stress lines and drifting to the carpet and bed with soft sighs, sends me spinning beyond hope, beyond fear.

I am tired of hurting. I want someone else to hurt. I want them to know what it felt like as I watched my world come apart, saw the thing I loved most lying lifeless on the bed. To watch the letting go of urine, which stained her clothes, then the bedspread, then soaked through my own clothes to touch my skin. The feeling that the smell of shit is right for how I felt at that moment, and that I should be sitting in piss. What else should I expect?

But I hadn't expected any of it.

Tonight, heaving and sobbing in my mother's room, I flop to the floor and sit in French perfume and think I haven't come very far. I stretch out, too weak to get up. My fingers brush a envelope that has come to rest in the midst of one shattered tray. It's pale to the point of colorlessness.

Inside I find several pieces of paper. The top one is covered with old-lady writing. I glance at the signature and don't recognize the name, but curiosity wins out. I read it and am disappointed to find it's only a letter from some old aunt who thought that Mom might like to have the enclosed papers now that her father has died. The only interesting comment is, "I was instructed by your father not to forward the certificate to you until you had reached an age of majority (whatever that is), but I have used my own judgment in this matter." Two boring letters follow, but the third letter is entirely different.

Dear ——

I am pleased to inform you that my daughter has been accepted into the law program at the University. [*So he* had *lived that long!*] I had talked with the dean and felt her admission was assured, so it didn't surprise me that she was accepted. Her decision to study law does surprise me, though. I suppose, if she works hard, she might make a good public defender. Or maybe she should focus on family law so that she can work around her future family's schedule. Since your husband pursued a career in law and you live relatively close to the university, perhaps he can help her with her studies. She's a fairly good student, but she might need some direction or reminders to attend to her studies instead of social activities. Perhaps your husband could suggest a low-key firm suitable to a woman's career needs when the time comes.

I look forward to hearing from you soon and trust you are in good health.

With best regards——

I hold the letter in my hand and wonder. Why would a man say such ignorant things about his daughter? Of all of the mementos of her life, why did my mother keep this one? I think of how driven she is, and for the first time, I get an idea why. Did she keep the letter as a reminder of the mistakes a parent can make? I think of her letter to the college trying to wheedle me in, just like her father did for her. At least her letter for me showed some caring.

When I turn to the next sheet, I freeze. It's a death certificate for a little boy who lived only hours. Mom's brother. My uncle. He would have been five years older than Mom, this son her father always wanted. Were her brother's imagined milestones always dangled before her?

Why keep the letter and certificate at all? I stare at the black type blurred by perfume. Why keep the hurt alive?

Did she need a reminder of how hard she needed to work to please a man who (even dead) would never be satisfied? Or did she feel vindicated that she'd achieved more and done better than any parent could've expected? Will I ever know?

Not after what I've done.

I survey the room, dropping the papers on her bed. There is no way I can hide what I did. Nothing I can do to put it right. But I do pick up the broken glass and the trays with their bent handles. I restore the few bottles of perfume that remain unbroken to the vanity. I open the windows, walk on towels to soak up perfume.

Then I sit on her bed. Where did her strength come from? Maybe if I had her will to overcome obstacles, everything would be fine right now. I face myself in the mirror, this time looking for her strength. I find only her white skin, her rosebud mouth, her high cheekbones, and her straight nose. My mouth isn't as firm. My face isn't as confident. I am a lot like her, but I own the mass of black hair and my eyes.

I have to accept that I am not my mother I am me. I hear Aimee again, telling me to look at myself, to admit that I have good traits. Many of my so-called good physical traits she wouldn't recognize now. I have beanpole legs that look like they can't hold up my body. My butt is flat, with a few dimples that I know will always be with me. Still, I can come back from this. I can get back my looks. Aimee will never come back again.

I push my hair out of my face, take a deep breath, and say, "I was a lot to drag around, wasn't I, Aimee? The right clothes, the right hair, no pimples. Boys asking me out, but me not dating them. Me whining and crying. Me not taking you seriously enough, or at least thinking my life was as bad as yours."

I stop. I can't go further. It's enough. For now.

I gather up the towels and pull the bedspread from the bed. The letters fall to the floor and I stare at them, unsure of where to put them in all this mess. Finally, I pick them up and stuff them into my pocket, figuring I'll deal with them later. I haul the linens and towels downstairs and throw them in our supersized washing machine. Then I go into the kitchen and pour myself a bowl of cereal.

That's where they find me, when they arrive home, eating cereal at the kitchen table.

Dad greets me with, "What stinks?" He sniffs, doglike, his nose pointed in the air, then says, "This place smells like a bordello. Did you go out tonight?" He leans toward me with his hands on the table.

I breathe a little more quickly. They can't smell the perfume down here, can they? Then I realize it must be all over me. Why didn't I shower and change? I shift, and the papers crinkle in my pocket. It's too late to put them back now. As I kick myself for taking them, I try to focus on my answer. He only asked if I went out tonight. I shake my head no and grunt. Technically, I haven't lied.

I go back to eating my Lucky Charms as if nothing's wrong, but I watch Mom smell the air, as though testing a theory that's forming in her mind. Her head turns slowly on her thin neck, then it swings back to me.

"I'm going to change," she says, tugging at the neckline of her black dress, which is short at the thighs, tight at the waist, and scooped at the neck.

"Mom?" I start to tell her, but how can I explain? "Forget it."

Before she goes far, Dad starts sniffing again. "Are you

lying again? Tell me what you did. The truth. What did you do tonight?"

I hold up my bowl, idiotically trying to make a joke. "I'm eating."

"I don't mean at this moment, I meant while we were gone! Why can't you just answer me? Why do you make some stupid comment every time I ask you something? What did you do tonight?"

I look up, smile sweetly, and without really planning to make him angrier, I say, "Did you have a good time?" I can't seem to stop pissing people off, and I never stop when I'm ahead. Mom will be down in a moment, and the truth will be painfully obvious. Why do I have to make it worse?

His face explodes into red. He comes around the table, his arm raised. He's never hit me before, but he's been under a lot of stress lately. What is Mom doing upstairs?

He stops next to me. I keep my head down, staring at the green and pink and yellow and orange charm shapes floating in my bowl. I always save the marshmallows for last.

He doesn't move away, but his arm drops. I pick up my spoon and chase rainbows, clovers, and half-moons. When I have as many shapes as I can get on the spoon, I shove it into my mouth. I glance at him. As he stares at my bowl, I realize he's seeing me as before, when I was still little and begged for sugary cereal every morning. Or maybe he's trying to reconcile that cheerful little girl with the accused murderer at his side.

His face is no longer red, his eyes are filled with tears, and he's shaking. I look away and keep eating, so that I'm pretty much done when Mom returns. She brings the scent of her room with her. It has infiltrated the fibers of her white cotton robe, seeped into the silk of her nightgown, probably even invaded the rubber of her slippers.

She hesitates in the doorway, but I won't meet her eyes. Dad looks up, but he seems lost and doesn't notice that the smell that started this outburst has grown stronger.

"I think you should leave," Mom says.

"But—" he starts to protest, but even to him it sounds halfhearted, empty. I can see that he wants to leave, get as far away from me as he can. Maybe he wants to go to a bar and drink away the memory of who I used to be, or more likely, what I am now.

"I'll handle her." Her voice is flat. Her face is washed of makeup but not relaxed or smooth.

She must have forgotten her moisturizer, I think, as she takes Dad's arm, leads him across the room and to the front door. I hear their voices, and I'm sure he's crying. I don't know if she's telling him what I've done, or if he's telling her about his epiphany in the kitchen. More likely it's the latter. He'd go nuts if she told him the truth.

I dump my bowl in the dishwasher and realize that I didn't eat supper, so I shouldn't be so proud of my late-night snack. Still, I ate. The washing machine has finished, and I pull her bedspread and towels out of it. The stench is gone. I decide to dry her bedspread first and stuff it into the dryer, putting it on the least damaging setting, "Air."

Ten minutes pass, and she hasn't come looking for me. I hop up on the washing machine and kick my legs, listening to the hollow, metallic bangs for a while, but still she doesn't come. I open the dryer. The spread is soaked. No heat comes from it. I up the setting to "Delicates" and leave the laundry room.

She doesn't come.

I walk to the front of the house. Dad's car is gone. I creep to the bottom of the stairs. There's a light under her door, but I can't go to her.

So I toss the smelly sweatshirt I had been wearing into the laundry basket, pull a long jersey that I use as a nightgown over my jeans, then go back to the kitchen to wait for the spread to dry.

When at last it is, I wrap it around me, like a mantel, and walk up to her room. I hear nothing through the closed door, but I know she's awake. I close my eyes, reach out, and knock.

"Go away."

I wonder if she means forever, she sounds that hard. "I have your bedspread." I pull it off me, try to wad it into a folded bundle.

She doesn't answer.

I turn the knob, push the door. She's sitting at the vanity table. "I'll put it on the bed," I say. I shake out the spread, smooth the wrinkles while I watch her reflection. I put the pillows back, fluff them, wait.

She says nothing.

"Mom, I'm sorry."

She looks down.

"I don't know what came over me."

She puts her hand over her eyes.

"I cleaned it up as best I could. I'll buy you more perfume."

"Don't bother."

"Whatever kind you want. I'll use my allowance, get a job, use money from my bank account. I'll replace it all. I was wrong."

I wait, but she doesn't respond.

"I will, too." I stop.

163

She hasn't moved.

I sigh, then turn to go. "I'm sorry," I whisper at the door. And I am.

"Where are they?" she demands as I'm pulling the door shut.

I stare blankly at her.

"You know what I'm talking about. Where are my things? You'd think if you were so sorry, you'd have given them back." She's standing now, facing me, her eyes snapping.

I dig in my pocket. "I . . . I was afraid Dad would find them if I left them out." I'm stammering, wishing I never took them. I sound lame, and I can tell she's not buying it.

"So you read them. Don't you think he knows?" She snatches the letters and certificate from my outstretched hand, being careful not to touch me.

I let my hand fall. "Yes. No." When she doesn't do more than nod, I ask, "I didn't know you had—"

"It's none of your damn business. Get out and don't ever come in here again!"

I back up, hit the door, spin around, leave.

———

"I deserved worse," I say to Marge. I've told her about what I did in my mother's room the day before, but I don't tell her about the letters and the dead brother thing. Those are my mother's secrets to tell, not mine. I seem to be developing scruples.

"Did she deserve it?" Marge asks, and for a minute I'm lost.

"Deserve—Oh! What I did?"

She nods.

I look out the window, as though that would make me think better, but what I'm thinking isn't what I should say. What I should say is, "No, she didn't. She was never that bad to me." But what pops into my head is, "Why didn't she let me see that she was human before?"

So I don't answer. I revert to silence as usual.

"I take your silence to mean that you're thinking about it. But think about this while you do: What did your mother ever do to anything of yours that caused you similar pain?"

I meet Marge's eyes then. I have to, but I don't tell her about that cold dawn, how they brought me home in a squad car, then took me away again later, how Mom had stood next to Dad, allowing her eyes to glaze over. That shuttered look came over her face as the officer in charge talked. Then she had stepped back from where I stood, turned her face away. She didn't cry. She didn't say I couldn't have done what they were saying. She didn't touch me. She didn't even look at me. She didn't ask me if what they were saying was true, had I really killed my best friend?

What she had said was, "We'll need a good lawyer. I better get Chris on the phone." She left the room. I wasn't sure if she meant me and them—that we all needed a good lawyer—or if she and Dad did. My hands cuffed in front of me, I stood on my one good leg and watched her go, and wondered how long she'd be gone. Would she tell them to take the cuffs off? Accuse them of violating my rights?

What she yelled from the other room was, "Will she be tried as an adult or juvenile?"

"For God's sake!" Dad said.

"We can't answer that, ma'am," one of the officers said. "She hasn't been charged with anything yet."

The other said, "We need to take her to the station now.

We felt, though, since you folks live so close and what with your wife being a lawyer, that we should stop off here. We wanted you to know as soon as possible, and she wasn't in any shape to call. The other girl's parents weren't too rational either. Besides, it's easier to hear news like this in person, you know." He coughed.

His partner coughed.

Dad sneered, "Yeah, right."

"Will someone be following us to the station?" The officer in charge rose on his toes, rocked a moment, and peered into the room where my mother's voice whirled and explained, ground to a halt, then rose in astonishment. She could have been talking about an interesting cocktail party instead of her daughter being a suspect in a murder investigation.

And who knows, maybe she was.

Dad glanced behind him, then took his coat from the closet. "I will."

The cops turned me between them.

"Are those really necessary?" Dad tapped the cuffs. It was he who stood up for me. It was Dad who remembered who I was.

"A matter of routine, sir. Calmed her down considerably besides."

Dad nodded, unable to say more, and walked to the garage after calling out where he was going.

Mom didn't respond. She didn't call out, "I love you," didn't say, "I'll see you there."

And she hadn't. Seen us there.

Dad stayed at the station until I lost it and started crying, keening really. They couldn't get me to stop, and they called a doctor. But I wouldn't let the short little man near me. I had some idea that he was going to give me an overdose, a tit-for-tat kind of punishment. So I kept running away from him, and he kept waddling after me, never very close, despite the smallness of the cell. I don't think he wanted to catch me, and I certainly didn't want to be caught, which meant I kept running from one side of the cell to the other, where I'd crash into bars or cinder blocks, bounce off, and head in the opposite side.

I kept thinking, Where is she? Where is she?

I wanted Aimee. I wanted my mother.

Neither came, of course. And I had no idea where either one was. Both, I imagined, were in hell. Aimee for what she had done, my mother because of what I had done or was accused of doing and because she had to explain to all the important people in her life what a monster I was.

Eventually, the two officers stepped inside the cell, and I ran out of places to ricochet off. One officer tackled me, cracking my forehead on the cement floor, leaving a circle of black and a bump the size of a plum. The other officer held down any spare parts of me that were still able to move with a man twice my weight lying on top of me. The doctor gave me the shot.

And over their shouts and exclamations of pain and frustration, and while I kicked and screamed and told them to leave me alone, I heard Dad whimpering. My big, strong, swearing, angry dad sounded like the biggest wimp in the world. But more than anything else, it was the memory of his pain-filled voice that got me through the next few days.

Down on the floor, I couldn't see him. I couldn't see much of anything other than beige shirts and pants, but I could hear him.

"Don't hurt her. My God! Be gentle. She's just a little girl.

Don't hurt her! Do you have to do that? Is any of this necessary? Why don't you let me talk to her?"

They didn't answer him. They held me down and doped me up. Then stood and backed away from me as though I still might jump them, as if I had been trying to hurt them in the first place. Then they opened the cell, scurried out, and, almost as an afterthought, let Dad in as I was fading, or maybe he forced his way into the cell. Things were pretty blurry by then.

I saw his face float and drift above me, felt his hand on mine, felt his handkerchief swab at my tears and dab at the bleeding lump between my eyes, heard him ask for ice. I heard his whispered, "I love you. We'll get you out of this mess."

But what I kept thinking was, Where is she? Where is Mom?

I look back at Marge, hold her eyes for a long moment, so she knows that I mean more than what I say. "That depends on your perspective," I answer.

"My what?" She's surprised. I haven't said anything for so long, she's slipped her mental gears and has been thinking of something, anything but me.

"On how you look at things and from whose point of view," I say.

The timer dings.

Marge smiles, but confusion is in her eyes.

I want to add more, but she hasn't understood the rest, so I don't. I want to tell her that Mom thought she was doing the best possible thing for me. She was securing me the best lawyer money could buy. But what I needed was her presence and her belief that I hadn't done anything wrong.

And she hadn't given me either.

I walk home from Marge's. I'm supposed to be driving home with Mom—actually practicing so I can take the driving test—but after the perfume incident, my mom "forgot" to come and pick me up. From the nearby school parking lot, I can hear the marching band fumbling through the school's fight song. It's cooling off, which means that the anniversary of Aimee's death is approaching.

The other anniversary I associate with Aimee now is in February, the anniversary of the trial. At that time, I was jailed in our home. Newspaper photographers, local television camera crews, even a few tabloid reporters had camped at the end of our driveway, braving one of the coldest winters in a decade to catch a glimpse of me. I'm sure good old Judy Murphy, the old lady across the street, was collecting money from them for sandwiches, hot drinks, and parking spaces. There were cars all over her lawn, vans with satellite dishes on top in her driveway, and cables and cords running into her house. It was pretty obvious what she believed about all of this.

But then again, she never had liked me or Aimee or the rest of us. If you asked her, we used to cut through her yard and trample her flower beds to get to school quicker. The worst thing I remember doing was sticking my tongue out at her when she banged her window open one morning and yelled words shrouded in frost, hatred, and misunderstanding. We were hoodlums, she yelled, her breath billowing out like dragon smoke. We destroyed other people's belongings. Look at her yard. Look at that path we were making.

We stopped a moment, not long because that would mean

we could be identified and our parents called. We glanced behind us. There, marked in the half-melted frost, was a path of footprints, six kids wide. But it had already disappeared in the section of the lawn where the sun reached. We shrugged, laughed, and took off, our legs flying like race-horses. We jostled and tumbled through an opening in the back of her yard and burst into the street beyond. We didn't stop there. We raced on, hearts beating war cries that pulsated in each of our heads. A rhythm shivered through me, making me think we'd never slow down, never stop.

Kates stopped first, pulling up and dropping her hands to her knees. Her laugh was little more than a wheeze by then. Aimee stopped with her, and then Jason and Kyle gave up.

Chard still ran, though, and I matched him stride for stride, until we were truly racing, and I became serious. Not a soul in the fifth grade could outrace me, and if Chard was trying to beat me, I'd show him.

I settled my hips lower, stretched my legs until my leggings pulled taut and threatened to tear at full stride. I got off my toes and used my whole foot, shoving my body forward off the balls of my feet and splattering the road behind me with stones.

I don't know when Chard stopped. At some point I threw my head back and let my books fall, trusting Aimee to pick them up. I was going somewhere, escaping something far more crucial than Mrs. Judy Murphy and her ugly lawn, beating down something more insistent than the competition of friends.

When I was almost to the bus stop, I burst into laughter, and that is what ended the perfect run of my life. Laughter.

Today, as I slog toward home, pants drooping on me, ridiculous, nonfunctioning shoes clomping the pavement, I think of that girl. Her ease of movement. Her joy. I marvel that I was she.

I wonder what happened to her laughter. I left her joy of chasing the wind behind in Aimee's room that night. I literally haven't run since.

I glance behind me and up the street. The band has stopped playing, but it will take the kids a while to leave the parking lot and make their way home. Right now, there's no one around. I tug a shoe off, then do the same on the opposite side. I clutch the shoes to my chest, take one last look around, then skip a few steps, limping on the uneven pavement.

My pants flap, so I stop and roll them up. Then, feeling a bubble growing inside my stomach, I throw my shoes into a bush. I close my eyes, pull myself taut, tell myself I can win this race, shake my arms and legs to loosen unused muscles. Then I crouch, tucking my fingers under knuckles, bringing my hips and buttocks up into the air, stretching my back leg straight, feeling the tension.

Then I'm running.

Running like the old me, head back, arms pumping, stretching, pulling me forward through air and space. I'm not thinking of anyone watching me. I'm not thinking of who might be around to see me. I'm only thinking of going fast. I was once the fastest kid in my class, and that achievement carried me through the rigors of an entire year of school.

My bare feet make less sound than the friction of my too big pants, but I don't hear either. What I hear is the rhythm that pounded in my ears on that perfect day, before anything bad had happened, when we were still young and innocent and without doubt.

I open my mouth, allow a chuckle to escape, then a burst of laughter, then a full blown flood of hysteria.

They're all behind me—Kates, Aimee, Jason, Kyle, even Chard. None of them kept up. None has outstripped me, and I am queen of the race.

When I can breathe no more, when I am sobbing more than laughing as my body tries to turn my lungs inside out to gulp more oxygen, when my stomach churns with rushing blood and lack of energy, I find myself hunched over, one hand on a stitch growing more painful with every breath, one hand on a jiggling knee as I try to push upright and not cough up breakfast, lunch, and dinner.

"Walk through it," says a voice. "That's the only way to get rid of a stitch in your side."

My head jerks up. It's Hope's boyfriend. He's alone, thank God, but he's smirking, his football cleats tossed over his shoulder and his bag of stinking laundry clamped under an arm.

"That was quite a performance." Now he's smiling for real. "You should run track. You'd whip every girl's ass in school and in the state too probably."

I stand and start to walk, lopsided. I don't tell him that I could, that I did, that I may still. Karen's face flashes before me.

"Where were you going, anyway? Someone chasing you? Or were you just trying to outrun your past?"

I face him, feeling as though the lack of oxygen in my brain is slowing everything down, but it's not that. It's him. "No. I don't need to run away from anything."

He nods, twists the handle to his gear bag, looks up at last. "Don't hurt her. Don't let her suck you in. Okay?"

"Who?" I want him to say it. "Don't let who suck me in? Into what?" I hear other kids approaching, but no one is visible yet. He must be a fast dresser.

"Hope. Hope, all right! She deserves more than she thinks she does."

"Talk straight. Tell me flat out what you're saying." The cement, hot in the sun, sears my feet. I try to keep my hands away from my cheeks, which are mimicking the heat in my feet.

"No offense to you," he says. He flashes a smile, but it's gone before I can tell if it's a nervous smile or a smirk. "But I've heard about you, and you've heard about Hope, about how she tried to—" He stops.

I raise my eyebrows, turn my palms out. "I'm not exactly on the gossip network at school." Still, I wait.

At last, moving closer and looking around, he says, "She tried to kill herself—all right? And she doesn't need a friend like you. She needs someone who'll help her see what she's worth, that that death stuff is nuts. She needs someone—"

"Like you?" I ask, unable to keep the sarcasm out of my voice. "Haven't been too successful, have you?"

"Look—"

"No, you look. I don't have to explain myself to you or to anyone else. You don't know jack shit about what happened to me or my friend. You only think you know. Even if I did do what everyone thinks I did, why would I do it for Hope?" His face has changed. There's a recognition I hadn't seen before, and I think, Good, I'm getting through to him. "What is Hope to me? What do I owe her? She's not even my friend. I hardly know her. And I don't know you at all. And I don't want to be having this conversation."

I turn up a side street, to get far away from this kid who ruined what had been a rare moment, but I go just a few steps before I hear:

"Hey, Hope," behind me. So that was the recognition I'd seen on his face. "I've been waiting since band let out. Where have you been?"

I turn to see her facing me, holding some musical instrument's black box. She's in band, and he's in football. It would only be more perfect if she were a cheerleader. But I don't say anything sarcastic because Hope looks like my finger could go right through her skin to poke muscle, nerve, and bone. "Hope," I say, "I didn't mean—"

She whirls away from both of us and walks fast down the sidewalk, her heels clicking loud.

"You're a real jerk," I yell at him when she's gone. "You knew she was there, didn't you?"

"I thought, when you got going, talking about how she's not your friend, that she might want to hear what you had to say." He shrugs.

There are kids behind us, and I think about causing a scene, but I'm too tired. Instead, I say quietly, "And what about what you said? Do you think she wanted to hear that, too?"

He looks blank. "I don't think she could have heard me. Besides, I'm trying to help her."

"I wonder if you know what that means. You have no faith in her. None. And you just told her that. Think about whether that helps her. Why does she need to be my friend, the biggest misfit your school has, if you're so god-awful wonderful?"

"You're a fine one to talk about being a friend. You're a frickin' murderer!"

I open my mouth, then close it. Barefooted, it's hard to spin on your heel and walk away, but I manage. There's a murmur behind David, of surprise or shock or agreement, but I don't stay to find out which. I figure it was the latter.

What I haven't managed to figure out is why I care that Hope heard me deny her friendship. I never actually said we were friends, and the closest we came to friendship was planning to see a movie but never making it.

So why does it matter?

———

I don't say anything to Mom when I walk in, shoeless, an hour and a half late from my appointment with Marge. She's home early and is sitting at the kitchen table studying papers. She's wearing a sweat suit and has a towel around her neck, which means she has either exercised already or intends to.

I walk past her to the refrigerator.

She doesn't look up.

I pull out a yogurt and a can of diet soda.

She grunts, so she at least notices that I am making a show of eating, but I take the food upstairs and leave it on my desk.

On my bed, lying unzipped, is my duffel bag. Nothing is in it. It's the first time I left it home since the scene between Mom and Marge. I hadn't meant to leave it, but something in me had relaxed, and I hadn't thought about it until I got to school. But I figured it was safe. Mom is never home before me.

But she is today, and now my bag's empty of everything important to me.

I grab the bag, turn it upside down, and shake it until even

I notice the panicked squeaks coming from my mouth as I put more and more force into every shake.

I stop shaking the bag, although my hands can't stop trembling, and turn the bag inside out. Nothing. I fling myself around my room, pulling open drawers, dumping underwear, socks, and pants on my bed. Everything flies, but still I see nothing that I want.

My heart is racing. I toss books off shelves, dump puzzles and games on the floor of my closet, rip dresses from hangers.

But I find no ashtray, no photos, no razor blade.

Then I spot my notebook sitting on my desk where she left it. After all, the doctor did say I needed to have that.

Did she read it?

I go to my door and try to jerk it open, only to find it locked. I look at my hands as they twist the polished brass knob, watch my feet dig into the carpeting, feel my body throw itself against the door.

And all the while a little voice inside of me is saying, She's taken Aimee away to get even with me. The voice grows louder as my body bangs into the door harder and harder. My shoulder caves into the wood, but it's my flesh that's giving, not the wood. My parents made sure this house was built right, even changing a few things in this room without asking me. Like the lock on the door so that they can lock it, not me, on special occasions like this.

My heart pushes bile into my mouth with each slamming beat. There's sweat on my hands, blood on my knees where I've smashed them into the door. I tear off the poster Aimee gave me, but there's still a door underneath. No peephole like at the psych ward, the last time I found myself caged.

Then everything explodes.

I hear myself shrieking every ugly word I know, every vile

phrase. My head whams into the door once, twice, three times in a rhythm I can't stop. Aimee. Aimee. Aimee. My heart pounds faster and faster, then becomes a constant flurry of motion indistinguishable as a beat. My breath catches, jerks, grates my throat raw as I scream.

Suddenly, she's out there, listening, and I stop. I hear her breathing. I smell her fear.

"Give her back," I snarl. There is nothing human inside of me.

She stays silent, but I hear the soft whisper of cloth on the wall where she must be leaning. Feel the sweatshirt stick to her back as she slides down the wall in defeat.

"I'll never forgive you for this. I didn't keep your stupid letter and death certificate. What do I care that you can't get over your dad's being a jerk? I gave them back. I broke your perfume bottles because I wanted you to know how bad you make me feel every day that you don't treat me like a person. Every time you treat me as a case to be handled and then dismissed, I hate you more."

I wait, but she says nothing.

"I hate you," I repeat. My voice sounds dead. I have nothing left to say.

I back away from the door, dart to my closet, and grab sneakers and an old sweatshirt. I shove them into the duffel bag along with a flashlight and the soda. Then I go to my window and bang it open.

Through the door I hear her sharp cry, then silence.

I stick my right leg over the sill, then twist backward to grab the notebook and a pen on the off chance that she hasn't read my journal yet. I don't want her to have another chance. Then I dangle both legs over the edge. No drainpipe stands conveniently placed like in books or the movies so I can shimmy in and out. No ladder. No kitchen roof here or waiting friends like every other time in my life I slipped out of my house.

There isn't even blackness.

There is the failing light of evening, a golden glow that speaks of happiness and whispers around the trees in the yard, softening the carefully placed lawn furniture, gilding the pool's edges, melting the borders of reality.

I see the carpet of gray-green that is the grass already fuzzing with a dusting of dew, the misty blue paleness of the sky fading to purple before me.

I wish I could see Aimee, but I can't. Or maybe I won't. Maybe she's here, and I won't see her, won't take her hand and follow her.

I close my eyes and jump into the evening, wishing for more height than a second-story window so that at last I would be doing what I should have done that night, not Aimee. It was 'me who should have died, me who should have taken all those pills.

Or maybe it was me who should have withstood all she had lived through. Maybe if she had my mother, she'd still be alive. And maybe if I had had her stepmother, I could have fought back.

I lie on the ground a moment and think of that. If I had lived with her parents with my temper, could I have survived?

But I have no time for such thoughts if I want to escape.

It jolted more than hurt when I landed, and my left ankle twisted, but it's nothing that I can't live with.

I hobble to my feet and look up. I see my mother's shape at the window. Why she came in now and not earlier, I don't know. Maybe I made a noise when I landed, and she got worried. Maybe she even watched me jump, too afraid to speak.

But it doesn't matter because I'm gone now.

"Come back and talk," she says, her voice low. She glances at the houses on either side, at the lights coming on as people arrive home. "Come back, please."

I watch her misery, apparent in her leaning figure, bending toward me, even holding out a hand for a moment.

But I do not move toward her. I pick up my duffel bag and I walk away, slapping the spiral notebook against my leg. When I've walked beneath the neighbor's oak tree and she can't see me anymore, I turn around. If she had still been there, if I could have heard her crying, I might have gone back. But she's not. She has closed the window quietly, and as I watch, she draws the shade. She turns the lights out. She'll probably call my probation officer next, then Dad.

Automaton mother. Everything by the rules.

I can't stay, so I head out. I have only what's in my pockets and my duffel bag, no money, no place to go, except maybe Hope's, but I've blown that, too. I flee through the dimming light to a woods nearby, hoping to find my path before it's too dark. No one comes here. Rumors about cranky home owners prowling the borders keep people out. The few kids who live in this neighborhood don't care for woods and wildlife anyway. They care for soccer and cheerleading, getting high and getting drunk and getting laid before their parents come home.

But I come here often, since I no longer care about the things other kids want. I found a great place where birch trees grow out of wild pachysandra, and the light is golden and white, and I can think or not as I please. No one but me knows about it. That's where I'm going, to this spot I've claimed as my own.

———

The light has failed, as has so many other things. Dad is gone, wallowing in irrelevant memories; I doubt he'll be back or accept me for who I really am. Mom, well, she was never really there, was she? Aimee is gone and can't come back. Kates, Jason, and Kyle left without a backward glance. They could have tried to keep in touch with me. And Chard.

My fingers slide over a pachysandra leaf, feel its waxy smoothness that ends with edges that bite. I look at the opening in the trees above me, at the dance of dying leaves in a breeze so slight I can hardly feel it. There will be a moon tonight, a huge diaphanous moon that will rise as a golden globe three times its normal size, shedding a peaceful light.

But there will be no peace, no softness. Not for me. All I've got is a notebook and a flashlight.

I'm not cold as I sit on a log in my mini-forest. I can't feel anything anymore anyway. But I can't stop my mind from seeing Chard, from hearing him. Maybe Mom will call him and ask him to come and look for me. He won't find me; he doesn't know my haunts, not *Here*. My mother will have to call someone official by morning, if she hasn't already. But unless they bring dogs, they won't find me either. I can hide beneath the pachysandra, I'm so thin. I'm too still to be seen. I'm alone in the freezing woods, with only a notebook and my memories for solace.

On his fifth visit to the hospital Chard came fresh from

my mother's house, showered and shaved and with a hint of wonder in his eyes. Wonder at being here with me, and wonder at what she must have been saying.

She would have told him about my nonprogress with the shrinks, about the one who couldn't stand me and quit. About the one I refused to be in the same room with. Not about the one she fired, who gladly went away from us and our multitude of problems.

But I believed Chard was like me. He was me. He knew me best of all by now. He wouldn't listen to her; he'd listen to me, only me. So I waited for him that night, trying to look good in my hospital gown, longing to touch and be touched, to be held, and to be understood.

He slipped into my room between nurse's visits. No sooner had he kissed me than the rapid squeak of soft-soled shoes approached, and he had to duck behind the curtains. The nurse took my temperature, checked my machines, and gave me pills to take. I tucked them under my tongue as I did every night, acting compliant and tired within minutes of "swallowing" them. The nurses thought I'd actually taken them when, in fact, I'd let them fall onto the pillow and roll down under my shoulders. It was easier than trying to spit them out. That was too obvious. Since I still had tubes in my nose I was breathing through my mouth, and it was easy to drool them out.

Anyway, she left, the nitwit, and Chard came out from hiding. He held up a canvas bag. "I brought everything."

"Good." I snatched the bag from his hands and dug out the change of clothes, the bank book, and the bank card.

"Will you tell me what you're planning?"

"Isn't it obvious?"

"You're planning on running away."

"Bingo, but change the pronoun. First, we have to get me dressed without setting off any of these machines." I pointed to the feeding machine to which my nose tube was attached and to the heart monitor to which my finger wire was connected. "Those we have to disconnect last, but if we can, we should shut them off, not disconnect them." I peered at the heart thing. It looked simple to figure out. The feeding thing was going to be harder.

Chard was standing by the foot of my bed, his hands in his pockets. I looked at him and saw his brain working. Finally, he said, "You keep saying 'we.' Is that what you meant by change the pronoun, you and me? We?"

"Yes, dummy. Us. We're getting out of here."

He didn't say anything, just looked a bit like someone who's gone on one too many roller coaster rides.

"You love me, don't you?" I tightened my grip on the shirt he'd brought. It was purple, and it was Mom's, not mine. She wore it the first day I was in the hospital. He had raided the laundry, not my drawers, for clothes. I wondered whose pants he had brought, but I didn't look.

Instead, I met his eyes. They were huge and filled with tears. "My cup runneth over," popped into my head, but I don't think his cup was running over with joy.

"What?" I said. "You do, don't you?" I wasn't sure now. I thought of all the things Aimee had said about him, that he loved me, that he was mine for the taking, then I remembered how the two of them were together so much and how that used to bug me. Maybe he had loved her, not me. I tried to remember what he had said the other night but couldn't. I felt paralyzed, stupid, alone. "Go away," I muttered.

"It's not that I don't love you," he said at last.

I could see his legs as they moved around the bed, came close to me. "Then, what?" I asked.

"It's that I don't think running away is the answer. I've had a lot of time to think, you know. Just as much as you if not more since Aimee—" He sucked in air, then shot it out again. "It's just that I want to finish high school. I'm getting good grades, and I might even get a scholarship to the school I want to go to." He hesitated. "I think MIT is out, so I'm aiming for Michigan Tech. I want to make it. Can't you understand that? I want to be someone." He stopped, looked away. "I don't want to be a statistic. I want to be an engineer. If I do well enough, I might even be able to help my mom. Dad never seems to. When I'm through with college, then—" He turned to me. "Then I'll be ready for this."

"I want to be with you. To never again have to sneak to see you. I want to live the rest of my life with you. People can go to college after they're married."

"I want to be with you, too. I do."

"But?"

He sucked in another huge breath, then let it out slowly as though he were counting to ten or trying to figure out what to say. When his lungs were empty, he hooked a breath out of the stifling air around us and plunged on, "It's that I'm not ready for that, not now. It would be a mistake. It's a lot harder to be married and go to school. You know that. We can wait. We have our whole lives. Now that both our parents are letting us see each other, it'll be different. We won't have to sneak—"

"My probation hasn't changed, even if our parents have. How long do you think they'll keep letting us see each other? Until I'm out of here, that's how long!" I waved a hand, smashing the feeding machine.

He lunged and caught the thing before it toppled. He steadied it, then lay down on the bed, his body draped over me.

I felt his heart thumping into my shoulder, but still I couldn't look at him. Didn't he understand that to say no now meant there might not be a later? Didn't he look at me, really see me? Couldn't he tell what I had become?

Or maybe that was why that he was turning me down. Maybe he couldn't take me as I was. He wanted that wild, carefree girl who had once been able to outrun them all, the one who hadn't seen her friend die, who hadn't watched friends and family drop away into doubt first, then into belief. The belief that I was a monster.

"I'm not what you think," I said, between clenched teeth. "I'm not a monster. You think I did it, too, don't you? You think I killed Aimee!"

"I never said—"

"Get off me!"

"I don't think—"

"Look me in the eye and tell me that you don't believe I killed or even helped to kill Aimee." I wrenched my eyes upward to where his face hung above me, tried to lock his eyes into a stare down, but he couldn't do it.

He pushed back. "Why are you doing this? It's not about that at all. It's about us. About waiting for us to graduate high school first, for Christ's sake." He leaned down.

"Say it!" I said. "Say that I didn't kill her."

"You didn't kill her." His voice was fierce and low and angry. His hands gripped my shoulders until they hurt, but I didn't cry out. He shook me, turning my attack back at me. I closed my eyes, not wanting to see the anger and hurt on his face. "Look at me."

But I couldn't.

"I said what you needed to hear," he said. "I'll even tell you that I love you. I always have. I always will. But I want you to say something, too. I need you to say it. I want you to say that you didn't kill Aimee."

Everything in me stopped. He believed the lie just enough that he had to hear me deny it. He had doubts. He could deny his doubts to my face even as he said he loved me. But his doubts were still there. And if he doubted me, everyone doubted me. Tears slipped down my cheeks, fell onto my hospital gown. "You don't believe me."

"That's not true," he said. "I believe you now, and I believed you then. But I'll tell you who doesn't believe you: You! You don't believe that you had nothing to do with it. You think you did something that helped her. It's you who doesn't believe that you had nothing to do with her dying."

I whipped my head to the side, tried to escape his hands as they danced before me, pursuing my fingers as they flew through the air, beating at him, at his words. He chased my hands in an effort to still them, but I didn't want him to touch me. I flung myself away, nearly off the bed. He caught me by my gown, and I felt the flimsy ties giving in the back, then he let go, only to catch me again around the waist. His arms closed tightly, hauling me back and up, away from the floor, but not away from the yawning pit inside me. Everything shook with my sobs. I couldn't say what was running through my mind, around and around, in dizzying circles.

I didn't kill her! I didn't kill her! I had nothing to do with it. Why won't anyone believe that? I didn't kill her! I didn't!

But I said nothing.

He caught my hands, pushed my legs under him, and lay on me.

I twisted and turned. The heart monitor pulsed faster and faster.

"Say it," he demanded.

I tasted his tears as he pushed his face into mine, pinning my head to the pillow.

"Say it." The sob in his voice was so plain that I cried out.

But I couldn't say it. I can't say it. Because I was there. I was there, and I didn't stop her. Can't he see that? Can't anyone see that? That is why I can't say that I didn't kill Aimee, because I didn't stop her.

I didn't stop her.

———

A few minutes later, the nurse found us tangled up, all legs and arms, but finally still. Two messed up kids in a hospital bed. She backed out the door and called security. Maybe she thought he was hurting me. I was certainly crying hard enough, but he was crying, too.

Security arrived with about a dozen other people—doctors, interns, patients, all gawking at us from the door. At last my real physician arrived and looked at Chard standing against the wall with a guard holding his arms, his face almost dry, but the snot running from his nose.

Chard wouldn't take his eyes from my face. He forced me to meet his eyes, and I could hear him willing me to say it. His eyes still burn me when I try to sleep. But right then, all I could think of was how he had hurt me, how he had made me go back there and try to figure out what I had done and not done. Where I could have changed things or not.

The doctor walked between us, paused and studied Chard, then turned to me. "Do you know him?" He picked up the clothes lying scattered on the floor, the bankbook. He snorted when he opened it. He didn't wait for my answer. "How far did you think you'd get on three hundred fifty-six dollars?"

"It doesn't matter." And it didn't. Chard wouldn't go with me, and without him, I couldn't go.

"Son, I'd advise you stay away from her for a while. Do I have to call your parents?" It was a threat, not a question.

Chard shook his head.

"Are you going home now?" A command, not a question.

Chard looked at me. I felt his question in the air. It would be there until I told him what he wanted me to say. I closed my eyes, turned away. He wouldn't run with me, and I couldn't say what he needed to hear. We had reached a chasm in our lives that I was not sure we could cross.

From outside me, I heard him say, "Yeah, I'm going home."

Inside me, I heard him ordering me, "Say it."

I listened to him move away from the bed. I heard the people part at the door. I heard him stop, felt rather than heard the in-drawn breath of the spectators. I opened my eyes. He faced me. "I'd have gone if you could have said it," he said, then he shuffled past them all, his cryptic comment leaving them dumbstruck.

He was so tall, so straight in that last moment before he vanished. I watched him go in silence, knowing he was right, thinking he'd be there when I was ready, but not knowing if he'd wait forever.

I listened to the doctor bark orders, watched people scamper away, felt the nurse swab my arm with a cold cotton ball, smelled the biting stink of alcohol, then tasted pizza, just as I had when they had given me the deep tranquilizers after Aimee's suicide.

But it was Chard whom I saw, felt, smelled, and heard as I drifted away and beyond.

I shake my writing hand to ease the cramp and stare at the moon, which has risen higher. It pales and pales again, casting a bleaching light so bright I can turn off the flashlight. I sit on the log and try not to cry because with remembering Chard and how we parted, I have to remember Aimee, and that is the hardest of all.

I have not talked to Chard. He's called. He's even talked to my mother. But I won't. I can't talk to him. The question will always be there, the words he has to hear. He doesn't trust me. He won't take me as I am. He has to wait, and I can't wait.

Sort of like Aimee. She couldn't wait either. Everyone asked afterward what drove her to suicide, and we told them what we knew. But no one believed us. They thought there had to be more. That her life wasn't bad enough for her to kill herself.

People who have never come close to seeking death don't understand its promise of an end to life's struggles. They don't understand the precarious teeter-totter on which a suicidal person balances, shuffling reasons to live and reasons to die back and forth to avoid hitting bottom. They don't understand that when you're that low, when you can't see beyond yourself and your fallen-apart world, it's the little things that send you over the edge, not the big things.

And sometimes it is the littlest things that keep you going, too.

For the longest time the little thing that kept Aimee going was her cat. No one cared for that fat football of a cat like she did. She once asked me what I thought of her cat, and I answered, "She's a lazy cow. Why do you have her?"

Aimee stared at me in disgust, hands on her hips, then she gathered the ball of flesh she called a cat to her, and started flicking through the TV channels.

As channel after channel passed before my eyes and the silence grew between us, I knew I had flunked a test. But later I realized that it was a good thing I flunked it. If I was unworthy of caring for her cat, then Aimee had to keep living.

But Aimee's cat died. And it died on the same day that Aimee's dad walked out and left her with her stepmother for two weeks without even a letter or a phone call.

He left her with nothing.

I think he had found out that Aimee's good old stepmother had the hots for someone else—he just didn't know who. He may have even spied on her to see if he could trap her with her lover—after all, hadn't he fallen for her in much the same way?

But he came home after two weeks, because the perfect stepmother didn't leave the house except to go to work and church and shop and chauffeur the kids. So there was nothing to prove.

By then it was too late.

Aimee slept at my house the first weekend he was gone, and she was a wreck.

"This is nuts," she said, smoking a cigarette and chewing gum at the same time. "He can't actually think I like being in her house?"

"'Course not. Do you think he has another woman?"

"Get real. I don't think he'd risk losing her. I can see him getting all self-righteous and leaving her, but him screwing around on her? She's got him too tightly wound for that." She shoved a hand through her hair. The cigarette still burned between her fingers as they clawed through snarls she hadn't the energy to comb out. A trail of ashes, like thick gray hairs, settled on her dark hair.

I sighed and looked away as her hand returned to her mouth. She drew in a deep breath, then coughed it out.

"What about her? Maybe she has someone in her life?" I said.

She looked up quick. "Well, we know about her, now don't we?"

For a second I thought she was talking about how her stepmother had stolen Aimee's dad from Aimee's mother, but then I realized she wasn't. I shivered, hesitated, finally said, "What do you mean, Aimee?" I didn't want to know, but I saw the red in her eyes, the white around her lips, the sunken cheeks marking a new weight loss. I had to ask. Had to hear it told. For Aimee.

"I've pretty much told you." She stared out the window and blew a long trail of smoke that floated from her lips to her hair, then spread into the air, thin curls of smoke heading for the crack in the window.

"Is it worse lately?"

"What?"

"You know."

"Say it."

I froze, unable to speak, and stared at her. Even then I couldn't say the important things. I couldn't face ugly truths. It seems to be a family trait.

Aimee had never really been explicit about what happened in her house. She dropped hints, some as big as a mall parking lot, but she never said outright what was going on. She and her stepmother didn't get along, that I knew. In front of people, her stepmother was as nice as sugar caramelizing on a seared pan, but I had always known she abused Aimee, hit her, knocked her around. But now, as I looked at Aimee's eyes, at her cheeks, at her shaking hands, I wondered if I knew anything. What do any of us know about each other?

"You tell me."

She snorted, choked on smoke, and went into a coughing fit. "What do you want to know? The details?"

"No, Aimee. I thought she knocked you around. Hit you, stuff like that."

"Yeah, she does if I don't do what she says."

"Is she mean to you? I mean, does she say mean things?"

She blew another frond of smoke at me. "Don't all parents?"

"Point taken," I said. I waited, but she just continued smoking. So I said, "Aimee, don't you want to talk about it?"

"No. You know what I want to talk about? I want to talk about my cat. That's right, my cat. And you know what? No one wants to talk about her. 'She's just a cat.' 'You can get another one.' 'She was old.' 'She was sick.' No one says, 'Wow! You and that cat go back a long way. She remembers what it was like before, when your real mother lived with you, when your dad didn't walk around with blinders on, when you knew you were safe in your own bed. She slept with you night after night then. Curled into a ball behind your knees, her purr vibrating into you, soothing you even when your parents fought. And when your mother left? When she ran off? Did your cat try to tell you that everything would be okay? Did she act like nothing bad had happened?' Tell me that! Tell me why people don't act like cats, and then I'll—"

She stopped, her shrill voice echoing. She looked at me for a long time, or at least what seemed like a long time, before she fell against me and cried.

I held her, rocking, wishing I could purr, still not sure what I was supposed to do to make her feel better. I rubbed my hands up and down her back, cooing and stroking her, like I'd seen Kates do to a hurt child. She rocked with me a while, then she stiffened.

"Don't touch me." Her voice came from some inner place I had never glimpsed.

I took my hands away. "Sorry. I just thought—"

"Well, don't think." She stubbed out her cigarette in her fancy ashtray, the one she'd stolen from Chard's mom. "You can have this." She thrust it at me.

"I don't smoke."

"Keep it anyway. Smoking is soothing, and maybe you'll learn the habit someday. Later. After."

"After what, Aimee?" I felt a dread deep down.

"Nothing. Did I say *after?*"

"What does she do to you, Aimee? Tell me." She needed to say it. Her eyes were hollow, empty of feeling. There was something dead inside her, something cold and frozen that never felt the heat of anything, not my love, not the joy of beautiful days, not the warmth of our circle of friends. She hid it most of the time. But it was the only thing in her eyes when I asked my question.

She rubbed her hands over her arms, ran them up inside the shoulders of her sleeveless top, snapped her bra strap. "Nothing that unusual. Lots of girls do it. It helps them when they get married."

She sounded strange, so far away—not in distance, but in time. She sounded young, childlike.

I gulped, turned away, decided I didn't want to hear any more. But I had pulled a key stone loose on a mountain of rock that had built up inside Aimee, and it was crashing around me. Images I'd never dreamed of tumbled from her white lips, of her stepmother and her filthy games. "Games," she called it when Aimee was young, then "preparation." Now she used threats—that she'd tell Aimee's dad about it, that she'd touch her brother like that. Threats Aimee knew were real. Because Aimee had seen her destroy her family, had seen her drive her mother away across the country, had seen her steal her brother's affection from her, had made Aimee into a problem child for her father. And all the while her stepmother remained an icon of her church, her community, her family.

No one would believe Aimee. Not a soul.

Things like that don't happen. Things like that never happen, especially in families like theirs.

"Have you ever told anyone?" I whispered. "Haven't you told your mother?"

"When?" she snapped. "The last time I saw her I was fourteen. I was never alone with her. There were always other people there, friends, family, my brother. And he praised the bitch so high that Mom began to believe she'd done the right thing. By then she'd had four or five boyfriends. Later, I'd try to call, but she was always on her way out, always with someone. I don't think she answers the phone when she's alone. So now I have an unavailable mother and a stepmother who makes me feel so ugly and dirty and ashamed. I mean, what guy would want me? I'm a lesbian."

"You are not!"

"What am I, then? I don't even know. What am I?" She rocked and rocked and rocked.

"I'll kill her," I said. "Chard and Kyle and Jason, even Kates would help. We'll kill her."

"Don't be ridiculous." She sounded tired. She unsnaked her legs and stretched them out before her—long, slender, shapely. She saw me looking and pulled the blanket over them.

"Then I'll tell my parents. My mother will help you. She's a lawyer." I didn't add that she would love such a sensational case and the renown it would bring her, especially if she won. "All we have to do is prove what she's done."

"And how are you going to do that?"

I hesitated. "Well, you'd have to tell your story."

"And who'd believe me?"

"Believe you?" I echoed. I believed her. What was not to believe? But I knew what she meant. There was no physical proof. There wouldn't be semen to test for. Was there any way to test for female stuff? Secretions? Probably, but that would mean telling, and Aimee's empty face told me that she wasn't going to do that. "So what do we do?" I asked, twisting her around and looking her full in the face.

She met my eyes without tears, without regret, without pain. "What I've been trying to do all along. Die."

My mind always stops when I remember her simple response, "Die." It's too hard to face. It's almost dawn, and I'm stiff and cold. I stand and walk around carefully. The moon set around four, and it's too dark to see much more than outlines against a paling sky. The ground is a mass of dark, darker, and darkest, although I can see the path's outline as I pace. As I walk up and down the slender path I've worn in the ivy since we moved here, I don't want to trip and make a bunch of noise or hurt myself. I have something to do before I turn myself in or am found.

I sit with my back cradled by three birch trunks, chew my

pen, and force myself to go beyond Aimee's "Die." I see Kates's, Kyle's, and Jason's faces again as I told them what Aimee had said. What she had told me. They stared blankly at me, and I knew then she'd told them enough that they suspected something long ago, just never had it confirmed. All the innuendo I'd missed, the shadowy figure at the door in the night. Where had I been? Was I that blind? Or did I just not want to know? Did I figure that being her friend was enough to counteract what was happening?

"She's talking about death, you know. Killing herself."

They nodded. I felt Chard's arms tighten around me. He was sitting behind me, holding me so I didn't chicken out of the meeting I'd called. I'd told him the day after I cried all night with Aimee, after I'd watched her fondling the razor. I'd hidden it in my duffel bag when she finally slept.

"We have to watch her. We have to help her. She says no one will believe her," I said.

"What if we went to the police?" Kates's voice was earnest, her eyes serious.

"They know us, remember? We're the town jokers, the goof-offs, the screwups," Kyle said. The Shih Tzu incident, the Suitman stuff, broken windows from kick the can, and dozens of complaints of noise, vandalism (not true), and disorderly conduct (I was not drunk and Aimee was wearing her underwear when we were caught swimming in someone else's pool) all melded into an insurmountable barrier between us and the authorities.

"What about Kates?" said Chard. "We could send her. She's the straightest of us all." He didn't mention her rescuing the baby, but we were all thinking of it.

"I can't," she whispered. "Not alone." She clutched her

hands to stop them from shaking. Even in the midst of her "fame," she'd stayed anonymous. She stuck her hands between her legs, but they still trembled.

We looked away. None of us blamed her. For the first time, I wished for Kates's cleaner, more boring life. Then I could go to the police.

"What about your mother?" Kates said after a moment, turning to me. "Can't she help?"

I looked up, ashamed. "I tried to tell her this morning, at least part of it. Not about what kind of abuse or anything, just that Aimee was being abused by her stepmother."

"What did she say?" Jason asked, leaning forward, speaking for the first time.

I hesitated to say the truth. "She asked where I get all these wild ideas from, and why kids today think it's funny to destroy the lives of the adults who have sacrificed so much for them." She talked about a few of her cases then. One involved a kid who had sued his parents for custody of his sister, claiming abuse. Turned out he was the abuser. In another case, the parents were blamed for some horrendous crime their kid had committed because they "should have known" about it beforehand. Then there was a divorce case in which the kid had lied about his father's supposed abuse so he could live in California with his mom. The father actually went to jail for a year before my mom proved the kid was lying.

So Mom had some basis for doubting my story, what with my record of mischief and her recent cases, but she could've given me a chance. She could've checked to see if I was telling the truth. Heck, she hardly even knew Aimee's stepmom, so why was she defending her? Was it because they were both professional women with careers? For my

much lately. Your grades are suffering, I'm sure." Mom shook her head. "It's ridiculous how you expect us to bend over backward for you. We're having a party here Friday. You can go stay at her house then." Mom almost always allowed me to go to Aimee's, school night or no, because then I was out of the house, not sulking at the kitchen table. Her double standard never occurred to her, I guess.

"It's just one night," I pleaded. "Can't she come tonight?" Aimee's dad still wasn't back, and I was afraid of leaving her alone when he wasn't there.

"Does this have to do with what you said the other morning?" Mom set down her teacup and practically skipped across the kitchen, she was so delighted with herself and her deductive reasoning. "If it does, you're being silly. I'm tired of all your games," she said.

Games. I drooped, unable to think fast enough to find the excuse that would bypass her arguments.

Games. Why is everything a teenager wants a game to adults?

———

After all my years of disrespecting her job, it turned out that Mom was a master of the high-stakes legal game that was the trial for my life. Whenever a witness said something remotely different from what they'd said earlier, she leaned forward and extended her yellow legal pad to the head lawyer. He was the guy she'd called when the police took me that night. He always read her scribbled notes immediately and usually followed up on whatever she'd written within the minute.

Mom didn't sit at the table where I sat with my lawyers.

She commandeered a seat behind us, arriving early and plunking her briefcase in the chair she wanted. Aimee's father and stepmother reserved front row seats, too, only they did it with coats and sweaters and their seats were always on the other side of the courtroom. They often looked my way, but I never looked at them directly, only watched them scurry around my peripheral vision like a pair of rats loose in the house at night.

A lawyer always sat on either side of me. A bailiff stood at each exit, and one took up her position not too far away from me. Her presence told me that I was not going anywhere until the twelve people fenced off in the jury box said I could. And, in case they were remiss in their duty, I should remember that the black-robed judge had some say in whether I could walk unshackled from that room, too.

Mom explained all these "necessary evils" to me in a pretrial meeting, but I pretended to ignore her. I'd been ignoring her for weeks by that point. Still, she came to most of the meetings—many more than Dad did. Reporters liked nothing better than to catch a picture of us going into our lawyers' office. I was quite the freak show, and Dad was uncomfortable around freaks and reporters both. Besides, there were layoffs and downsizing at the plant and, according to Mom, his job was threatened. He kept his job, at least, despite the time he took off to attend pretrial hearings, psychological analyses, the trial, and all the other crap I put them through. He never complained to me, although he started going in earlier and earlier to compensate for the midday breaks. Maybe all of it did hurt his career, and that was the real reason for the transfer *Here*.

Did Mom upstage that hotshot lawyer in the strategy or

research meetings? Or was he just humoring her because it was her daughter's trial?

I'll never know.

I do know that she became addicted to the game. She even took a leave of absence from her job to play it to its end point.

Did she win?

I picture her silhouette in my window and her slow closing of the pane after I'd jumped. I imagine her moving through my room to the door, past the trinkets left over from when I was little. Did she wonder why I still have the black, almost furless stuffed cat? Did she remember who gave me the Pooh music box? Is she surprised I haven't boxed up my collection of Beatrix Potter figurines, or rather that I haven't broken them? Does she know anything about me? Or am I just another case to be handled? A high-profile, career-enhancing case?

I don't know.

I do know that when they announced the verdict, she almost leapt over the brass railing separating our table from the visitors' seats. She went straight to her hotshot lawyer pal and hugged him. She kept saying, "Thank you, thank you."

Dad stood beside her, shaking lawyer's hand after lawyer's hand. I stood behind the huddle of grown-ups with the young lawyer who didn't quite count, I guess. It was he who first told me congratulations. He shook my hand as if he had no elbow, and for an instant I thought he couldn't believe I'd gotten off. But then he smiled, and his eyes showed he was glad.

Over his shoulder, I watched Aimee's dad rise, stiff-jointed and with head bowed. He raised his head long enough to meet Aimee's mother's eyes for a moment. His eyes dulled, his skin grayed, and his shoulders stooped in that moment of locked eyes. Then he turned away, took his second wife's arm, and silently shoved their way out of the courtroom, never slowing down long enough for his current wife to comment. She left with her mouth open but silent.

It was the first time I had seen Aimee's real mom in the courtroom. She stared at me for what seemed like a long time. Maybe she was remembering one phone call too many when she didn't have time for Aimee. Maybe she was wishing she had bought her a plane ticket. Maybe she was just wishing I was dead and not Aimee. I couldn't read more than grief and regret in her face as she focused on the reporters jostling her with microphones and questions. "No comment," she said. "I have nothing to say." Then she darted under someone's outstretched arm and was gone.

Then someone spun me around and I felt the air move as people rushed in and out of the courtroom.

It was Mom I now faced, but before she could say anything—if she intended to say anything—there was a sharp cry of, "Turn your heads!" and a sudden brilliant flash, followed by dozens of others.

The pictures show a shocked me, too stunned to smile. Dad is floating in the crowd, relief all over what you can see of his face. Mom, however, stands poised and beaming in the picture, as if she had just won a million dollars instead of another couple of years with me under her roof. Her arm encircles me in a possessive gesture, but what she said to me was, "Don't say anything. Let the lawyers answer all questions. We'll get out of here as soon as possible." The moment for congratulations was past.

I ducked my head, then craned around to see if any of the

people I longed to see were there, but if Chard, Kyle, Kates, and Jason were there, they were in the crowd of people shoving for the exits. Gradually, even the reporters darted out the doors, cell phones pressed against their ears, mouths jabbering away.

We were left standing in the courtroom, accepting the tense congratulations of the prosecution team. Then we gathered whatever belonged to us in that ordered, nearly empty room.

"God, I can't wait to get home and put my feet up," Mom said. "Thank you again. We couldn't have done it without you." She shook the hotshot lawyer's hand.

She dug a knuckle in my side, and I said, "Thank you," in almost a whisper.

The lawyer smiled, as had the young man earlier. "It was worth it—if you keep your nose clean. Take care of yourself." He chucked me under the chin as if I was a four-year-old. He obviously didn't have kids.

"She will," Mom said.

Apparently I was a little slow in the response department, but I echoed her nonetheless, since I was still in the dutiful daughter mode, brought on by being in a courtroom. "I will." I looked at Dad. "Can we go home now?"

"You bet," he said. He took my arm, and, after a quick hug and a swipe at his eyes, he began guiding me to the main exit.

"Wait," the young lawyer said, and Dad stopped, dropping my arm when he turned. "Go out the back. The bailiff says you can. You'll avoid the press that way."

I smiled for the first time in weeks. A hand took mine, and I allowed myself to be steered out the side entrance and down a maze of corridors, following the woman who could have just as easily been leading me to jail instead of to freedom. By the time she opened a door to the daylight, I had almost convinced myself that the not-guilty verdict was some kind of joke. I expected to see a police van waiting to take me away, but there was only my parents' black Mercedes, brought around by a lawyer and still running.

We ran for it, and when we were safe inside and heading for home, I realized Mom wasn't sitting up front beside Dad. She was sitting next to me. It was her hand that had led me through the halls—her hand that still held mine.

I didn't withdraw it until we pulled into our driveway, only to discover that the reporters had beaten us home. Dad grabbed me around the shoulders, scrunched me down, and forced me through the crowd like a back-hoe operator forces the scoop through earth. He slammed the door when we were inside.

We'd left Mom outside with the reporters.

Which is where she stayed until they all went away. It was her moment in the sun. The doubting of the verdict hadn't begun yet, and it still wasn't obvious, at least to me, that we'd have to move.

But before we moved, she had that one glorious moment of being able to stand tall again. Even the hardest reporters' questions she'd deflected and made harmless. She knew what she was doing.

Even if it didn't do us any good in the end.

My body jerks as I wake. Sharp pains shoot up my fingers as I pull them from between my legs where I had stuffed them for warmth. The sun is up, blinding me with its slanted rays yet casting no warmth.

I take no comfort in the sleep that ended my remembering, because someone else is here in my secret place, someone with a slender waist and neck, whose long braided hair curls snakelike over her shoulder then crawls over her chest. She holds a thin metal rod, which, as she raises it to her mouth, I see is a flute. The light shimmers, refracts from the silver before I hear the notes. It was her music that woke me.

I listen to three songs, all played with no lilt, before I move or speak. I want to have some idea of her mood, my flute-playing intruder, this person so involved in herself and her sadness that her music must be played alone in an unlistening wood.

I wonder about the path that led me to this almost secret place. Was it really a path of my own making, or had someone been here before me, often, marking a path faintly between the trees?

The girl's flute falls into her lap. Her head collapses onto her chest. She straightens after a moment, turns her head, but she still doesn't see me.

So I stand with an abruptness that silences the few birds singing in the trees and sends some of them into flight.

She jumps up, faces me, her flute clutched in one hand like a weapon.

My suspicions are confirmed. It's Hope. "Hey," I say.

And she responds, "Hey."

"Come here often?" I ask and think I'm an idiot to begin with a pickup line.

But she doesn't notice or doesn't care. "When I want to be alone."

I nod. "Yeah." I point at her flute. "You're in the band, right?"

She looks at the flute like she's never seen it before. "Yes, although I dropped out for a while last year. I thought it would be fun to watch the football games instead of being in the band. You don't get to see much of the game, and you have to hang out mostly with the band members, you know. I just rejoined. I don't know if I'll stick with it, though," she adds in almost a whisper.

I nod, although I don't know about being in a marching band. "Don't you have friends in the band?"

She eyes me, then makes a decision and sits back down on the fallen log. She slides to one side, and I sit beside her, trying not to trip with my half-frozen, sleeping feet. I bite a cuticle, waiting, but I don't expect an answer.

But she gives me one. "I did have friends. In the band, I mean. Then I stopped doing much with them, and they gave up on me. I was busy being friends with the kids who count. When that didn't work out, then, well, then I tried to commit—" She stops, sucks in air, then continues without looking at me. "I tried to commit suicide, and now none of my new friends seem to be able to talk in full sentences to me, or at least they can't do it without their pity showing through." She slams her music book shut. *Hits of the Eighties*, the cover reads.

She's all backward, I think. Mad when she should be sad, sad when she should be happy.

Hope twists her flute apart. "Did your friends abandon you?"

"Some kids—"

"Of course not. You moved away, but I'll bet they stood by you. I'll bet it was your friend who everyone whispered about and hated. Maybe not hated, but it was her who everyone thought was sick. Not you. Pretty little you. Rich little you."

"I don't have to take this." I hop off the log as if it were infested with fire ants.

"Yes, you do. The police are looking for you. I'll tell them where you are. How does it feel to be the one hurt? To have people talk about you like you're a clinical case, as though you're not even there?"

I laugh. I can't help it. She has no idea who I am or what I am. "First off, I didn't know you were there, yesterday I mean, and second, I'll bet I've been a clinical case a lot longer than you have."

"Hah!" She practically throws her flute into its case. "What's wrong with you anyway? First you're in school, then you're not, then you're back—for what, two days? Then you run off. My dad listens to the police channel—" I hear the implied "endlessly." "We heard your mother's call last night and the police's response. They put a lot of people on your case awfully fast. Was it because of who your mother is? Hotshot lawyer?"

I sit back down, rub the inside of my arms where the bruises from my recent hospital stay still creep in purple down my veins. "No," I say. "It's because of my history, I'm sure. Might come in contact with another loose wire, another nut who wants my services. Then again, maybe I set all this up to meet someone who wants—" I stop and glance at her. I can almost see where her mind is going. My empty stomach nibbles at me, making my hands shake and my head ache. At least I blame it on my hunger, but there is something too familiar in Hope's eyes. Something I'd seen in Aimee, or rather not seen—an emptiness. Lately I've seen this hollowness reflected back at me late at night in my own mirror. I shudder and take a different angle. "My mother doesn't work for the police. She defends people. She hardly ever prosecutes them. No money in public service, you know."

Hope checks to see if I'm joking, then decides I am. Her laugh is tinny and momentary. We drop into a silence that neither is willing to break. It ends with her shivering the kind of shiver that starts deep in the gut and vibrates outward, leaving you weak. "You must be cold," she says, and I nod, even though she means that she's cold. "Want to come over to my house a while?"

I figure, why the hell not? I'll be found soon anyway. "Sure." I stand, pick up my duffel bag, and we set off down the path I had claimed for my own. When we've almost reached my house I see that the path continues inside the edge of the woods, passing house after house until it reaches the thick woods at the back of our development. My path is only an offshoot of this longer trail.

I discovered nothing new.

Hope turns to me. "I could walk along the street, but I've always liked walking in the woods better. Don't you?"

I don't say anything, just follow her to the end of the woods and onto a street that's blocks from my house. We cross the street and head up another. "He lives there. We've known each other forever."

I figure she means her ex-boyfriend, David, and I gaze, as instructed, at the white-and-green house, then follow Hope, thinking only of food and a bathroom. I really need to use a bathroom.

Hope's house is nothing like mine. There is no grandness, no frilly pretensions such as a huge hallway and funny-shaped windows with no curtains. Her house is simply a house. It has a kitchen, a dining room, and a living room. The one bathroom is toward the back, by the bedrooms. There are two bedrooms and an office of sorts. I peek into it on my way to the bathroom and see old sports trophies. Dead fish are mounted on wooden plaques. There's a large, shiny CD player/tape recorder on a table, and a reclining chair—old, ratty, and grease-marked where a head has rested for years. Beneath the single window is a desk with everything precisely placed on it, like on a desk in a furniture store, not like on a desk that is being used. On the left side of the desk is the police radio. I imagine the family gathered in here, listening to disasters and crimes and hopelessness. I don't think they broadcast follow-up reports on the radio, so listeners never hear that the criminal has been sent to jail, the fire victim recovered, or the widow of the car-accident victim remarried.

I shake my head and slip into the bathroom. This is the room where she tried to kill herself. I sit and pee. She draped her hands in the sink, didn't she? I try to imagine her dad coming in and finding her, and that makes me wonder where they are—her parents, I mean. And I wonder why she's not in school.

I return to the kitchen armed and ready for anything she dishes out. I don't have to take her crap. I can give it back. "So, if you're such a goodie goodie, why aren't you in school today?" I say.

"I have to drive my dad to the doctor's office. My mom's at work, and my dad should be home from his walk soon." She says it like it's a stock response, one given over and over to the same question, so there has to be more to what she says than what she's telling.

I sit at the table in the breakfast area. It's not really a room, just a space between the kitchen counter and the living room. A larger table stands at the near end of the living room, which counts as the dining room. Everything smells closed in, locked up, airless. The table beneath my hands is smooth, with no crumbs, no sticky patches. As I accept a cup of coffee from Hope, she runs a wet cloth before me, clearing any stray dirt before I put the cup down. She brings a bowl and a box of cereal, and repeats the swabbing. The milk and sugar arrive along with a spoon, and she runs a dry cloth over the table to remove any dampness.

"I don't expect perfection," I say. "Or is it that you want to be sure I don't leave any fingerprints?"

She colors and moves back to the sink, where she looks out the window. "Habit," she says. "It's just a habit. Sorry."

I eat without talking, not wanting to destroy what little feeling of friendship she has for me. I'm not even sure she likes me. Maybe that's why I feel so weird here with her. She doesn't like me, and some early-warning device is telling me that she's trying to use me, like Aimee used me. Maybe that's why I'm so mean to her.

Then again, I think as I watch her stare out the window, maybe I'm paranoid and maybe she's just lonely. She said all her old friends abandoned her after her suicide attempt. That is something I can relate to—losing your friends. Sympathy seeps into me like water into a rock, but then there's a noise outside the kitchen door. Someone is in the entryway.

"Here he comes," Hopes says quietly. She moves toward the door but doesn't open it. Her whole face goes still, not a happy stillness, but an expectant, dutiful blankness.

Suddenly I have the creeps. Not again. I can't take another evil stepmother.

But it's not an abuser who fumbles with the knob. It's not Aimee's stepmother with her quick, clattering step that walks through the door. It's a man in sneakers too modern for his brown pleated pants and baggy flannel shirt. It's not the impeccable preacher who walks in, but someone who has missed loops with his belt and whose hair part is slightly off.

You could bet Aimee's stepmother wouldn't be caught dead in those dark glasses either, especially inside.

But I, of course, don't get the significance of the sunglasses in the house until he pulls his cane in behind him and leans it against the counter. "Hope!" he yells.

"I'm here," she almost whispers.

"Oh, sorry." He faces her and waits, his head leaning forward and his lips puckered.

She pecks his cheek, which he accepts as his due with a shrug. "I have company," Hope says.

"Not David, is it?" He swings around, searching for sounds.

I cough, but Hope beats me to the introduction. "No, it's the friend that I told you about. She's new at school. Do you remember?"

"Ah, yes. The new girl." He doesn't ask for my name as he holds out his hand with a smile, and he doesn't connect me with the girl they listened to the police search for on the radio last night. "Still, you'll have to bring David around sometime." He turns toward me. "Do you know David?"

I glance at Hope.

She says, "David is not my boyfriend, Dad. We broke up, remember?"

He wrinkles his forehead. "Yes, well. You could get back together."

"And pigs may fly," Hope mutters.

I look at her dad, but only a passing flicker of pain tells me that he's heard.

"When is your appointment?" Hope asks. "Mom didn't tell me."

"Eleven, I believe. She said to pick her up so she can come home to fix lunch, so don't make anything. Did you do your schoolwork?"

"Yes. We're going to my room, okay? I'll come and get you at quarter of." Hope pulls me through the door. I look over my shoulder and see him sit heavily in a chair, then strain to reach his feet. But then we're around the corner, and he's gone.

───

"I hate him!"

"He seems nice enough to me," I say.

Hope looks at me as though I'd produced a bag of worms and started eating them, dirt and all. "He didn't have to be like that. He wouldn't follow his diet, wouldn't take his medicine. He doesn't even exercise. He walks twice around the block at a very slow pace and calls it exercise." She rips off a piece of fingernail with her teeth and spits it at the wall. She hasn't stopped pacing since she closed the door behind me. Pace, two, three, four. Bite, twist, rip, spit. Pace, two, three, four.

"You're making me nervous. Sit down."

She stops pacing and pulls her finger from her mouth, but she doesn't sit. Instead, she goes to a mirror on the wall and starts undoing her braid. When it's undone, she rakes a brush through her hair as though she's trying to rip it out.

I feel unsure of the role I'm supposed to be playing. It's

been a long time since I was the healthier or stronger person in any relationship, and I don't know what to say next. It doesn't occur to me not to play a role, to be myself, to say, "Hey, sit down and quit trying to make yourself go bald!" in the old bantering style I had with Aimee. That didn't work with her either. Besides, I've become the queen of avoidance lately. Or maybe I'm the princess. My mother's the queen. Watching Hope's hair fly around with built-up static electricity, I toy with asking her what she thinks of Marge's prim and proper hairdo, but she might not see my humor. Instead I say, "So where does your mom work?" Which is a big mistake.

"The fucking pharmacy. She's a cashier, for God's sake, and she can't miss work. We need the money and the benefits for me and her. Her insurance won't cover him. Previous condition, I guess, but the government does, so we should be thankful. That's all I hear. Be thankful. It could be worse. Pray for him. Pray for everyone. Say the rosary. Well, fuck the rosary!"

My mouth must be hanging open a foot, but she doesn't care. She noticed my surprise the first time she swore, and it's only egged her on. Too late, I clamp my mouth shut.

"That's right. Fuck them all." But her level of anger has dropped with each word until her voice is little more than a worn-out recording.

"You don't mean that. I mean about your parents. He's kind of sweet."

"What do you know?"

"You're right. What do I know?" I sit and stare at the wall. There are no posters decorating the walls—there is, as a matter of fact, nothing on them. A single nail over her bed pokes out to remind her of what had hung there once.

Hope follows my eyes and notices the bare nail as though for the first time. "We're Catholic, you know."

I stare harder at the nail and imagine the crucifix that should have hung there. "No reason to know," I say. "We're whatever is fashionable."

She nods. "Maybe that would be better. Not to have such strict rules."

"Oh, there are rules, they just change all the time. I must know fourteen different versions of the Lord's Prayer and a million other prayers besides."

"In my thoughts and in my words, in what I have done and what I have failed to do." Hope is tracing the white scars on her wrists. The ragged bumps catch the light, almost glisten.

"What?"

She drops her hands, then puts her arms around herself in a tight hug. Still she shivers. "I've sinned."

"What do you mean?" Even Aimee didn't get this weird. She said exactly what she meant. ("All that's left now is to die. Will you help me?")

Hope sits down on the floor, as if she hasn't the energy to make it to the bed or the desk chair. "Well, you've seen part of why I did it. I'm supposed to, expected to take care of him, don't you know? Daughter cares for elderly parents. But I think he's going to die soon. He still doesn't take his insulin, not without me or Mom reminding him, and do you know what's up the street? A convenience store. That old one, where everything is dusty except the candy and cigarettes and milk and bread because those are the only things that anyone buys. He walks up to the store, buys a candy bar, and walks just long enough to eat it. Every day. Every fucking day. And Mom? She has to work, but she comes home at

As he makes the crossing, Hope's mom starts banging and clattering as she gathers items from all over the room. Onions from the refrigerator, pans from beneath the stove, a cutting board from a drawer, butter from the refrigerator, flour from a canister, and milk from the refrigerator appear—in that order. Mom would have been freaking out over the inefficiency, but no one here notices or cares.

"You finished your report?" Hope asks, to explain my presence.

"Yesterday," I say because I don't feel like playing along.

She narrows her eyes, then pours a coffee, which she takes to her dad. "I meant the other report. The one on the wildlife indigenous to the forests in this area."

Which I take to be a threat that she'll expose my secret hiding place in the woods, but I don't think she'd do that. For one thing, she would be giving up her secret spot, too. "Yeah, toads, salamanders, and snakes. I once saw a whole mess of snakes all twisted together, just writhing in the plants and half under a tree stump."

"How unpleasant," Hope's mother says. She's slicing onions, big thick slices, and layering them in a pan lined with store-bought pastry. I have no idea what she's making. "What did you do?" she asks.

"I lost it after watching them for a while. So I took a pointy stick and started poking them, kind of popping them really. When they still didn't come apart, I bashed them with a log. After a minute of that, I came to my senses and walked away."

"Oh." She carefully sets the knife down on the other side of the kitchen.

"Are you planning on studying wildlife, amphibians, or reptiles in college?"

What a diplomat Hope's dad is. I kind of like him. "No."

He nods. "Those snakes. I'll bet that was some sort of mating thing, or maybe it had to do with body heat. Snakes are cold-blooded, you know."

"Maybe I should do a report on it."

"Maybe you should," Hope says. "But I thought you had to do a book report on a classic novel—for lit credit." She doesn't notice that she's changed what kind of report I'm supposed to be doing, nor do her parents. They seem oddly enthralled with whatever she says, as though they never want to disagree with her or question her about anything.

"*Lord of the Flies*," I say.

She rolls her eyes. "Mom, do you need any more help? The table's set, and Dad has his coffee."

"No, dear, why don't you and your friend run along." There's relief in her voice. "I'll call you when lunch is ready."

Hope turns on me when we get to her room. "What are you trying to do? Paint yourself as a psychopath?"

"But isn't that what I am? Antisocial, psychotic, paranoid? Ask Marge about it. You know, the psychologist we share. I call her Marge. It fits her, don't you think?"

And suddenly she's laughing. "It does. I don't know why, but it does." She drops to the bed and snorts between laughs. "What do you think she'd say about me?"

"I don't know. Do you cooperate at your appointments?"

"Of course."

"Kiss-up. How often do you go?"

"Once a week. I used to have to go more often, but then she said I was making progress."

"Progress. What's that?"

"Telling her what she wants to hear." And just as quickly as her laughter started, it's gone.

"Kiss-up."

"Maybe, but how often do you go?"

"Way more than that. But I use the time to write novels in my head. So it's not a complete waste, and since I don't have hobbies or friends—"

"You could have. You used to have friends, and lots of people would be nice to you if you'd only try being nice to them."

"Why bother? What do they have that I want? I'm assuming you mean guys? Because no girl in the entire school, besides you, has even met my eyes or said hello."

"You could try to make friends," Hope insists. "But you won't. That's why they don't say hello. You never try to be friends with anyone. And why do you think everyone is after something or that you have to get something from everyone else? Can't people just like you?"

"Tell Marge to explore that theory with me. She'd love to have guidance on how to get through to me. I never talk. To her, that is."

"Who do you talk to? Don't you need to let some of it out sometime? I do, and since most of my friends don't talk to me anymore, I talk to Marge. If I didn't, the pressure would just keep building up. Sometimes I think I'm going to burst." She stops, and her eyes go all unfocused.

I move to the door and lean against it, facing her, my hands pressing the wood behind me as though I could force it to disintegrate. "I don't have to talk to anyone, about anything," I say. When the door remains solid, I shove my hands into the crooks of my bent elbows to stop my fingers from shaking. I know all about the pressure she's referring to, about the pain that piles up until there's a huge weight pushing against my mouth. It comes from my head—all those "what ifs" and "should have beens." But lately, those thoughts have started to crush my heart. I feel it caving in. Aimee as I last saw her flashes before me, and the burning in my head makes my eyes throb. I force Aimee down, back to the darkness, where I can handle her.

I make myself see Hope, not Aimee. I blame this girl—small, frail Hope—for my pain, but in her dark eyes, I see a reflection of it. There are three blind people in this house, I realize. None of us can see where we're going, where we'll end up.

Hope is prattling on, still talking about friends or her lack of friends. I'm not listening, and she stops abruptly. "How do you stand it?" she asks. "You're so alone."

I shrug, determined not to let her in. "I'm a survivor," I say and try not to think of how often I've heard that phrase used in reference to me. I hunch my shoulders forward as though to make my chest a smaller target. There will be no getting inside of me.

But somehow she does.

"How'd she do it? Why did she do it? Were you there?" she asks, her eyes gleaming like a lobster's on a plate.

I feel the rage building in me, the feeling of complete violation. How dare she ask that? How dare she think I'd tell her about Aimee? But then it all vanishes as I turn on her. There's no idle curiosity in her face, no rubbernecking at an accident scene. She wants to know, like I do, how she had the strength to draw the razor across her wrist. She wants to know if she could do it the way Aimee did, since the way Hope tried failed. She wants to know what the difference is between her and Aimee and if she has what it takes to go either way. To die or to live.

I spin away from her and press my forehead against the door. I don't have the answers. I can't say what she wants to hear. My hand fumbles for the knob, but Hope grabs my hand, pulls it away. She's got a finger to her lips. Is she telling me to forget she asked, not to tell her? But then I hear her mother calling us for lunch. Hope wants to know, just not within hearing of her parents.

With the sound of her mother's voice, normalcy returns, and I realize that Hope's situation isn't the same as Aimee's. Aimee and I were alone, and she had it all planned. She meant it to happen. Hope is not alone, nor does she have a plan, just a morbid, frightening curiosity that I don't have to deal with. Her mother and father are out there, waiting for us to eat lunch with them. They'll take care of her. I can eat, then bolt for the woods. I don't have to stay here any longer than that, and I won't. For her dad, I'll eat lunch with her to make it seem like she has a friend.

I reach out a shaky hand and turn the knob. "After you," I say. I follow her out of her bedroom and into the dining room, where the smell of onions knocks me flat. Onion pie is what we're eating for lunch.

———

Lunch is a lesson in looking elsewhere. I cannot, nor would I want to, stare at Hope's dad. Hope's mother doesn't glance at him, yet she manages to help him. Like when she slides his saucer beneath his descending coffee cup. He acts like he doesn't notice.

Hope does notice, even though she pretends not to. Her face ranges from diaper white to volcano red, and again I think that his blindness is new. Did it happen before or after Hope's suicide attempt? There's no way to ask. If it happened before, I can almost understand how she thought she couldn't go on, given what she's already told me, but if he went blind after, I wonder why she did it. Onion pie served to your friends, especially ones who say they're not hungry but are obviously underfed, can be embarrassing. Still, it's not suicide material.

The coffee spills suddenly, and with it goes Hope's dad's composure. I hadn't guessed that his easygoing attitude was a façade, but he jumps up and knocks his chair and plate over. His face is a shiny crimson all the way to his hairline, and his hands are clenched. He yells, "Damn!" then, "Damn!" again as he hears his plate topple and his chair hit the floor.

Hope's mother slides her chair back almost without sound and murmurs indistinct words at him. I can see he only hears pity in her soothing tone, the kind one would use to talk to a child.

For a second, I'm convinced she's swearing, in so soft and comforting a voice that you can't understand her. Who would blame her? There's a mess of onions, still crisp and sharp-smelling, stewing in the spilt coffee. A drip, drip, drip tells us that the stinking liquid is escaping through the crack in the table and splashing onto the carpet, staining it.

Hope's father dodges his wife's hand, almost as if he could see it moving toward him to guide him. He steps away from the table, facing us—his wife with her thin, futile napkin in her hand; his daughter, who is still eating; and me, who never did start eating. "Damn it all to hell," he says, his voice aching with regret and loss. He lumbers toward the wall, touches it, moves gracelessly to the hallway opening, and vanishes through it. A moment later, the door to the study slams.

Hope picks up her plate and mine and carries them to the sink, where she dumps them. She grabs a roll of paper towels and a wet sponge, which she hands to her mother, who takes them without expression. "Gotta study," Hope says as she passes me, and I take my cue and rise to follow.

On the way to Hope's room I pass her mom. She looks as though she's holding her shoulders down to keep from shuddering. Her mouth is tight and her nose pinched, but there is no anger in her face. Instead, she looks surprised. Surprised to be here when all this time she thought she was heading someplace else.

The demand in Hope's face that I follow and the way she doesn't even think to help her mother clean up make me gag. Without a word, I change direction and walk outside. I close the door quietly, but I don't look back. I don't want to see Hope's face, and I don't want to see her mother grubbing under the table, but I do in my mind.

Still, I don't go back.

The woods would be too obvious a hiding place this time, at least to Hope, so I don't go there. I crouch in the bottom of a phone booth for a while, thinking I might call Chard, but I'm not ready yet. So I walk past my high school, where Hope says I have only to smile and I'll be accepted. There's Karen's office, but what if she's not there? Or worse still, what if she is, and her offer to help me get back to normal vanishes in the face of my latest escapade? So I stroll the sidewalk across the street, almost daring someone to turn me in.

But no one notices me, even though there are kids milling around on the corner smoking. The smell sends me back to times with Aimee. I don't want to go back there mentally, so I almost, but not quite, run to the mall. I power walk. I don't feel so light on my feet anymore, and I don't want to get another stitch in my side or see another kid's face laughing at me. There's nothing to laugh about, and there's no one to laugh with me. I try to remember what makes me laugh, but I can't. There's only my mother and my betrayal of her—in her eyes—and Hope and her dysfunctional family life, and Aimee's family hating me, and Chard and Kates and Jason and Kyle, who last I heard was home, safely on the path to normalcy, whatever and wherever that is.

Chard had called, the day before the perfume incident, with the news of Kyle's release. I didn't answer, so he left a message.

"Hey, babe." His voice is so soft I know he's not really mad at me, but his demand to say I didn't kill Aimee still hangs between us, so I didn't pick up even then. "I know you're there. Pick up, would ya?" He paused, but not for long, because then the machine would cut him off.

"Well," he continued, "thought you'd like to know Kyle's home. I saw him yesterday. He's cut his hair. Short. Real short. He's got a buzz cut actually. He said the staff had to do it because when he wasn't right—his words, not mine—he'd pulled a bunch out. Now he says he likes it."

Another second-long pause.

"He seems okay. No wisecracks about girls, though, so I guess he's not completely back to normal. Not healed, his mother said. He's got a shrink, too, and his parents are going, too. His mom said he's taking some medicine and that's why his affect is so flat. I wanted to ask what she meant, but she didn't want to go into too many details and seemed just about ready to cry the whole time. I thought you might know what that meant—*affect*. Maybe my mom can tell me.

nervous. More likely he's a paying, long-term customer with no real problems so he has no possibility of recovering, and he's known to change doctors because of situations like these.

He says, "I've never. Tuesday at four then," and stomps out without seeing if that time is good for Marge.

The receptionist nods at Marge and checks the appointment book. She reaches for the phone and dials. I'm not sure whether she's canceling the next appointment so Marge is free to spend more time with me, or if she's rearranging Tuesday's schedule. When Marge closes the door and I'm within the inner sanctum of her office, I ask Marge which is it, today or Tuesday?

Marge gives me a weird look, as though to say, "Is that why you've interrupted my day?" but she says, "Both." She sits in her chair and turns a page in her yellow pad. She scrawls at the top, checks her watch, scribbles again.

I sit, sticking my hands between my knees because now that I'm here, I don't know why I came, and I'm cold. I'm always cold. I worry about what will happen after I say what I came to say. I wonder if it will matter. Will it help Hope, or will I just look bad to everyone, like someone who's always trying to point out flaws in other people so that her own problems aren't so obvious?

Surely Marge'll call my mother, or the receptionist will, and then I'm screwed. As I stare past Marge's head at the window and the tree branches arching across it, I know I need more time. I'm not ready to go home and face whatever it is Mom has to say to me, whether it has to do with her stuff or my stuff, or whether it has to do with my future status in the family. Dad's gone. She could easily leave me, too. She could send me to some home for troubled kids, which actually means "trouble kids," the ones no one wants around anymore.

Still, I'm here, so I suck in a breath and say, "You aren't doing Hope any favors, you know," which isn't the most tactful way to begin. I see her face tighten, and I wonder if skin can crack from tension and anger.

"How exactly am I not doing her any favors, and how exactly do you know this?" she says.

So I tell her how I spent my morning. When I come to the part when Hope talks about sinning and how she was stroking her scars, Marge winces. When I describe how Hope feels trapped and by what, Marge shakes her head. But when I tell her how she won't leave the subject of Aimee alone, she waits until I've finished, then excuses herself.

The receptionist is surprised to see her, and I wonder if Marge caught her doing her toenails or something. The receptionist probably figured she had the remainder of the afternoon to goof off, what with me, the runaway, turning up and all. "I've called all your appointments—" she says, but Marge cuts her off.

Her voice is low, but the receptionist, usually the model of tact, blurts out, "But how do I explain?"

"Think of a way," Marge says, then comes back into the office. She closes the door and smiles. "Problem taken care of. I'll be seeing Hope's parents later on this evening or tomorrow at the latest." She sits at her desk, laces her fingers before her, and says, "Let's talk about you."

"That's not why I came. I came because Hope needs more help than you are giving her, and I thought you ought to know."

"Unlike last time, when you thought you could handle it

alone." She pauses to let her meaning, i.e., Aimee's suicide, sink in, then she continues, "I'm glad you sought help this time."

"Yeah. Unlike the fucking last time." I stand and walk to the door. "You really shouldn't have bothered to cancel your appointments, and I think that maybe you aren't the best shrink in town. But I do hope that you won't let Hope down, no pun intended." Then I walk out.

The receptionist drops her jaw when I stride past her and out of the waiting room, moving quickly because Marge is probably on the phone right now with my mother or maybe even the police, telling them to come and pick me up, that I'm somewhere in the vicinity of her office and I can't have gone far.

I'm standing at the elevator, staring at my feet, waiting for the door behind me to burst open and Marge to come running after me, when I decide not to go far at all. I think of the office upstairs. Marge used to have a partner, but the guy recently left to move across the country. He had this sweet smile whenever I passed him. I used to think I could talk to him if he was my shrink, but that was probably my hormones talking—he was handsome for an older guy.

When the elevator arrives, I press the button for the lobby, then I hop out, so if Marge checks, she'll think I went down. The stairway door is unlocked. The passage is dark, so I walk cautiously, not wanting to make noise. The door at the top of the stairs is ajar, and that is my only light and my hope. I can get that far, whether or not I can get into the empty office.

I push open the door and check out the reception area. Some cans of paint and file boxes are heaped on the desk. A different doctor's name is on them. Must be a new tenant moving in. Luckily, they're not here yet. There are two doors, both unlocked. One goes to a kitchen area and then a bathroom, the second goes to the empty office. Rolls of wallpaper stand in one corner. I find a refrigerator with a pint of milk due to expire today, two apples, and a yogurt past expiration but not opened, so it's probably okay. I can make coffee after Marge and her receptionist leave, but I don't dare do anything more than take an apple and the milk and lie on the sofa in the office until then. It's quiet and lonely with the bare shelves and empty desk facing me, but I like it. I wonder who the new tenant will be as I eat the apple and drink the milk. Then I snuggle into the cushions for a nap.

———

When I wake I see, to my horror, two eyes gazing at me from outside the uncurtained window. The empty shelves look like coffins stacked against the walls, and the day has almost given way to night. Shadows have crept everywhere. I panic instantly, decide it's Aimee come for me. Then, in as short a time as it took me to panic, I realize it can't be Aimee. The eyes, though, have to belong to someone or something.

I jump up, and the eyes pull back, almost disappear, then press forward against the glass again.

I tiptoe along the walls of the room until I am leaning against the window frame. Shaking, I peer into the glass and see a spray of white beneath the eyes and two pointy ears tufted in white.

It's a cat, although how a cat has managed to trap itself on a third-story windowsill, I don't know. I glance out and see hints of the same trees I've stared at hour upon hour from the office below. That must be how the cat climbed up. I don't know why it won't climb down.

"So, pussycat," I say, sliding a hand along the window frame until I find the latch, which I undo. I push the window up slowly so as not to frighten the animal, which wobbles, then catches its balance. When the window is open about six inches, the cat squeezes under the glass and leaps to the floor as if it belongs here. It circles the desk, then finds the nearly empty container of milk tipped over and dribbling onto the hardwood. The cat crouches and drinks. I fetch the yogurt and another apple from the refrigerator after setting the coffeepot to brew.

"So I have a companion for the night," I say, sitting on the couch and allowing the cat to jump on me. It purrs, rubs its head against my hand, then settles on my lap after several test turns. It opts for the couch between my legs, finding my legs, perhaps, too thin to balance on. "I'm eating though," I tell the cat, and I scoop yogurt into my mouth.

It looks up at me, then squeezes its eyes most of the way shut, tucking its paws beneath its chest.

So this is what Aimee saw in her cat, I think as the gentle vibration of the cat's purr begins. The animal lowers its head and seems to sleep, unconcerned about being with a stranger.

And then it dawns on me.

I could have given Aimee another cat. Something new for her to hold on to and love. Maybe it would have helped. But I didn't think of that then. I only thought of what I would have wanted, something that might have helped me, and that hadn't been enough.

I balance my journal on the arm of the sofa. It's hard to write this way, but I don't want to disturb the cat.

On that night, the night I had wanted Aimee to sleep over but my mom refused because it was a school night, I sneaked out of the house at ten. My parents were stuck in their own ruts: snoozing in front of the television after coming home cranky and exhausted from his conference (Dad), and buried in the office studying some new legal twist a case threatened to take (Mom). I left my lights off, figuring that by the time they went by my room—they never came into it—they'd think I was asleep. I wouldn't be expected to show my face until the next morning around seven, seven-fifteen if I was running behind.

This was the last night we needed to stand guard, because Aimee's dad had called to say he was returning the next day, Friday. We, as a group, were going to talk to him then.

I called Aimee before sneaking out so she wouldn't be surprised when I showed up. That's how I found out Aimee's stepmother had canceled her Bible study group to "be with" Aimee that night. But her stepmother was gone by the time I arrived. She'd gone to meet Aimee's dad. Aimee was waiting for me in a long blue gown that fell almost to her toes. "My latest gift from the bitch." She twirled, and the dress fluted out around her thin calves, showing sneakers beneath. She saw me looking at them and said, "Didn't get any new shoes with it, though. Can't be too generous, can we?" She hiccupped.

"What's it for, and where's the liquor?" I asked, moving past her to the kitchen. Every bottle in the house was sitting on the table, arranged by size and color, not type. I picked up the gin and rum, trying to judge how much she'd drank.

"Homecoming, and you found it." She pulled a cigarette out of her purse.

"Is this your parents' liquor?"

"Hell no! I called the store and had it delivered." She

chuckled as I rolled my eyes in disbelief. "We should have the rest of the gang over tonight to live it up."

"You don't need to live it up. You need to sleep." Still, I poured myself a cranberry juice and vodka.

Her thin face turned watchful. "I don't need to sleep. I need to have some fun. Maybe fuck around, but you're the wrong sex for that." She lurched toward the phone. "I should call—"

I grabbed the phone away from her hand. "No one else is coming."

"Chard," she said, her voice losing some of its slur. "He's always good for a fuck."

"Cut it out." Her language alone told me she was in a strange mood, and nothing else she was doing made me think otherwise. She'd twirl one moment, watching the crushed velvet ruffle and swirl, then she'd collapse on a chair and stare sullenly into a bottle before upending it. All the bottles were missing their caps, and she drank from whichever bottle was closest.

"Why should I cut it out?" she said, drinking from a nearly empty bottle of schnapps. "Who's going to make me? If you won't have him, he's got to find someone else. Doesn't he? Don't we all? Miss Pure? Huh?" Despite her steady pouring of alcohol down her throat, there was no trace of a slur in her voice now. Hard-edged, it slashed me. Even though I knew she was lashing out, trying to hurt someone else like she'd been hurt, I couldn't stop the anger rising in me.

"I said—"

"I said," she mocked, swaying and waving her hand at me. She looked so grand in the dress, so in charge, until I looked closely and saw that she had two different colors of eye makeup on, green on her left lid, brown on her right.

233

"Cut it out."

"Cut it out." She stopped and turned to the window. "I don't think I can cut it out." She pushed her sleeves back to her elbows and eyed her thin wrists. She prodded her skin as if she were looking for an opening.

She had such tiny bones, such white skin.

I grabbed her arm. "Aimee! Stop talking like this. It's not right. You have a lot to live for."

"Name something."

"I'm going to call your mother." I picked up the phone and shook it at her.

"Which one? The one who left me on her husband's altar, or the one who met me there? I already tried calling the former, but she's out. More than likely with steady boyfriend number seventeen. They probably went to a boob-and-ass show in Las Vegas, which means she'll be out late. I left a message. She'll call me in the morning, if she's home by then."

"She will," I said, but Aimee barreled on.

"And mother number two, the one we all know, love, and cherish, has gone to meet her delinquent husband and convince him that he's crazy, that there's no one else, and that she loves only him. He called right after the gift part of the evening was over, but before I could express my thanks. I still owe her my thanks." Aimee sat down with a thump. Her chair tilted, but she didn't fall. "He's been in Maryland the whole time, visiting some college buddy and lying low, waiting for her to miss him."

"Did you talk to him?"

"Oh yeah, but he didn't invite me down like he did obedient child number two. My brother went with her. Instead, dear old Dad asked me about school and dating. I told him I was fucking Chard, and the bitch took the phone away."

I felt my stomach boil. Was she serious about Chard? Her face was blank, oddly out of sync with her uneven makeup, but she kept on talking, so I couldn't ask her about Chard. I couldn't ask her about anything. She wasn't listening. Not to me.

"So I went upstairs," Aimee continued, "and got on the phone in their bedroom. I told him about my cat dying, and he said that's too bad, but at least she went peacefully. He might as well have said, 'Oh good, now your stepmother doesn't have to get allergy shots anymore,' which is what he was thinking, I'm sure. She probably slipped the cat something to kill it because she was tired of sneezing and being poked in the arm."

She drew a breath, and I jumped in. "When are they coming back?"

"Hopefully never. None of them should come back. They should all die in an accident, and then I'd be free of the bunch of them. Assholes one and all."

"Aimee!"

"No one to say what a pain in the ass I am, no one to say what a liar I am, no one to whisper how beautiful I am at two o'clock in the morning. Won't it be lonely?" She looked up at me, and her eyes were open so wide the eye shadow disappeared. Then they squinted, and a bark came out of her mouth. I think she was laughing.

"Sounds like it," I said, crouching next to her. "But you'll have us. Chard, Kates, Jason, Kyle, and me. You won't be lonely. You aren't alone."

"Yes, I am. Yes, I will be lonely tonight," she sang softly.

I took her arm and guided her toward the steps. I had already lifted the skirt of her dress so she wouldn't trip. "No, you won't," I said. "I'm here."

"Don't you want to know who I'm going to Homecoming with?" she said, sinking to the steps. She leaned forward with her hands between her knees, and for a second, I thought she was going to puke, but she didn't. Her head lifted as if someone had pulled it up by her hair. "Don't you? Don't you want to know?"

I bit my lip, trying not to be drawn into her game. Aimee wasn't normally mean when she drank, but she must have drunk a lot before I arrived.

"Chard, sweetie. I'm going with your Chard," Aimee said. "Called and asked him tonight. Yup. Called and asked him. Figured it's never too soon to find a date for Homecoming. I thought I should act fast, before someone else snapped him up." She leaned against me, one arm draped over my shoulders, the other clinging to the banister as I struggled to get her back on her feet. "Should've claimed him when I told you he was yours for the taking." She laughed again, tugged her skirt free of my hands, and darted up the rest of the stairs.

When I'm ninety, I don't think I'll feel older than I did that night, dragging myself up the stairs to her room, wanting to leave, but knowing she needed me. Knowing she was lying, but doubting at the same time. She had asked him to the Sadie Hawkins dance. She went to his house all the time. Chard had known all about the abuse when I hadn't pieced it together. What if she wasn't lying?

She was lying sideways on her bed, her dress wadded up beneath her so that most of her legs stuck out. I sat next to her and slid her zipper down.

"Boy, is this familiar," she said without raising her head off the comforter.

"You have to undress so you can sleep. You'll ruin the dress otherwise."

"What do I care? I can weasel another lousy dress out of her."

"You should shower, try to sober up, then sleep. Take off the dress. I'm going downstairs to make coffee. Good and strong." I didn't add that I needed it.

From downstairs, I heard the shower running. I dumped my drink down the drain. I didn't think drinking alcohol tonight was such a good idea anymore. The rest of the liquor I stuck hodgepodge in the closet where her parents kept it.

Later, they'd find my fingerprints all over the bottles and say that it was me who started Aimee drinking.

The coffeepot was ready to brew, as though someone had set it up and then forgotten to turn the timer on. I plugged it back in and switched it on. I washed my face at the kitchen sink, dried it on a dish towel, and stared at myself in the black glass of the window above the sink. I felt drained, washed up, and unable to cope, and I'd been there less than an hour.

Maybe Aimee would fall asleep from the liquor. Maybe she'd pass out on the bathroom floor, bang her head, and need stitches. I could call an ambulance, check her into the hospital, and say she was an alcoholic. They'd have to keep her for the rest of the night at least, and I'd be free of any responsibility for whatever else she did, said, or made happen.

But when I went back upstairs with the pot of coffee, I found her dressed in her pajamas, sitting on her bed in a scrunched-over ball, rocking back and forth, and crying. I set the mugs of coffee on the desk.

"I'm such a bitch," she moaned into her hands.

"Don't I know it," I said. I lifted her head with one hand. "Here, drink this. You'll feel better."

"I'll throw up."

"Drink it."

She took a mouthful, then pretended to gag and puke.

"Are you done yet?"

Aimee unwadded herself, turned, then swung her legs up under her. "You're not much fun tonight, are you?"

"Neither are you." I sipped my coffee, not taking my eyes from her white face. Now that she had showered away all traces of her makeup, she looked awful.

"Maybe that's why Chard doesn't go for you. You're no fun. What happened to your drink?"

"I want coffee," I said, focusing only on the last part of her comment.

"You should drink more. People would like you better."

"Like Chard, I suppose?" I closed my eyes, sighed, and turned away. I balanced my cup on my legs. I'd fallen into her game.

"Maybe," she said, warming her hands on her cup. "Maybe it's too late for that."

I didn't have the energy for this, not tonight, not ever. I took her cup away, and she let go of it like a tired child. Then I leaned her back on the bed none too gently, pulled the spread off the other bed, and covered her up. "Sleep," I said. I turned off the light and lay down on the empty bed.

"Yes, Mommie," she said to the darkness. Her breathing slowed, then became inaudible. She fell asleep.

I finished my coffee, then peed. When I came back to her

room, she had rolled over and was facing away from me. I climbed under the covers of my bed and allowed myself to sleep.

———

I woke to see Aimee creeping back into the room. The front of her pajama top was wet, as if she had spilled water on herself while washing her face, or maybe she had tried to clean some puke off of her. Which was possible, given her condition earlier. I sat up and watched her walk. She was steady, not tripping or banging into anything.

She saw me sit up and sank onto her bed. "I'm scared," she said, like a child who's woken from a vague but frightening dream. "I'm scared," she repeated.

I struggled out from beneath my tangled sheets and blankets and sat next to her. "I'm here." I had woken to the memory that she'd been pissing me off before she fell asleep, and I wasn't sure why. I did know, looking at her in the light from the streetlamp outside, that I didn't want her to be in pain anymore. She was big-eyed, quiet, almost stunned, but underneath there lurked something that made me uneasy. I put my arm around her and pulled her against me. "Everything will be fine," I said.

And I thought I was right. She looked like my old friend, not like the stranger she had been earlier.

"I know," she whispered. "I'm glad you're here." She rested her head on my shoulder. She didn't smell of puke, so I guessed the water came from her trying to bring down the swelling and redness in her eyes. She wasn't crying at least. "I'm sorry I'm such a bitch, and I don't—" She stopped.

"Don't what?" I asked.

She yawned and said, "I don't think I could have come this far without you as my friend. Will you stay with me tonight? One last time?"

"What a weird thing to say, one last time. Of course I'll stay. Tonight and any night you need. But why should this be the last time?" Something inside me jerked awake, something I had let sleep or maybe was hiding beneath my anger. Warning lights, sirens, bells, everything started clambering in my jittery mind.

Before I was concerned about Aimee. Now I was terrified for her. "What do you mean, Aimee? One last time?" My hands shook as I twisted her shoulders so that she faced me.

She looked blank, unaware of what she had said.

"What do you mean?" I asked again.

"I need to end it, and I can't. Not without your help. Not without you here. It's so dark and scary doing it alone."

I grabbed her wrists, then dragged her to the desk. She hadn't cried out, and neither wrist felt wet or sticky, so I didn't think she had slashed them, but I had to be sure. The light blinded me as I clicked on the desk lamp, but immediately I could see there was no blood, no gaping wound. So this was still just talk.

"No, Aimee. Not that. I can't do that. You're my best friend." I closed my arms around her. "I can't live without you. I'll help you live, not here, if that's what you want. I'll support you any way I can, tell them I've seen her come for you, tell them I've seen her beat you, tell everyone about what happened until they believe it, but I need you alive. We all do. Chard—"

She snorted. The light had made her blink, but if anything she seemed more groggy than before. "I'm not your best friend. Chard's your best friend. And don't kid yourself. Remember scary problem number fifty-nine? Overpopulation results in worldwide famine and epidemics. We either (a) survive, or (b) die." She yawned again and leaned against me, heavier this time.

I stroked her hair, although I wanted to yank it out by the roots I was so mad at her for twisting everything.

"You're good at that," she continued. "Surviving. Not me. But you know, I can't do it alone. Just can't. So you'll have to stay. Please stay."

"Aimee, I can't take this. Snap out of it. Your dad will be home tomorrow, and we're going to tell him what's going on. You don't have to tell him, we will. We'll support you one hundred percent."

"Then support me how I want you to support me. I can't do it your way. Hell, I can't do it at all. I'm tired. Tired of everything. And none of this—" She waved an arm at her room, but her hand flopped on the end of her arm like a dying fish.

I shivered watching her.

"I have to sleep. But you have to stay with me so I can do this," she murmured.

"Aimee, I will not help you. You have to fight, damn it. You have so much going for you. You just wait. Things will look brighter in the morning. You'll come home with me. I don't care what my mother says, and you'll see, things will be better. Hell, you might even meet Mr. Right." I glanced at her, knowing that I sounded like an idiot, like someone offering comfort without meaning any of it. But I meant all of it. Things would get better. They had to.

"I just want to sleep. Guys are pains in the asses. I'm going to lie down." She didn't say anything about Chard, but I wasn't sure whom she was referring to. I needed to be sure she wasn't talking about him. I was obsessing and hating myself for it.

"All guys? Even Jason, Kyle, and Chard? Aren't some guys worth it?"

"Nothing is worth it anymore. Let me sleep. You have to stay, though. Have to stay. Help me do this, okay? And everything will be all right."

"No. I will not help you kill yourself." I still didn't, at that point, have much of a clue about what exactly she was talking about. Did she mean help her slice her wrists? Hold her hand while she did? Watch her die?

I remembered the razor blade I had taken from her. I didn't want to spend the rest of the night staring into the darkness, making sure she didn't sneak off to find another to use. I'd check the bathrooms for razors now. "I'm going to the bathroom to pee. Pull yourself together, Aimee," I said as I stood up.

She flopped over onto the bed like a doll stuffed with beans.

"Bring me the bottle on the sink," she muttered without raising her head. "I want to take something."

My mouth went dry. Drier than when I had found the razor in her hand and saw her pretending to cut. Drier than when she had asked me to help her die. Then I felt nausea sweep over me, and the saliva ran wild in my mouth. I swallowed and swallowed again, edging toward the door, trying not to hurry. Trying to see her and leave the room at the same time. "What bottle?" I called, with my foot out the door, my body ready to bolt for the bathroom.

"Bottle on the sink. Very important. Bitchy stepmother

should never leave sleeping pills out with kids in the house. Never. Never. Never. How many times will they replace her lost pills?" Aimee started to laugh, a deep gagging laugh. She coughed, sat up a moment, then rolled back onto the bed.

I raced for the bathroom. I didn't walk into or stop in any other rooms. I told the police that. I told the court that. I wasted no time trying to discover what she was talking about, but even then, I thought I just needed to hide the bottle, that she hadn't taken anything or done anything. She needed me there to do it. She said so herself. What else could she mean by "Stay with me tonight? Help me die?"

On the floor of the bathroom were a billion pieces of glass. Since she had left the smaller bathroom light on, I managed to see it before I stepped on it. My hands sprang out from my sides and grabbed the door frame, halting me midstep. I stood panting and stared.

The mirror over the sink had been shattered. I saw my eyes, wide and startled, in a dozen places when I bent down. My nose, big and little, my hair, and my cheeks fragmented as I swung my head from side to side in disbelief.

The noise of Aimee breaking the mirror should have woken me, and maybe it had. But then, why didn't I remember anything before she crept back into the room? I racked my brains, trying to figure out when she had done this. How she had done this. Her feet hadn't been cut, so she hadn't walked in the bathroom. Then I saw that mixed with the mirror's shards were pieces of the drinking glass that usually stood on the sink. She must have thrown it at the mirror.

I also saw fragments of what appeared to be one of the family photo albums. Judging from the little I could piece together of the pictures, it was her father and stepmother's wedding album. Every picture of her stepmother had been cut into tiny fragments. The pictures of Aimee's dad and brother were mostly intact.

There were no remains of Aimee anywhere.

But the bottle was there. A little brown plastic bottle, the kind that holds antibiotics. I strained forward, so tense everything shook, but I couldn't reach it.

With my body wrenched sideways to close it, I tried to shut the toilet lid so I could stand on it and grab the bottle. When I looked down, I froze. Inside the toilet bowl floated three or four slashed versions of Aimee. All had been carefully cut from a larger picture, and all had been sliced into ribbons. I reached into the water and pulled out one of the mutilated pictures.

I was almost unaware of my tears as I picked up the bottle. There was no rattle of pills, no weight to the bottle at all, and the prescription label had been soaked in water or something so that I couldn't read it.

"Aimee!"

I felt devoid of hope.

"Aimee!" I screamed again, feeling as though my limbs were being pulled in opposite directions like a puppet in a warped play.

I thought of all the things she had said earlier that had infuriated me, and I wondered if it was part of her plan, to make me so angry I wouldn't pay attention to what she was doing.

Whether that was true or not, she had already carried out the other part of her plan.

She had already taken the pills.

My head cleared in a spasm of guilt. Here I was standing

and staring at broken glass trying to figure out if she lied about her and Chard.

I needed to get to Aimee. I needed to get help.

Panic overwhelmed me, and I lunged for the door, landing on a shard of glass. I stopped to pull it out, with blood seeping across my fingers and down the insides of my hands. But I didn't stop to bandage the gash in my foot. I didn't wince or hobble when I ran. That would have taken time, and I had none.

"Aimee!"

She wasn't answering.

"Aimee!" I shrieked from the door of her room. I held up the bottle for her to see, but, of course, she didn't see it.

She was lying facedown on the bed, an arm sprawled above her. Her back rose, fell, rose, fell, but slowly, too slowly.

I rolled her over and came face to face with despair. A long slug trail of vomit slithered down the side of the bed. I had planned on making her throw up, but she already had. It was the only thing I knew to do that would slow things down and get some of the drugs out of her system.

No pills were visible in the slime. How long did it take to digest them? Could all of the poison be in her system already? Had she chewed them to get them into her body faster?

"Oh God! Oh God!" I cried, my hands dancing through air.

"Aimee," I said louder, closer to her ear.

She didn't respond.

I pulled her mouth open to shove my finger down her throat, thinking maybe she hadn't thrown up enough. If she did it again, maybe the pills would come up. "Try again!

Throw them up! Come on, Aimee! You've got to be okay." I pushed her up, and she slumped forward.

There was blood on the bed, and I searched her body for wounds, then the room for something to wrap whatever was bleeding on her. It was then that I saw my trail of bloody footprints on the floor and realized the blood on the bed was mine.

Then I saw the phone.

I lowered Aimee back onto the bed and jumped for the phone. Aimee groaned, and I turned back to her, grabbing her shoulder, slapping her face lightly, trying to get a response. "How much of this stuff did you take? Answer me! Answer me!"

But she didn't. She couldn't.

. She didn't groan again.

The phone. I picked it up, tried to dial, but somewhere in the house Aimee had left a phone off the hook.

"Damn you!" I screamed. "Damn you for this!" I was hobbling and crying, snot ran down my face. I raced from room to room.

I did, too. Whatever the police and her parents' attorneys say, I did check everywhere I could think of for the disengaged phone. I didn't save her, but I did that. My bloody footprints were everywhere in the house. Everywhere. Not because I freaked out and was chasing Aimee to make her take the pills. Which some asshole newspaper reporter said I did. Was he there, or was I? I was checking for a phone that worked. I even crawled under tables and beneath beds to make sure the phones I found were plugged in.

And all the phones were on the hook. Except the portable. Which I couldn't find.

The clock said four A.M. Maybe some insane commuter would be up or I could wake one up. I opened the front door onto an empty street as if to run out, but then I turned back.

Here is where I failed. Because I thought of Chard and then of Kates and Kyle and Jason, and they were all too far away to help me.

But here is where I made the wrong choice, did the wrong thing. I should have kept going, but I wasn't thinking, I was reacting, and what I reacted to right then was leaving Aimee alone when she had begged me not to and explaining to my friends, to Chard, that she had died alone.

I would check on Aimee first. I had to see if there was anything else I could do, should do before I abandoned her to find help.

So I spun around and slammed the door. I flew back up the stairs, three at a time—according to the report and the footprint analysis. I was planning on making her drink something before I left. Anything. Coffee. Her full mug was still on the desk. I'd force some caffeine in her to counteract the pills, but who was I kidding? A cup of coffee against a bottle of sleeping pills?

I raised her head, tried to support her with my shoulder while I cradled her from behind. I opened her jaw with one hand and dumped coffee through her lips with the other.

Her throat didn't respond to the cold coffee dribbling through her pried open lips. She didn't swallow.

I tried to make her vomit again. That's when her bladder let go.

Later, in court, I learned that this is a normal part of death when someone takes sleeping pills. At the time, I was horrified, disgusted, and positive this was not a good sign.

I hugged her, with a finger on her pulse, trying to be sure she was still alive, thinking I'd do mouth-to-mouth until I found the phone, not even understanding that I couldn't do both.

When she shit, I knew I was done for. I wouldn't have my best friend anymore. I was screaming, shrieking, moaning. *Keening* might be the right word for what I was doing, but I don't remember exactly.

Aimee's window was open partway. It always was, and I thought someone would hear me. Some jogger, somebody walking a dog. I couldn't see the clock. Couldn't let go of Aimee. She was gurgling now, and I thought I should lay her down. So I draped her unmoving body, heavy in its stillness, across my legs, where it weighed me down and put my legs to sleep.

My screams weren't even making Aimee twitch.

I had forgotten all about escaping out the front door, running away to find someone else to take care of this mess. Someone who knew better what to do. All I knew, lying there listening to her labored, slowing, ending breathing, was that I was losing the dearest thing in my life, and there was nothing I could do.

Nothing would stop it. Even if I managed to find help now, looking at her bluing lips, I, who had never seen death, knew she was beyond help.

"Help me! Oh, God! Don't do this. Don't take her. Chard? Kyle? Jason? Kates? Where is everyone? Why doesn't anyone come? Why is this happening? I hate you, Aimee! I hate you!"

I screamed on and on, and eventually, when Aimee's eyes were fixed and dilated, when she was cold and blue and filthy and beginning to stiffen up in my arms, someone heard.

There was a pounding on the door, but I would have had to let go of Aimee to let them in. And I couldn't.

I just kept screaming, incoherent rages against God and country, and everyone in between.

The pounding stopped, and shouts rose up from the ground below the window, and all I could do was moan, "She's dead. She's dead. Aimee's dead," in a hoarse whisper that was grotesque in itself.

Then a car pulled in, and car doors slammed.

I figured it would be the police, and they would help me. They would take Aimee away and take me home. They would call her parents. Then I could get a pill of my own that would take away the sight of Aimee's twisted legs wrapped around mine and the smell of shit and urine mixed with vomit and coffee, and maybe the police would do something about my foot, which throbbed and still bled into a puddle on the yellow spread like an ever-growing, ever-blooming flower.

I quit screaming. I quit moaning. I waited, watching the flower spread and grow, my eyes glazed over. I slipped away. I stopped thinking, stopped reacting like a human being. I became still, cold, dead inside.

I still feel that way most of the time.

Sometimes, though, I feel the opposite, filled with a rage that's uncontrollable and unknowable to anyone else. When it wasn't the police who walked into the room, but Aimee's father and stepmother, who had come home because they couldn't get through on the phone and were worried sick, the rage appeared for the first time.

The police report says I dropped Aimee on the floor and charged her stepmother. I remember her face, the shock and horror mixed with the smug satisfaction of knowing she was safe, that Aimee wouldn't tell. I still don't know if she cared for Aimee in her own sick way. But something snapped inside me when I saw her.

I don't remember trying to kill her, though. The report states that I lunged for her neck, screaming and ranting. According to the first newspaper story, I tried to kill Aimee's stepmother, *too,* but a concerned neighbor pulled me off her.

I've told the rest, in bits and pieces. About Mom and her concern for the best lawyer. About Dad watching while they drugged me up. Someone, sometime stitched up my foot.

Then it was the psych ward for me.

I didn't go to the funeral. I wasn't allowed.

I did hear where she had hidden the phone—on her stepmother's pillow, covered by blankets and tucked into the arm of her teddy bear. The paper reported the facts, but no one understood the significance of them. Even when I told them what the significance was, they didn't believe me. They accused me of hiding it earlier in the night, before I had cut my foot, because there were no bloodstains anywhere near her stepmother's bed. There were no footprints by the bed because there was no phone on the bed. Not normally anyway.

When they found it, the phone had long since quit bleating its recorded message: "If you'd like to make a call, please hang up and dial again."

But Aimee had completed her call.

———

It feels weird to be woken by a cat. It's especially strange because I didn't think I'd been sleeping. Remembering, yes; channeling, perhaps; but sleeping, no. But my pen's lost in the cushions and my journal's lying on the floor, so I must have slept.

I've never had a pet, especially a cat that likes rubbing her little black, wet nose into my cheekbones and hands. She's even nibbling on my hair.

The cat, a small cream and tan female with pale blue eyes, swishes her mocha-colored tail in my face and blinks slowly. Then she pushes her face against my hands. I don't move, so she thrusts again, harder, which is almost funny since she weighs maybe six pounds and couldn't bump anything awake, let alone knock it over. Still, she has my attention, and I reach for her.

I do what I saw Aimee do a million times. I bring her tiny, purring body to my face and rub her back. To the cat this must be some kind of primitive scent-marking ritual, but it feels right, this touch, this physical sharing.

I think again of how I could have given Aimee another cat. Which might have prevented her suicide, or at least delayed it.

Or I could have searched her house for danger signs instead of letting her piss me off with all that Chard crap. I might have found the pills. Or the phone. Hell, if I'd have seen that phone lying with her bear on her stepmother's bed, I would have known Aimee was doing more than just talking about suicide.

But shouldn't I have known that anyway? Isn't talking about it one of the major warning signals? But *nooo*. I screwed that up, closed my eyes to it, thought I had it all under control.

But I couldn't control Aimee. That should have been obvious from her car accident and all the other bull crap she pulled. The phone is just one of many hints I have to anguish over. I had a blind spot with Aimee, a carryover from our third-grade friendship when she was the cool one, the one with all the right friends and all the neat stuff. I looked up to her. She could do nothing wrong, especially not this wrong.

That night I didn't know that I shouldn't still be admiring her, looking up to her, worshiping her.

Maybe my hero worship was part of the pressure that wore Aimee down and made her give up. Maybe living up to my expectations was one thing too many. But I'll never know for sure, and part of me still won't accept the truth about Aimee. That she was not and never was perfect.

The cat curls on my lap, tired of my halfhearted petting, and sleeps. I watch her ears twitch, and I remember Aimee's final sleep, how deep it was, how permanent.

I'm crying, splattering the messy pages of my journal.

What if I hadn't gone to her house alone? What if I had made my mom or dad come, or one of the other kids? What would have happened then?

Someone else would share the blame. We could have slept in a tag team so that Aimee was never alone. One of us could have gone for help while the other stayed.

But only Chard and the other kids knew I was there, and none of them could stay with her. I keep reminding myself of that, but it doesn't sink in.

It doesn't matter.

My teeth roam the inside of my cheek, looking for places to bite, and I discover several raw and swollen places that I've already chewed. I clench my teeth, force them away from my flesh, but before my next thought is formed, my fingers find a hangnail and rip it back. A tiny square of blood forms where the skin had been.

I sit on my hand, and the cat blinks twice before she lowers her head again.

My original plan, to have Aimee sleep over, would have saved her. Maybe Aimee would have done it some other time, but I don't know that. I will never know it. She said she couldn't do it alone, and I didn't understand until afterward that she meant she couldn't die alone.

But here's the hair-splitter. She did die alone. I gave her nothing but arguments during her last few waking moments, and I left her alone for much of the time when she was unconscious.

So even there, I failed her.

Helped her die, my ass, I think, standing up and dumping the cat on the ground. She regards me with disdain, then cleans her paw as if to say I have a lot to learn about having a cat. But I'm not thinking about her.

I'm watching Aimee die. Yes, I watched her die. But I didn't do it willingly. What did I get out of supposedly helping her to die? A stint in the psych ward, a court trial, during which I may have been acquitted, but I'm still guilty in the public's opinion. Hardly a reward. I was also ruled psychiatrically unstable and put on probation, since I wasn't acquitted of the breaking-and-entering charges. There was no proof that Aimee let me into the house.

Loneliness.

That's what I've gotten from Aimee's suicide. Loneliness, and not just because she died, which is awful. I am cut off from my best friend forever. She also took away all of my other friends and even my family. She even tried, during that last night, to take Chard from me.

And now I'm sobbing and shaking because that night, I believed her. I believed that she and Chard were lovers and that he didn't care for me. And I believe, at last, that she could do that to me: she could have taken him as a lover to make me go along with her plan, or to make me overlook what she was doing. She was capable of that. I can see that now. But I should have known that Chard wasn't capable of it, not with all he knew—the stepmother thing, etc. But she convinced me.

It was part of her game.

Rage scorches my eyes, and I can't see. My heart pounds a loud, staccato rhythm as it strains in my chest and burns as though it's about to burst. My hands clench, my mouth opens as though to scream. I squeeze my eyes shut against the knowledge of who I was and what I let happen. Because a part of me did allow it.

I need to admit that. When Chard testified, I searched his face for signs that what she said was true, that he was her lover.

But he looked the same.

I want to scream more, longer, louder than I have ever screamed. If Chard denied what I claimed Aimee told me about the two of them, then everything else Aimee said was suspect, including what she said about her stepmother. I can see at last why they called her a liar.

I sink to floor and drop my forehead on the windowsill. Its cold roundness presses into my flesh. The feeling of the trim digging into my skin is concrete. It is discomfort but not pain. It is something I know. I can prove it. But Aimee? I can't prove any of what she said was true. Ever. I want to bang my hands against the window it until it breaks and sets me free, but I can't.

I can't.

I can't. And not because I would be found and forced to go home before I'm ready, but because I can't stay mad at Aimee. I want to, but I can't. She was, is, my friend, and she needed far more than I could give her. I couldn't or wouldn't understand what she needed, so maybe she's wherever she is now, screaming silent screams of anger back at me because I didn't help her. I only watched and acted bigger than I was, acted braver. But I was scared shitless of every sad and angry word she said. It terrified me to imagine her in a coffin and dead and not on the other end of the phone when I needed to talk.

So I didn't think it could happen.

Friends don't commit suicide. They don't die.

We'd sit with Aimee like a parent whose kid has chicken pox, and when the outer signs, the pimples, were healed, then she'd be cured. Right? But the chicken pox virus lives in your body forever, and when you are exposed to the virus again, later in life, it sometimes shows up as this gross and painful rashlike thing called shingles.

I think the same thing happens to people who want to die. They never get rid of the bug. They can only try to get help for it and find some way of looking at life that gives them hope and strength. If they're real lucky, they find the joy in life, whatever that is, because I don't think I've found it yet. But some people have, and you can see it in their faces. Their happiness is visible.

But how was I to know all that then? I can only grasp the edges of it now, like a cloak of silk fluttering forever at my fingertips.

It's almost daylight. Only my second night on the run, but I feel like I've been running for years—at least since Aimee's death. I close my eyes and think of all the "should haves" and the "should never haves," but I need to admit that I, at the time of Aimee's suicide, didn't know what else to do.

I thought just being there would be enough. That having a friend in the house would be enough. She would talk; I would listen. In the morning, I'd turn her over to her parents, her father specifically, and later the whole gang and I would come and confront her stepmother. Then we'd call her mom out in Las Vegas and tell her to get her act together and come be a mother.

Aimee had other plans, obviously. She had tried to ask for help in some ways, but no one took her seriously enough. Not even us. Not even me.

That, Chard, is why I have a hard time saying what you want me to say. Because if I had been smarter, if I had been less sure of myself and my ability to save Aimee, if I hadn't been jealous—which is exactly what she wanted me to be—if I hadn't believed she was perfect and that shit never happens to people you know, then Aimee would be here. All of these ifs made me blind to Aimee, more willing to accept her pain as something she needed to bear. If I had run out of the house when I first realized she had taken the pills and the phone was hidden, if I had called someone when I found her drunk, combative, and depressed, if—

I sigh, unaware of why the cat is licking my chin until I push her away. Then the tears splash onto the sill, my knees, and my journal.

If. What a word.

What I really need to say is that if I had been God, I could have stopped Aimee. But I'm not, so I couldn't.

The hardest question of all is, Why didn't God?

About an hour and a gallon of tears later, I pick up the phone, grateful that the renovators have turned it on. The cat is curled in the chair so I can't sit, but this call won't take long. I actually have two calls to make. I dial the first number slowly, but I dial it.

He answers, which I think is a miracle because his mother always jumps for the phone first, in case it is a creditor she doesn't want her husband to know about. Maybe she's cured of all that?

Anyway, I'm stalling, and he's saying, "Hello? Hello?" I've got to say something, so I finally open my mouth.

"I didn't kill her," I say, holding the mouthpiece close to my lips because there is life in the office below, footsteps and drawers opening and shutting, and I can't be caught yet. Not yet.

"I know," he says, and I can hear his smile. "I know." He stops, but I can't say anything yet. "When can I see you?"

"Is it legal?"

"Was it ever?"

I giggle, something I thought I'd never do again, and say, "First, I have a few things to tie up. Then, I'll have to see where I'm at, living-wise. I sort of broke probation."

"Your mom called looking for you, but she didn't explain much, just that you'd run off. Since she didn't call back, I figured it all blew over. Guess not, huh? What did you do?" He sounds tired but not mad.

"Sort of blew up and ran away, and I'm still hiding out."

"Oh, Zoe," he says.

"Say that again," I whisper.

"What?"

"My name." I think of my name and how it's been Aimee I've had in my head for so long and how she's gone or diminished now. But I am not her and she is not me.

"Zoe, Zoe, Zoe," he chants, and I hear his mother ask if that is who he's talking to, and he says, "Yeah. And you can't stop me. She never did anything wrong, and you know it. You also know that it wasn't us who was wrong in all of this mess, especially since Kyle. It was you guys, you hypocrites."

"Hang up the phone," his father says. I picture him hulking on one side of the table like a bristled up German shepherd.

"No!" Chard says. Then he says to me, "Zoe, call me again. Later. I'll be here. Promise."

There's a click, but no dial tone, so I say fast, before I'm cut off, "I will, but don't argue with them. Okay, Chard? They don't understand. They never will. But if we could have turned to them, maybe Aimee would still be alive, and none of this would have happened—"

"Exactly, Zoe," Chard interrupts. "And since my father put you on speaker phone, he got to hear what you said, too. Happy, Dad?"

"We don't have to listen to this," Chard's dad says, his voice about fourteen decibels louder than necessary.

I hear Chard snort and say, "You never listen. Zoe is finally getting better, and all you can say is, 'I don't have to listen to this.'" He stops.

A minute of silence follows, during which I clutch the phone. "Chard?" I choke out at last.

"Yeah?"

"We didn't listen a whole lot better either."

Then, for the first time since that night, his mother actually talks to me. "Is that how you kids felt, Zoe? That we wouldn't listen?"

"Feel," I say, trying to talk around the marbles of fear in my mouth. I pause, then I say, "Sorry, that's how I feel."

"Have you told your mother all of this crap?" Chard's dad says. He's talking quieter, but he's not going to go down this path of mushy nonsense. "I'll bet she doesn't believe it either."

And I wish I could be there to see the look his mom sends him, because the next thing I hear is her saying, "This isn't about Zoe's mother, it's about us. Listen to them."

I hear a blustering curse, then a sigh. From Chard's dad, I think.

His mom continues like it's a refrain they sing a lot. "At least I'm willing to admit my mistakes. Are you?"

There's another minute of silence, which I can't stand. "I am," I say into the quiet. "I—we—should've given you a chance. We didn't because you had other problems to worry about."

"That doesn't mean we wouldn't have tried to help." From her voice, I can tell Chard's mom is crying. I hear a grunt, and I'm sure she's poked her husband.

"Yeah, right," he says in that offhand agreeing voice grown-ups use when they don't want to admit someone else is right.

"We miss her, too," his mom says next. "We miss Aimee."

A thud signals that a door has closed, then Chard's mom says, "Chard, Zoe, it's almost time for school. Call each other back when you have more time to talk. Come visit us, Zoe, and I, for one, will try to be a better listener."

I hear a click, and panic sets in. I didn't have a chance to say good-bye to Chard. Surely this is a dream? Chard's mother siding with us? Maybe even Chard's father?

Then I hear Chard. She only turned off the speaker phone. "I'll come to see you next weekend. Will that give you enough time to figure out where you'll be at?"

"I don't know if I'll have much say in it. I pissed off my mother totally this time, and I told the shrink that she was letting one of her other patients con her into thinking she was better when she's really getting worse. I'd say she's suicidal. So I doubt my shrink will take kindly to me from now on."

"We all need to hear that stuff sometimes."

He's probably referring to me, but I just ramble on, "I thought it would be better if this time I didn't try to solve everyone's problems. I couldn't solve Aimee's problems, I'm not going to try to solve Hope's."

"Hope?"

"No one you know. The patient I was talking about. She's just a girl who heard my history and thought that I'd help her, too."

"But you didn't." He sounds so careful, like he isn't sure about the truth.

"No, Chard. I didn't help her, and I didn't help Aimee. I didn't do anything to help Aimee actually commit suicide, but I didn't help her live, either. That's something I have to live with, and, I guess, so do you. We tried. We all tried, I know that. But what we tried was not help, not really. We should have picked up a phone and called the police, a hospital, a crisis center, God only knows what else, until we found somebody to listen. But we didn't."

"No." His voice is a whisper really, but I hear it. "I can't stop thinking about that. How about you?"

"No," I repeat, just as softly. "So this time, when Hope started acting freaky, I got out of it and turned her over to someone who knows what to do. And I hope it works. But if it doesn't, I won't have to feel guilty about it. That's what I find hardest to take, Chard. The guilt over Aimee. The 'what ifs.'" I stop, then add, "And I don't quite get why it had to happen at all. Why God let it happen. But I don't think anyone will answer that for me."

"Zoe?"

"What?"

"You sound a lot better."

"I've been doing a lot of thinking since you left."

"Obviously." I hear the smile in his voice.

"Chard?"

"What?"

"I've got to go. I need to call someone else."

"Who?" He sounds surprised, like he's the only person that matters to me.

"My mom."

"I love you."

"I love you, too," I say, and I add to myself as a reminder, *And I didn't kill her,* because I still need to be convinced. I know it, but I don't believe it. Not yet.

———

I hesitate after hanging up with Chard. Should I call or go see my mother? I wish I knew what time it is, but there's no clock in the room. What is that phone number that tells the time? I can only think of 911, and that isn't it. So I wait.

Then it dawns on me that if it's late enough for old Marge to be in her office, it's certainly late enough for Mom to be in hers. I glance down at my clothes. I'd only provoke an argument if I went to her office like this. I'll go home first. I doubt anyone is watching the house. If they ever were.

As I head for the door, the cat sits up tall, stretches, then hops down from the chair. She rubs against my legs, mewing in this weak, soft voice I wasn't expecting. She seemed demanding last night, but she has never meowed at me before. I bend down and stroke her. "You'll have to go someplace else when we go out. I'm not allowed to have pets. You'll get hair on—"

I stop. Why should a little hair matter? I'll care for it. Clean her litter box and feed her. Mom can't complain about a little ball of fur if I straighten myself up and act right. And I intend to.

I'm not Aimee.

So I scoop the cat up and open the door.

And there sits Marge. She isn't what I expected, obviously, and I nearly drop the cat. Instead, I hug her tighter. "Oh, hey!" I say, pretty stupidly.

"Hello," Marge says. She sips from her coffee mug. "I was wondering who our new tenant was."

"How did you know?" I don't finish the question, just leave it hanging, but she knows what I mean.

"The coffeepot was on, with an almost full pot in it. We clean it out at lunch every day. Neither of us drinks coffee past then. And I heard footsteps this morning, so I decided to slip up here and investigate."

"You didn't call the police?" That's what I would have done, given the strangeness of the situation.

"No. I thought I knew who I'd find."

"Were you right?"

"What do you think?" She raises her eyebrows and stares at me. She doesn't glance at the cat.

I sit in the chair across from her and don't answer. The cat settles herself on my lap, bobbing her head as I stroke her. Up, down, up, down. "How's Hope?"

"I haven't spoken to her."

I look up, my mouth open and dry. "But I told you—"

"Yes." She sighs. "You told me that she was talking crazy. But she denies it, to her parents anyway."

"So you're just going to ignore it? Pretend it didn't happen? Well, if you do and she kills herself, you're to blame. You and her jackass parents who, like all parents, won't admit that anything's wrong." I think about jumping up and running out. But I don't. No energy, I guess.

"No, I'm not going to ignore it. She's coming in this morning with her parents, and we're going to discuss it."

"Discuss it." I can't keep the disgust out of my voice.

"You don't know what's best always. You can't think that you do."

"I don't!" My voice rises. "That's why I told you. *You're* supposed to know what's best. Everywhere I go people say, Why didn't you just tell a grown-up? They would have helped. They would have been able to get her the help she needed. Like a psychiatrist. But what do you quote-unquote grown-ups ever do when we tell you stuff like this? You say that the person denies the problem or that we misread the situation or that we don't know what's best. Did I misread Aimee's intentions when I told my mom about how desperate she was? Or did my mom?"

Marge's mouth is open. But I can see she's not going to say anything.

"Hypocrites. You're all hypocrites. To admit Hope still has

a problem would mean you failed. Wouldn't it? And you can't admit that because then you'd look bad, but by all means, please tell you if something seems wrong. You'll handle it. You know what you're doing."

I stop, mostly for breath, but also because the cat is looking at me like I've lost my mind and she's not sure she wants to stay on my lap. "Whose cat is this?" I ask.

Marge is trying to shift gears and failing. "I don't think I'm failing Hope. She's responsible, in the end, for her own actions," she says, ignoring my question.

"That's how you justify it, then?"

"Justify what?"

"When a patient dies, commits suicide, bites the big one, and you missed it."

"Look—"

"I asked you, whose cat is this?"

She throws her hands in the air. "It's a stray. It's always on the back porch or in the back yard. It catches mice, and sometimes my receptionist gives it milk. We've called the pound, but they never come to get it. Happy?"

I nod. I am beaming, I'm sure.

"You don't think I can help Hope?" Her voice is almost beseeching, but she does not meet my eyes when I turn back to her.

"Not with your current attitude. She's not responsible if she's sick, even if she denies it later." I feel like I'm a million years older than yesterday. I wonder if I'm talking about Aimee here, and if that means I should forgive her, too. And maybe me. Because if Marge doesn't get it, then how could I? "I would rather be wrong and Hope got a lot of extra help than be right and Hope dies because no one helped her."

Marge looks up. "What really happened that night?"

"I wrote it down last night. Most of it, anyway, and most of what I think and feel about it. That's what happened last night. I looked backward."

"That was very brave."

"That's bull. I had no choice, and you know it. It's what you wanted me to do all along, what I needed to do if I don't want to end up like Hope. And after seeing her dancing around all the pain in her life—just when did her dad go blind anyway?—I didn't have a choice. So, in a few days, after I've talked to some people who deserve to hear about that night first, and write out the last part, then I'll drop the notebook off, and you can read it."

"Do you want it back?"

I stare at her. "Of course. Do you think I'd trust you not to publish it in some psychiatric case-study book or something like that?"

She laughs, actually laughs. "No. I doubt you'd trust me to do anything right."

"Damn straight," I say, but I'm smiling, too. Because I do, trust her, that is. I just don't want her to know it. "And what about Hope?"

"Her dad went blind about three months ago, and yesterday they found out that his left leg will most likely have to be amputated."

"And she tried suicide when?"

"Before that." She picks at her nails. "It's a lot more stressful now. She doesn't have much support at school either."

I take a chance. "She has this guy named David."

"They don't date anymore."

"That's Hope. He'd have her back in a second, I think."

"I can't make her date him."

265

"You can make her see what she's doing and why. Then all that other crap will take care of itself. And friends should never be left out. Never. It's awful lonely in here." I tap my head. "And the voices aren't always to be trusted. When they take away your friends, too, it does weird things to you."

"Is that what happened to you?"

I shrug, then meet her eyes. Her hand is stretched halfway across the table, and for the first time I realize how long we've been talking, and without a timer, too. "It would have been different if I only lost one, you know?" I feel the thickness in my throat and the burning in my eyes and look away. "I wonder if that's what happened to Kyle? Loneliness. It's a thing, you know, not a feeling. A big, ugly thing that moves in and takes over until you forget how to live without it, but you can't live with it either." I stop and wipe my eyes on my sleeve. I want to leave, not talk anymore, but she has more questions.

"Will you call Chard? Or the others?"

"I've called Chard." I wave at the door behind me. "Sorry about not asking first."

She smiles, then catches sight of her watch. I still haven't touched her hand, and she draws it back to check the time. "Hope and her parents will be here any minute. You can stay as long as you want. I won't tell."

She's not so bad, is Marge, I think, but I don't say anything.

"Will you come to your next appointment?"

It sounds almost like an invitation to a party or something, but it's not. I think about the guilt and sorrow, the empty space inside me where Aimee used to be. And I think of Chard and how he wants me whole, not halved. So I nod. "Not as many times a week though, okay? I want to join this track club. They run together to keep in shape and I don't know what else." I don't mention Karen's offer, or that I'm going to take her up on it.

She nods. "Call and set up the times. Maybe twice a week, and a sport would be good for you." She doesn't say that it will keep my mind off things, but we both know it will.

"And I'm keeping the cat."

"Good." She glances again at her watch.

"Go to Hope. I'm okay."

She passes through the door and down the stairs, and I've still not thanked her or touched her hand.

I tiptoe down the stairwell. I can see Hope's car parked in front of the building. I glance up at the windows, certain for a second that I'll see Hope on the other side of the glass, waving and smiling her gratitude.

But of course she's not there, and she'd probably spit on me right now, if she even guesses I'm the one who ratted on her, which I'm sure she does. She has about as many friends as I do.

I tuck the cat inside my sweatshirt, and she pokes her head and front paws out of the top but doesn't try to get away.

"You like me, huh? Well, there's at least one other person you have to charm, and she's a tough one." I don't worry about Dad. He doesn't fit into my life in the same way somehow, and I wonder if that is how Mom feels about him, too. Not that I don't want to see him, just that he's happier living alone in his little messy apartment forty miles away. He'll have to keep a litter box, too. I won't leave the cat with

267

Mom when I visit him on the weekends. Mom would forget to feed her, or she'd take her to a kitty shrink and mess her up real good. Tell her catnip was bad for her or something.

My house looks deserted, as does the entire street. No kids are out, but they wouldn't be. School's in session. Except you'd think somebody in this huge subdivision would have little kids, ones who don't go to school yet. I almost wish they did. Then I could baby-sit. Make some money, because this cat is going to need a fancy collar. Her eyes and coloring remind me of something, which comes to me as I climb the front steps. A feline husky. That's what she is. "Can you stand the cold like those dogs?" I ask. I have my key. I don't know if I forgot it was in my pocket or if I took it in one of those subconscious moves Marge likes to talk about, but there it is in my hand, and now it's in the door.

Silence greets me.

What did I expect? A homecoming party? A bunch of people standing around a crisis hot line, brainstorming about where I've been or where I'm going next?

Not a chance.

I set the cat down and pull my shirt over my head. Shower first, then food, then some money, then the store. The cat won't wait too long for a litter box and some food. She sniffs my mother's potted rubber trees, and for a second, I think, "Go ahead. It'll probably kill them." Then I yank my shirt back over my head and take the cat outside to the garden, where she politely does her business, then scampers back to me.

Inside, I hurry through my shower and get dressed. Then I raid the stash of cash in my desk. I have sixty bucks. Surprise, surprise. Having no friends and no place to go has one advantage: I have spending money.

The cat, who needs a name, is curled on my bed asleep, so small and white you wouldn't see her if you didn't know where to look. I close the door and hurry to the store. I agonize over brands and soft versus dry food and scoopable versus regular litter, then run home. I want the cat set up so well Mom can't complain. But she will anyway.

I burst into the house and stop cold. Mom's keys are on the hall table, her purse sits on the floor. I hear footsteps upstairs, moving from room to room, then I hear her voice. She's on the phone.

"I'm certain it was her. No. She's gone again. Her door was open when I left; it's closed now. Someone took a shower, or rather she did, and her clothes, the ones she was wearing, are in the hamper. The hamper, for Christ's sake! Like she—"

But she doesn't finish her sentence because I'm standing in the doorway with a couple of shopping bags filled with kitty supplies nearly dragging on the floor.

"Oh. I'll call you back." She takes the phone away from her ear and presses the Off button without taking her eyes off me. "Where were you?" Her voice is a croak.

"Places," I say.

"Don't start—" She stops. Bites her words, and closes her eyes. Breathes so deeply she swells to twice her normal chest size.

Her struggle for control does something funny to me. It reminds me that I came back to try again. She is trying, too. "I was in the woods, then at Hope's, then Marge's," I say, my voice still tight. I glance around the room and don't see my stuff. Come to think of it, the ashtray and other things weren't in my room either. Couldn't she have at least put them back? I fight the increasing speed of my breathing and master it, at least temporarily.

She looks puzzled by my answer.

"Marge is my shrink. It's a nickname I made up for her." I'm going to have to stop calling her that. "I stayed at her office last night."

Her mouth tightens, and her grip on the phone becomes a stranglehold.

I have to defend Marge, so I say quickly, "She didn't know I was there. I sneaked up to the office above hers. The empty one. Did you talk to her? Marge, I mean?"

"She said you stopped by yesterday, but ran out before you said much."

"When did you talk to her?"

"Just now." She looks at the phone as if she expects Marge to be dangling from the cord or something.

"Did she mention Hope? Is she okay?" I ask.

"Why wouldn't she be?"

Suddenly I don't want to talk. Of course Marge didn't tell her about Hope. She can't even tell my mother anything I say. All this dancing around the subjects we should be discussing, the things that still hang in the air between us. Was your dad abusive, or just mean? I want to ask. Or did he basically ignore you? Did he remind you that all his hopes died with your brother? Is that why you work so hard even now? To prove him wrong?

My arms are tired, sagging. I want to set the cat paraphernalia down. "I—"

"Zoe? Can we—"

"Can we what?"

"Can we try again?" She walks over to her closet and opens it. She bends down and pulls out a plastic bag. "It's all there. Except for—" She stops.

"Except for what?" I drop the shopping bags on the floor

and snatch the bag from her hands, which, if I'm not mistaken, are shaking. I paw through it, but I know what she's going to say.

"The razor blade. I threw that away." She stops and waits for me to look up. "I was afraid of why you were keeping it. Afraid that you'd—" She breaks our stare, turns away.

"Afraid I'd use it?"

She nods, and I nod, too. I don't say it's okay that she threw it away, but it is. It was time. "The other stuff? My journal? Did you?" I let my question hang, trying to see in her eyes if she read it before putting it on my desk just two nights before. It seems so much longer ago.

"Your stuff is all there. And I didn't read the journal." Her voice is not defensive. She sounds like she's presenting facts in a case. She doesn't apologize. Maybe she can't.

But I can. "Mom?"

She swivels her head up and around but does not turn her body to face me. "I want you to know I'm sorry. I was wrong to even go into your room, let alone—" I stop, then go on when my voice is steadier. I don't want to sound pissed or like I'm just saying it because I have to. I want to sound like I mean it. "I was stupid," I say, and then I pick up speed until my words are falling faster than an avalanche and I'm not sure if I sound sincere or not. "I've been stupid. I'm going to change. Can we just not talk about it a lot? I'm sorry about the letter and the perfume." I sniff. I can't even smell the stink anymore. The power of money and professional cleaners.

Behind me, I hear a meow. Then a bag crackles as the little cat pushes her nose into the plastic. I stoop to pick up the cat. She smells my nose, tastes my chin, then snuggles into my arms. Mom is staring.

"I'm keeping her," I say. There is no room for argument in my voice, but I don't think I'm being unusually demanding or crabby. In fact, I sound just like her. "She found me last night." Was it only last night? "At Marge's. I realized, last night, that there were things I could have done that might have changed what happened. But that is true of everyone who knew her."

"You mean Aimee?" Mom, the anti-pet freak, reaches out and taps the cat's head. It's not quite a stroke or a pat, just a tap. Still, the cat pushes her head against Mom's hand.

"Yeah, I mean Aimee. But I didn't kill her. I didn't even help her die." I wait, stroking the cat because I can't look at Mom. I need her to say that she believes me, that she always believed me, and she has to say it on her own. She has to admit to her mistakes, too. If she can't, I can always try Dad, I think, as her silence stretches. He seemed more willing to bend last time I was there, even acted like he knew they were wrong about Aimee and me.

Mom turns away from me and the cat, and she sits on her bed, or rather allows herself to drop to the bed. She's all stooped over and old-looking. "I should've listened, I suppose," she says, and I can barely hear her. "I could've tried to help Aimee. Hell, I could have let her stay over that night, then you wouldn't have had to sneak out, and she wouldn't have been able to carry out her plan." Her voice grows hard, angry, and I wonder who she is mad at.

The words she chooses strike me as wrong. *Aimee's plan?* Her death, you mean, Mom, I want to say. But she's trying, so I nod, and don't say anything. At least for now. Because, at last, she believes me.

She looks at me, and her eyes are full of tears. "I know you didn't—"

And it's enough. I sit next to her, and I'm crying, and she wraps one arm around me, which is one more than she's used in years, and we stay that way for a long time.

But she pulls away at last and swipes at her nose and dabs at her eyes. She already looks like she wasn't crying, but she was. My shoulder is wet.

"No more running away, okay?" she says. "I didn't know if you were okay, or if you had—" She looks away, and I know exactly what she means. If I had killed myself someplace or been raped or murdered. But the killed-myself part is what shows most in her face. That fear must be a big one with her since Aimee. She pushes her shoulders back with a huge breath and continues, "It's awfully hard not knowing where you are, what may have happened to you—" She reaches for another tissue and blows her nose with this perfect little snort.

"I can't. I won't," I say, ignoring the tears on my face until she forces a tissue into my hand. "Who would take care of my cat?" I waggle the cat in her face, and she nods with only the corners of her mouth curved up.

I can almost hear Aimee, see her saying the same thing to someone somewhere. Was it to me? It seemed so real for a second. Then she's gone, and I don't see Aimee anymore.

"So you want to keep this cat?" The old Mom, who worries about appearances and success, has returned, I think, as she pulls her jacket on while looking at herself in the mirror, flicking her collar into place and checking both sides of her face for makeup damage. This is her freaking-out stance. The one that says, I'm perfect and I know what's best for all of us.

But Dad is gone, and I nearly left. Maybe she has changed, too.

Still, I expect her to say I can't keep the cat, that it would mess the house, eat the plants, get fur on everything, make people sneeze, smell awful.

But she doesn't say any of that. She bends over me, and she doesn't smell like anything but soap and maybe some flowery deodorant, and I see that she hasn't yet replaced any of the perfumes I ruined. She pats the cat's head, then suddenly hugs me with the cat squashed between.

"Yeah. I want to keep the cat," I say. Even though the answer is obvious.

"Well, it will need a name, and you'll have to take care of it." She glances at the plastic bags heaped by the door. "But I see you already know that."

"I'll think of a good name for her." I don't tell her that I have already thought of one. Perfume. It fits the exotic-looking feline in my arms, and it will remind me of where I've been and what I don't want to be. I'll tell her all of that later. In a week or a year, depending on how well we do. "Mom?"

"Yes?"

"Do you have to go to work?" The question pops out of me, as unexpected to me as it is to her. Visions of our mall dates crowd through my mind, but I try to ignore them and imagine us here all day. Sweats and slippers, popcorn and kitty chow, rolling balls of yarn for the cat. But that is unlikely—ever.

"Of course. I put off an important court date until this afternoon so I could search for you this morning." She blushes. "But I won't stay late tonight. We'll have Chinese or pizza. Whatever you want."

I take this with a bit of skepticism but try not to let it show. What is late, anyway? Eight? Ten? Bringing home enough work for three or four hours and doing it at the table? Does that count? But she's trying, so I change the subject. "Can I see Chard again?"

Her shoulders droop, but only for a moment. Then she squares them up as if a voice in her brain is saying the same thing as the voice in mine: Don't let it get to you. She's trying to get along, so don't ruin it. And I wonder as she checks her nylons for runs if this will ever come automatically, this urge not to fight over everything.

"Oh, Zoe, one thing at a time, please," she says in her businesslike voice. Then she sighs as if she knows I won't let it drop—not this time. "If his parents say it's okay, then I don't—"

"I talked to his parents this morning. They said it's okay. We want to get together next weekend." I try to sound as matter-of-fact, as this-is-how-it's-going-to-be as I can.

She's almost at the front door, her purse and keys in hand. As she looks back at me, I think of all the things that went into making her this careful, tight-hearted woman. I wonder what I don't know about her, if I will ever know everything about her, and if I want to know everything about her. Like how she's not sure she wants to know or talk about all the things that are a part of me. I wonder if I'll have a daughter for whom I'll have to decide what is right and wrong, and if there will ever be a time when I'll have to admit to her I made a mistake when I thought I knew perfectly well the best way to handle things.

But none of this wondering shows on my face, or at least I hope it doesn't.

She shakes her head with exasperation, maybe even frustration, but not with anger. "Always pushing for one more thing. First a cat, now Chard. What will be next? Yes, you can see him if his parents say it's okay. It never was me who said you couldn't see him, you know." And I see something in her eyes I never saw before. I think it's recognition. Maybe she sees that I'm a little like her, always pushing for one more thing, one more success, and maybe she likes that about me. Likes my track trophies, likes my surviving this.

"Thanks, Mom."

I don't tell her what will be next. It's Karen and learning to like me again, and it's that track club and learning to let people in once more, and it's Hope and being the friend to her that I should have been to Aimee, and living to learn from the past.

But she doesn't need to know all that now.

I watch as she walks away, her spine straight and her shoulders squared in her tailored suit, as though she has a heavy book balanced on her head to remind her to be careful and prim and proper. As though that wasn't the way she always was and she has to work at it. Maybe, I think, she does know about the chances I need to take, like helping Hope or being with Chard. She just doesn't want to do that anymore.

It's my turn.